Not According to Flan

by

Karen C. Whalen

The Dinner Club Murder Mysteries
Book Two

This is a work of fiction. Names, characters, places, and incidents are either the product of the author's imagination or are used fictitiously, and any resemblance to actual persons living or dead, business establishments, events, or locales, is entirely coincidental.

Not According to Flan

Cover Art by *Kim Mendoza*

The Wild Rose Press, Inc.
PO Box 708
Adams Basin, NY 14410-0708
Visit us at www.thewildrosepress.com

Publishing History
First Mainstream Mystery Edition, 2017
Print ISBN 978-1-5092-1464-8
Digital ISBN 978-1-5092-1465-5

The Dinner Club Murder Mysteries
Published in the United States of America

She slipped outside into the warmth

of the early September, blue-sky, Colorado day to check on her puppies sniffing around their new territory in the backyard. Leaning over the deck railing facing the lot to the east, she gazed into the bottom of an open excavation where a basement was being poured. Someone had parked a tractor down in the dirt, and near it a white cowboy hat lay on the ground. A man's hand stretched toward the hat's brim. Had someone fallen into the pit?

Jane bounded down the deck stairs and out the wooden gate, only stopping for a moment to secure the latch. She rounded the corner of her new house and rushed to the adjoining lot, pausing near the edge of the concrete that formed the basement's foundation.

A man was shoved against the corner of the foundation wall. His torso and legs were partly covered with dirt. The cowboy hat concealed the top of his head. His left hand almost touched the brim, as if he were about to take off his hat and say "Howdy do." A large manila envelope lay a foot or so away from his other outstretched hand.

On the envelope tall, block letters spelled out: "Jane Marsh—welcome to your new home."

Dedications

To our sons, Drew and Garred,
and daughters-in-law, Lisa and Joy
~*~

Also to the dinner club members:
Mary and Dean Harris,
Sandy and Russ Van Houten,
Barb and Pete Buchanan,
Cindy and Owen Hamilton,
and Michele and Dave Bollig

Chapter 1

Slam! Chink. The brown packing box fell off the dolly with the tinkling sound of glass on glass. Jane sighed as the mover stacked the box labeled "kitchen" back on the dolly and thumped down the basement stairs with it.

Never mind. She'd sort it out later. She slipped outside into the warmth of the early September, blue-sky, Colorado day to check on her puppies sniffing around their new territory in the backyard. Leaning over the deck railing facing the lot to the east, she gazed into the bottom of an open excavation where a basement was being poured. Someone had parked a tractor down in the dirt, and near it a white cowboy hat lay on the ground. A man's hand stretched toward the hat's brim. Had someone fallen into the pit?

Jane bounded down the deck stairs and out the wooden gate, only stopping for a moment to secure the latch. She rounded the corner of her new house and rushed to the adjoining lot, pausing near the edge of the concrete that formed the basement's foundation.

A man was shoved against the corner of the foundation wall. His torso and legs were partly covered with dirt. The cowboy hat concealed the top of his head. His left hand almost touched the brim, as if he were about to take off his hat and say "Howdy do." A large manila envelope lay a foot or so away from his other

1

outstretched hand.

On the envelope tall, block letters spelled out: "Jane Marsh—welcome to your new home."

Jane's hands flew to her throat. "Ethan," she breathed.

Her eyes took in the three cement walls rising out of the dirt floor and at the rear, a crumbling slope of dirt spilling into the pit. Starting toward the back slope, she hesitated. The soil might not be stable. She lifted two planks, plunked the long ends of the boards into the pit, and climbed down.

The smell of turned earth filled her nose as she skirted the tractor, a small, front-end loader. Falling to her knees, she lifted the cowboy hat, then dropped it. She felt the man's wrist for a pulse. It wasn't there. Then her hand moved toward the envelope with her name on it, but she drew back.

After yanking a cell phone out of the back pocket of her worn jeans, she punched in 9-1-1. "A man fell into a construction pit... I'm pretty sure he's dead...no, he's beyond help." The dispatcher asked for the address, and she gave it to him in a shaky voice. "Yes, I'll stay on the line." The makeshift bridge was harder to get back up than it was to get down. After making it to the top, she crossed the lot and rushed through her front door.

"Caleb!"

"Yeah? Whatzup, Mom?" Her grown son appeared from the kitchen. He was almost a foot taller than she, but with the same slim build and a cap of the same rich brown hair.

"Ethan Valrod. The construction manager for the builder. He fell into the basement pit next door. He's dead." Breathless, she took a deeper breath to stop her ears buzzing and her heart pounding.

"What the?" Caleb's eyes widened and his mouth dropped open.

"Ethan Valrod's dead. I've called 9-1-1 already and they told me to stay on the line." Jane lifted the phone to her ear, but the operator was silent. Legs shaking, she led the way, and Caleb followed her out the door.

Her son stationed himself on top of the foundation, hands clenched to his sides, while taking in the sight below. She plucked at his sleeve. "Are you going down to look?"

He nodded his head and descended the plank. In only a few moments he was back, dragging her by the elbow over to the concrete curb where they sat together facing the street.

After hearing a voice spluttering from the phone, Jane spoke into it. "I'm all right. I've got my son here with me now. We'll wait together." She hit the mute button and shifted the phone from her right hand to her left.

Caleb slid a folded piece of paper out of his tight jean pocket and handed it to her. "I forgot to give you this."

In a tremulous voice, she read out loud, "Mrs. Marsh, I stopped by to give you a welcome packet with the keys. I'll come back later." Ethan Valrod's signature was scrawled across the bottom. She gazed into the distance for a moment.

Caleb lifted his hands, palms up. "It was on the counter when I got here. The movers set a box on top of the note, and I didn't want it to get lost, so I put it in my pocket."

"Okay, thanks." Swallowing hard, she darted a quick glance over her shoulder, but no one else was around. "It looked like someone used the tractor to cover the body with dirt."

"I noticed. And there were marks on the ground, like someone rolled his body into the corner first."

"Did you see the blood on the tractor bucket?"

"Yeah." Caleb gave his mother a pop-eyed stare and she returned the look.

Her ears seemed sharper than usual. The dogs barked from the other side of the fence. A plane's engine droned from overhead. Police sirens approached from the next block.

Moments later, two police cars screeched to a stop at the curb. Caleb and Jane catapulted to their feet as she told the dispatcher, "Thanks. The police are here now," and disconnected.

The officers exited their cars and strode over to them. Jane gave one the brief facts as the other scaled the boards into the pit. He came back and issued the command, "Wait in the house."

Not needing to be told twice, they dashed inside. Jane explained to the head mover, "We found a man dead next door." The movers' eyes flew back and forth between one another, but they didn't pause in their work and continued to bustle about, unloading the boxes and furniture under Caleb's direction. In fact, they appeared to progress quicker than ever.

She found the stainless steel, drip coffeemaker and yellow coffee cups in a box in the basement and started a pot. Before too long, the head mover approached Jane with a clipboard. "We're all done. Will you sign the invoice, please, Mrs. Marsh?" She signed it. Watching from the front door as the movers loaded the dollies into their truck, she stepped outside when a policeman came over. The men gave the officer their names and contact information, then they climbed into their moving van, backed out of the driveway, and drove down the street and around the corner.

It was done; she was moved in. No going back now. Had she made a mistake leaving her comfortable home to move to this northern suburb of Denver where she didn't know anyone? And where a person was killed right next door...

Her eyes were drawn to the neighboring lot. More officers had arrived and were carrying tall measuring sticks and staking yellow crime scene tape around the perimeter of the foundation. Several police personnel were down the block canvassing the area.

One of the officers approached her. "We need you to fill out a statement."

She led him inside to the kitchen where he handed Jane and Caleb each a form.

"Would you like a cup of coffee?"

When the policeman declined, she sat down at the counter to read the instructions with her own coffee cup cradled in her shaking hands. She whispered to her son, "What should I write?" Caleb was starting his last year of law school, and even though Jane was a paralegal, she relied on him for her personal legal advice.

"Just write about finding the body," he murmured, taking a seat next to her to complete his own statement. Soon they both set down their pens.

The officer asked, "Did you see anyone next door or on the street before you found the victim?"

Caleb answered first. "I heard a tractor engine start up a couple hours ago. It sounded like it was idling, but not for long."

"Did you see who was operating the tractor?"

"No. I was in the house waiting for the movers to arrive. I didn't even look out the window."

"What about you?" The officer turned to Jane.

"I had just gotten here. Maybe ten or twenty minutes before I found, you know, the body. This may not be the time to ask, but um, can I have the welcome envelope with my name on it?" Jane felt her face flush.

"Not yet—"

"There's supposed to be a set of keys with it." She drew Ethan's note out of her pocket and handed it to the officer.

He read the note, then tucked it into a plastic evidence bag. "How did you get inside the house without a key?"

Caleb spoke up. "I used the garage door code. The door from the garage into the house was unlocked, and I came in that way."

"There were no keys in the envelope." The officer's gaze ran down the length of Jane's statement lying on the counter.

Jane's brows furrowed. "Were they in his pocket?"

"No—"

"No? I need to go look for the keys." She jumped up so fast her stool fell over.

The officer put his hands on his hips, his feet spread apart. "You can't go over there. Anyway, we've examined the whole area and didn't find any keys."

Jane's eyes pinged about the room. Her voice sounded shrill to her own ears. "Someone else got to

Ethan before I did and took the keys out of the envelope. Or maybe he lost the keys and thought he'd dropped them in the pit and went down there to look for them. Or...was he shoved in? And the killer has my keys!" She was pacing, and her voice had gotten loud.

"Mom, your imagination's getting the best of you." Caleb spun his stool around and stopped her with his hand on her arm.

The policeman picked up the statements from the counter. "Do you have somewhere else to stay tonight?"

"What? I can't stay the first night in my new home?" Her stomach tightened into a knot.

"Call a locksmith." The officer's lips were pursed together in a tight line.

Caleb got out his cell phone. "I'll find one."

"So, it definitely wasn't an accident, was it?" She thought about the blood on the tractor bucket, the attempt at concealment, the yellow crime scene tape fluttering in the breeze. Would there be a taped outline of the body in the dirt, too?

"We're still investigating."

"He was murdered..." Her voice trailed off into a moment of silence.

The officer glanced away and didn't deny it. "Do you know if he had enemies?"

"No. I only met him a couple of times to talk about the house. I didn't know him."

"All right. Here's my card. Call if you think of anything more."

After the officer picked up their statements and left, Caleb squinted at his phone. "I found a locksmith. But I can't believe...another murder."

"I know. How likely is it I would find another dead body?"

"At least this time you can't be accused of anything." Caleb swiveled back toward the counter and let out a long sigh. He rubbed the top of his head causing his short brown hair to stand up. "Don't get involved, Mom. I mean it." She noticed the back of his T-shirt for the first time. It read, "I told my therapist about you."

She waved her hands around. "All right. Fine. But before you phone that locksmith, let me call the construction office to find out if they have the keys."

Even though she let the phone ring over and over, there was no answer. So, Caleb talked to a local locksmith who said he could be there within minutes. "Do you want to stay with Erin and me at our apartment tonight?"

Her lips trembled as she peered past her son through the open window at the dogs sniffing along the fence. It was tempting to escape into the safe arms of family. But she forced her lips still, squared her shoulders, and jutted out her chin. "Thanks for the offer, but my dogs don't get along with your cats, and I can't leave them here alone. I'll be okay with new locks on the doors."

The locksmith arrived and rang the bell. Even though she had expected him, her hand jerked, spilling her coffee. Cranked tight like a Jack-in-the-box, she popped out of her seat and scurried down the hall to let him in. It didn't take long to drill out the old locks and install new ones. He handed her a key and two extras, along with the bill, and Jane gave one of the keys to Caleb.

Just as the locksmith left, Erin walked in the door and hugged her mother-in-law. "I'm shocked. Caleb called and told me what happened. Don't let this take away the joy of your new home. I brought you this." A petite, young woman with auburn hair and a shy smile, she handed Jane a miniature, yellow banner with teal letters that read, "Celebrate the Small Things."

"I love it. How thoughtful you are. Just the colors I chose for the house. Thanks so much." Grateful for the ordinariness of being given a house-warming gift—on such a day as this—her stomach unclenched a little, and she breathed easier. "I'll remember it as my first bit of decorating in the new home."

While Jane and Erin put glasses away in the kitchen cabinets and Caleb finished assembling the dining room table, the doorbell rang yet again.

A young couple faced them on the front porch. "Hello and welcome to the neighborhood. I'm Tara and this is my husband, Justin. We live two doors down the street, on the other side of that lot." Tara's head tilted toward the crime scene, causing her straight, long blonde hair to stream out and cascade down her arm. Justin stood very still. He was over six feet tall, with a shaved head, short whiskers covering his chin, and a lean, athletic build.

"Come inside." Jane introduced the neighbors to Caleb and Erin, who were standing behind her in the entry hall. Tara gave Jane a heavy plate covered with plastic wrap.

"Thanks so much. Let's sit down in the living room, if you can make your way past the boxes." Jane led them down the hall, set the plate on the kitchen island, and gestured to the couch and chairs in the adjoining family room.

Justin perched on the edge of the sofa. "We won't stay long. This must be a hectic day for you. And with that Ethan falling into the basement pit next door..." He glanced sharply at his wife, then away.

"Did you know him?" Jane's eyes moved from Justin to Tara.

The young lady slid closer to her husband. "Everyone knew Ethan. His dad owned the construction company that built all these houses around here." She flicked a long strand of blonde hair over her shoulder.

Justin cleared his throat. "And his brother, Steven, too. Their dad passed away last year, and Steven and Ethan run the business. I guess just Steven will now."

Jane said, "I met Ethan a couple of times after I signed the contract to buy the house, but I never met his brother."

"I hope it's all right that we stopped by after all the excitement next door. I'd already made the flan for you, so I thought I might as well bring it over." Tara patted Jane's beagle on his head as he nosed in her lap.

"A what?" asked Erin.

"A flan..."

"How nice." Jane caught her daughter-in-law's eye.

Tara got up from the sofa. "We're leaving so you can get back to your unpacking."

They followed Jane's new neighbors to the front door. "Thanks again for the, uh, the flan."

"You're welcome. Bye now."

Caleb shut the door after them. "Don't neighbors usually bring a cake? What's a flan?"

"It's like a custard with a sweet, syrupy sauce over

the top, like a glaze. Do you want to taste it?"

"No, thanks." Caleb turned to his wife, and Erin shook her head as well.

"Are you going to be all right by yourself tonight? Do you want to stay with us?" Erin tapped Jane's arm.

Jane leaned against the wall near the front door. "Caleb already invited me. But as I told him, I can't leave the dogs. Thanks for asking, though."

"Try not to think about that man's death, Mom. And lock the door behind us when we leave." Caleb edged closer to his mother, put his arm around her shoulder, and gave her a squeeze.

Erin made a face. "What a way to be introduced to the new neighborhood."

Jane was able to smile a little. "Yes. I wanted change, but not this."

Erin gave Jane a hug, then the young couple proceeded down the driveway, got into their cars, and drove away. After shutting and locking the front door, Jane turned around to gaze down the length of the hallway in the unfamiliar house, quiet now. The beagle, Nick, and her white terrier mix, Nora, plopped down on the floor at her feet. She inhaled the new-carpet smell.

She brushed her hands down her jeans and marched along the hall into the master bedroom. The dogs jumped up and followed her. The movers had assembled the bed, but she needed to find the sheets and blankets. While walking through the bathroom into the master closet for bedding, she realized the shower, a clear glass-enclosed cubicle, was visible from several windows in the bedroom and from the picture window over the tub. There was no bathroom door, other than for the separate toilet space. What had attracted her to the house were the immense windows and open rooms. Now it was a problem, since she didn't plan to install blinds until the next day.

"How am I going to take a shower?" she asked the puppies at her feet. "It's already dark outside, so I guess I can shower without the lights on." The pups thumped their tails on the floor as if in agreement.

After making the bed and locating a pair of pajamas, she turned all the lights off, shed her clothes, and climbed into the shower, letting the warm water stream down her hair and body. The minty-fresh smell of the soap wasn't enough to calm her. What if the killer came back and tried to unlock the door to get inside the house? Would he be frustrated that the key no longer worked?

Her scream rent the air as a beam of light darted through the bathroom window. She dropped the shampoo bottle with a loud thud causing the dogs to bark and jump around. The light ran across her bare body, reflected off the shower door, then the mirror, and blinked out of sight. But it was only the glare through the window from the headlights of a car driving down the street. Did one of the neighbors get a glimpse of her nude? She got out of the shower, dried off, jerked her nightgown over her head, and crawled into bed, wet hair and all.

The next thing she knew, she heard a rattle, maybe the jouncing of a doorknob.

Grabbing her cellphone, she hit the flashlight app and pointed it around the room. Her dogs' eyes glowed in the light. Reminding herself no one could get in the house, that all houses had their own noises and she wasn't used to this one yet, she patted the bed and the dogs sprang up next to her.

Yes. She'd made a terrible mistake moving here. Why, oh why, did she leave her comfortable, familiar home of twenty-plus years? This house wasn't home. There were no memories here, no sense of safety and security, no one but herself in the empty-feeling house, with the unpacked boxes, unadorned walls, and uncovered windows. She shivered under the blankets and blinked as a hot tear ran down her cheek.

Was Ethan murdered and who did it? She needed to know. Otherwise, a "For Sale" sign was going up.

Chapter 2

"Are you kidding me? You found a dead body again?" Cheryl scowled.

"Well, yes." Jane fingered her dark brown hair, sprayed stiff in the shape of "Victory Rolls" in the 1940's pin-up girl style. She brushed a white dog hair off her red and white polka-dot, halter dress and caught a glimpse of her red, peep-toe shoes. The Gourmet Dinner Club group had made plans months ago to meet at the Annual Colorado 1940s World War II Ball at the Boulder Airport on Saturday night. Even though she had moved into the new house only the previous day, she wasn't about to miss this event.

Cheryl set down her glass of wine and yanked her chair closer to the table next to the outdoor bandstand. Similar to the women who took their husbands' jobs at factories during the war, she was outfitted as "Rosie the Riveter" in overalls and a polka-dot blouse, her hair tied up in a scarf. "I suppose you're going to be nosy and snoop around to find out how he died."

"Well, I do want to know. I won't feel safe in my new home with a murderer out there. I called the police twice over the weekend to find out the status, but they wouldn't tell me anything." Jane shook her head, every rigid hair still in place.

Cheryl's husband, Bruce, said, "Of course they didn't. Anyway, how do you know it was murder?" He was wearing saddle shoes, black pants with suspenders, white shirt with the sleeves rolled up his forearms, bow tie, and a fedora on his head. In the true newsboy style, he threw back a short shot of scotch from a flask kept in his pocket.

"It was murder. The police all but said so." Jane tensed her lips into a pout.

"Don't tell me you're going to get wrapped up in a murder investigation again." Doug, another member of the dinner club, dragged a chair over. He was tall with an upright bearing, wearing Navy whites and a sailor cap perched on top of his fiery red hair.

"I can't help it, Doug. Not only am I worried about a murder next door, I'm curious about what's going to happen to the neighborhood. There are several empty lots and half-finished houses and the construction manager's now dead."

"Oh, that's your excuse, is it? Not because you have an overactive imagination?" Cheryl knew her too well.

The band ended the song, "Oh, Lady be Good," and began to play, "Take the 'A' Train." A male dancer lightly lifted his partner in the air over his shoulders and swooshed her back down, her feet sliding along on the floor between his legs. They made it appear easy. But more impressive to Jane was an elderly couple dancing with less energy, but in perfect unison, on the other side of the dance floor.

"So, what've you done to investigate so far?" Bruce was likely interested, since he was a former police officer who now taught criminology classes at the university.

Jane was quick to answer. "It was easy to find the

Valrod Construction Company website on the internet. It even had a page with the history of the business. Harold Valrod formed the company in the 1980s, and he passed away last year. His son Ethan took his place as CEO, and his other son Steven is on the Board of Directors. Ethan's the one who was killed."

Cheryl poked a strand of her chestnut hair under her headscarf. "Some people give their kids names that sound alike."

"These two could've been twins. Steven appeared identical to Ethan in his picture on the website. There was also a photo of a Gina Valrod, but she didn't resemble the two men."

Doug's better half, Olivia, leaned forward at the table. She was wearing a World War II Army Auxiliary Corps nurse's uniform with a matching white cap. "So you have some suspects already? Steven and Gina Valrod. Sibling rivalry maybe? The first murder in history was committed by one brother against another."

"That could be. There was a probate dispute after their old man died." Jane's eyes narrowed, her back stiff and her fingers pinched around the stem of her wine glass.

Cheryl asked, "How do you know that? Never mind. I guess as a paralegal you know how to ferret this stuff out."

"I found a record for Valrod Construction Company on the bankruptcy court website. Anyone can find it because it's public record. Not only a bankruptcy, there's also a dispute concerning Harold's estate. I'm planning to stop at the courthouse because not everything's on-line."

"Bankruptcy? What happens if your builder goes

16

out of business?" Olivia's eyebrows raised in disapproval. Jane gave an elaborate shrug.

Doug smoothed his red mustache as he shook his head. "Jane, keep out of this investigation. Don't forget all the trouble you got into before." Jane scowled at being told what to do. He pointed at the platform on the other side of the dance floor. "Look. Frank Sinatra, Bob Hope, and the Andrews Sisters are taking the stage."

"You mean their impersonators." Bruce glanced at the platform and back.

Olivia flipped her hand in the air. "Tsk. Do you see those students with tattoos all over their arms and shoulders?" Probably from the university, several sported blue hair and facial piercings—definitely not a vintage style. But both young and old were enjoying the ball.

The two dinner club couples took the dance floor, leaving Jane to hold the table. Twice widowed, she usually brought a date, but had recently broken up with her boyfriend. Impatient for her friends to return, she sipped on her crisp white wine in a self-conscious way and watched the crowd.

Once the song ended and Jane's friends regrouped at her side, they all peered into the sky as a Douglas dive bomber flew over the airport followed by a C-47 transport plane. Two parachutists jumped out and floated to the ground with the majestic mountain peaks in the background.

When the ball drew to a close, a General Patton impersonator drove to the bandstand in a World War II jeep to announce that the war had ended. The band struck up a celebratory tune, balloons and confetti fell onto the throng from above like it was New Year's Eve, and the world's longest Congo line formed on the dance floor as thousands of people joined in.

Doug and Olivia kissed in the famous pose of the nurse and sailor.

Once home, Jane hung up her polka-dot dress and put on a robe. She extracted a handful of hairpins from her thick, brown hair. After rubbing the glabellar frown lines on her forehead above her dark eyebrows, she discarded her robe and climbed into a soothing shower to wash out the gummy hairspray. She had installed the blinds that day and could now shower with the lights on. But her shower was brief, because the dogs ran barking out of the bedroom and scratched at the back patio door.

She jerked on a thin robe and clutched it around her. Picking up a heavy flashlight, she skirted the oak sleigh bedstead and went out the bedroom door across to the picture window in the kitchen nook. She turned on the outside light and aimed the flashlight out the window, but saw no movement. "Hush, you two. I'm scared enough in this house without you adding to it." Returning to the bedroom in her bare feet, she climbed into her pajamas and slid under the cozy comforter.

This time, the dinner club group didn't seem as interested in the murder investigation. This time, she was all alone.

****

Driving the unfamiliar route to Limestone Heights after work on Monday, she glanced out the driver's side window at the full glory of the Front Range Mountains. Even from this distance, the mountains' grandeur appeared as perfect as a painting with the robin-egg blue sky above the white-topped peaks. She rolled down her window and let her hair blow in the breeze on this warm fall day. The drive was different and new—out of her old routine—with black-eyed Susans growing along the roadway and smells of baking, yellowing grass. She cruised past two exits with convenient gas stations, but no coffee shops, only a sign for a hay auction.

After she turned into her new subdivision, she made a snap decision to stop at the office at the construction company's trailer near the model homes. Jane opened the door. "Hello. Is anyone here?"

The realtor, a heavily made-up, older woman wearing a dark blue business suit, came around the corner from a back room. "May I help you? Oh, it's you, Mrs. Marsh. Is everything all right in your new home?"

"Hi, Margaret. It's all fine, except for what happened to Ethan the day I moved in."

"The family is saddened by this unfortunate event." Margaret had a grim twist to her mouth.

"Of course. I'm sorry for the family's loss."

"Is there anything I can help you with?" Margaret glanced over Jane's shoulder as a young couple entered. They appeared excited examining the site map on the wall.

"Yes. Do you know what's going to happen now?"

"What do you mean?" Margaret's eyes returned to Jane, then swept down her suit to the high heels on her feet and back up.

Jane lowered her voice. "The Valrod Company has filed for bankruptcy."

The realtor mumbled, "They're in the process of reorganizing, and the family's arranging to have the projects that are underway finished."

"The house next door to mine will be completed soon, then?"

"Certainly." Margaret's expression didn't entertain any doubt.

"I never got the welcome packet or my house keys. I had to have the locks changed."

"Give me the bill for the locks, and I'll make sure a welcome packet is dropped off at your house. It just has the phone numbers for the electric company, the HOA, garbage pick-up and stuff like that. And your warranty information." Margaret turned from Jane to greet her new customers.

"Thanks." Jane left the construction trailer and drove through the subdivision to her street. "For Sale" signs dotted the empty lots between the new homes. Evidently Valrod Construction was trying to sell the unbuilt lots to another builder. This all happened fast— Ethan had been killed only days ago. The developer of her old neighborhood did not have these types of issues.

A man on the front porch of the house to the west of hers shot up from the porch bench and ran into the house when Jane gave him a wave. She rolled her car into the garage, got out, then swept up a newspaper from her front step. Once in the door she tickled Nick and Nora under their chins as they wagged their tails.

She unfolded the paper and laid it on the kitchen counter. About to go to the pantry for dog treats, she did a double take. The newspaper headline read, "TWIN MISSING AFTER BROTHER'S DEATH." Gripping the page, she scanned the article, then slapped the paper down. The realtor at the construction trailer had to have known, but hadn't said a word.

She went into the bedroom and threw off her work clothes in exchange for jeans and a T-shirt. Even though she had sampled only one, thin slice of the custardy flan, she fed the leftovers to the garbage disposal, then washed Tara's platter. The dogs gobbled their treats as she rummaged in her pantry for chocolate baking squares, then tied a big apron around her waist. She melted the chocolate and added butter, flour, sugar, and vanilla to mix up a scratch batch of brownies. With the pan in the oven, she ate a granola bar and a few cubes of cheese as she tidied the kitchen. Then, when the brownies were done, she cut them up and arranged them on Tara's platter.

And with that, she bolted over to her neighbors' house and knocked on the door. Tara answered straight away.

"Thanks so much for the flan. It was wonderful and I'd like the recipe." Jane handed the platter of brownies to Tara.

"You're welcome." Tara's eyes widened when she touched the plate. "They're still warm."

"Just out of the oven. I couldn't return your plate empty." Jane gave her a smile.

Tara deposited the plate on the hall table and joined Jane outside. The two women sank into the Adirondack chairs on the front porch and Jane cleared her throat. "Did you read in the paper that Steven Valrod is missing? I didn't know he and Ethan were twins."

The skin on Tara's face blanched as she shook her head from side to side. "I don't get the paper. What'd it say?"

"Just that his wife hasn't seen him since Friday morning and the police want to question him." Jane leaned forward, elbows on knees.

Tara's voice shook. "What do you think it means?"

"He's been gone three days, no, four. Friday, Saturday, Sunday, and now today. It can mean only one thing. He killed his brother and ran away. He's probably in Mexico by now." Jane leaned back in her seat and tapped her index finger on her chin.

"Steven kill Ethan?" Tara had a doubtful look on her face.

"What do you think? You knew them better than I did, right?"

"I know there was quite a rivalry between the brothers."

"Was it serious?"

Tara's fingers twisted a lock of her long, blonde hair around. "I didn't believe it was…until now. Yet it could explain everything."

"Yes, it could. I always thought twins had a special bond, but I suppose that's not true in every case. What do you know about Steven's wife, Gina? The paper didn't say much about her." Jane knitted her eyebrows.

"I heard she plays a big role in the company, but I don't know what she does. She seems the bossy type."

"The website has Gina on the Board of Directors. Ethan was married, too, according to the newspaper."

"Yes. His wife is, I mean, was Kimber." Tara fixed her eyes on Jane. "What website?"

"The construction company site. And I thought Ethan was the construction manager, but the website said he was the CEO."

"Ethan was the manager when his dad was alive, and that's what everyone still called him. Why are you so curious about all of this?" Tara yanked her fingers through her hair, and tossed a strand over her shoulder.

"It's a mystery, literally on our doorstep. Aren't you curious?"

"Not so much." Tara pursed her lips.

Jane clutched the armrest of the Adirondack chair. "Maybe I'm jumping to the conclusion that Steven killed his brother and ran off to Mexico. Maybe Steven was so distraught by the death of his twin that he ran away to deal with his loss in private. Or maybe Steven was the intended target. They resemble each other, you know. So, someone kills Ethan, Steven gets scared and runs away to hide."

Tara didn't say anything for a few moments, then shook her head. "I'm back to thinking it was an accident. Ethan fell in, broke his neck, and died."

"But how did Ethan's body come to be buried under the dirt?" Jane searched Tara's face, but her neighbor looked down at her hands and shrugged. Jane pressed, "And how do you explain Steven's disappearance?"

"Like you said, he ran away." Tara blinked her eyes several times as she gazed up past Jane to the crime scene tape between their houses. She seemed so young, probably the same age as Jane's two daughters-in-law.

Jane gave her neighbor a light pat on the shoulder. "Don't worry. I'm going to find out who killed Ethan, and then we can both sleep soundly in our beds at night."

"Please don't stir up trouble. This is a nice, safe neighborhood and no one was murdered here. It was an accident." In spite of her words, Tara had an uncertain gleam in her eye.

"I hope you're right." Jane chewed on her lips for a moment, then stood. "Thanks again for the flan. I ate a slice for breakfast the day after I moved in."

"Oh no. Next time I should bring muffins to a new neighbor. That'd be more practical."

"It was delicious with coffee, and I appreciated it." Jane said goodbye and trotted the few steps back to her own house as a curtain twitched in the window across the street. After she unlocked the door and stepped inside, and even though she was only gone a few minutes, she stooped low to welcoming kisses from her puppies—licks up and down her cheeks.

****

She rode the shuttle bus to the federal courthouse on her lunch break the next day. It took the entire hour to get through the bankruptcy file. At the small work table, she thumbed past many of the pages, but examined the bankruptcy petition in detail. The twins' father Harold did not have a living spouse at the time of his death. Gina Valrod, Steven's wife, was listed as a separate beneficiary under the will, but not Ethan's wife, Kimber. The bankruptcy schedule described a loss to the company of several hundred thousand dollars as "theft" without any details.

She made copies of some of the records, including probate pleadings attached as exhibits to one of the motions, then shoved the copies into her briefcase.

After returning to her office, she dialed the police and left yet a third message. Three strikes and you're out. If the police didn't return her call, she'd give herself the green light to investigate on her own.

At noon the next day, Jane met her dinner club buddy. Cheryl always came up with fun plans for their lunch hour. She was the one who told Jane the City of Denver offered B-Cycle passes for riding the red city bicycles around downtown. It was like a mini-vacation to meet with Cheryl for a bike ride—a refreshing respite from work.

They pedaled their way down to the Cherry Creek bike path below street level, out of the wind. Wearing a skort and ballet flats, Cheryl appeared urbanite on her bike, but Jane had only changed from her work clothes into a T-shirt, yoga pants, and tennis shoes. Stopping to rest at the bike kiosk at the Cherry Creek Mall, they refreshed themselves with a drink from their water bottles.

"Cheryl, the construction manager's brother is missing now."

"Tell me all about it."

Her friend was a good listener, so Jane explained what she'd found out from the bankruptcy file as they sat side-by-side on a park bench next to the trail.

Cheryl offered another possibility. "What if Steven shoved his brother during a scuffle, and Ethan fell by accident, hitting his head on that tractor bucket?"

"But why try to cover up the body if it was an accident?" Jane chewed on a fingernail until Cheryl slapped her hand down. "The one neighbor I've talked to, Tara, knows a lot about the Valrods, but she seems young and scared. The realtor is tight-lipped and loyal to the family. I'll need to ask around the neighborhood, I guess. Maybe I can rally a group of concerned citizens."

"Why do you need to do anything, Jane?"

"I won't feel settled in the new house until the murderer is caught."

"Tell me again why you moved to Limestone Heights." Cheryl gave Jane a level gaze. "I wasn't surprised when you sold your house, but I was when you moved all the way out to the country."

Jane answered in a strangled voice. "I wanted to live in an entirely fresh, new place, one with no memories, nothing familiar." The empty nest syndrome was a big factor. First her oldest, Luke, had joined the Army after graduating from college, then he and Caleb had both gotten married within a year of each other. And she wanted freedom from the memories of Craig and Hugh, her late husbands who both died in tragically similar manners, causing her to be the subject of a police investigation. Since she was exonerated, it was time to put all that behind her.

"Well, now you're moved in, you need to make the best of it. Don't let the murder keep you from enjoying your new life." There was empathy in Cheryl's voice.

"You're right. I can't forget how excited I was for a new home that reflects just me, starting completely over." Jane turned her lips up in a grin. "You know the old adage, 'be careful what you wish for.' Well, I got the new house I wanted, but now I'm missing my old home."

Cheryl had a sad smile on her face. She glanced down at her hands, folded together, fingers interlaced in a tight grasp. She lifted them up to her chin, steepled her fingers, and touched her lips as if in prayer.

"What's the matter?" Jane's grin faded as a chill of foreboding washed over her.

"I have some news I need to tell you, but I've been dreading it."

Chapter 3

Jane grasped her friend's arm as her heart skipped a beat. "What's wrong?"

Still staring down, Cheryl took a deep breath. "Bruce and I are moving to Portland."

"What?" Jane gripped Cheryl's arm tighter. Her breath left her body, and she couldn't seem to take another.

"Bruce got a job offer he couldn't pass up. Head of the Department of Criminology at the university." Cheryl lifted her head, her chin jutting upward in a proud way, but did not look Jane in the eye.

"I didn't know he wanted a new job."

"He's always looking. It's quite a big salary increase."

"I guess I should say congratulations, but I'm going to miss you so much, Cheryl. When are you moving?" She sat back and folded her arms across her chest. How would she survive her lunch hours without her downtown buddy? And what would happen to the dinner club group?

"Bruce's job starts in two weeks."

"That soon." Jane's stomach dropped even farther.

"We'll be back in Denver all the time to see everyone. Since Megan's going to college at the university in Boulder, we'll be visiting quite a bit, I promise. And I think we're going to love Portland."

Cheryl's face lit up.

Jane willed her lips into a smile. "Of course you will. I have moving boxes you can use, and I'll help you pack, too."

"Thanks." Cheryl took a long sip from her water bottle. "I'm so relieved you feel that way. Megan's pretty bummed about it."

"It's natural for her to be upset about her parents moving so far away. What about your job?"

"It won't be easy to leave the museum. There aren't many like it." A hint of regret crossed Cheryl's face, then disappeared. "Anyway, I'm going to send an email to the group reminding them dinner club is at my house this weekend. It'll be our last time to host and I have a surprise in store."

"Another surprise?" Jane's eyebrows shot up. "I don't know if I can handle any more surprises. What is it?"

All traces of sadness gone, Cheryl's eyes danced. "Don't worry. It's just a little event I have planned for our dinner party. And on another note, can you meet me over lunch hour on Friday? There's an Open House at a loft downtown, and I've made an appointment to view it. I'd love for you to go with me."

Jane stopped raising her water bottle half way to her lips. "Why do you want to see a loft in Denver?"

"I want to compare it to what's available in Portland. We want to buy a loft there, if we can."

"Okay, I'm in. Just tell me where to meet." Jane took a swig, then put her water bottle in the basket on her bike. If she moved away from Limestone Heights, maybe she'd consider moving to a loft.

"I'll email you." Cheryl clambered onto her bike,

so Jane climbed on hers, too.

They steered their bicycles toward town, coasted under the overpasses, then pedaled hard up the steep hill to Speer Boulevard near the Denver Country Club. When they reached one of the kiosks in town, they clicked their bikes back into place, said goodbye and parted.

Jane tried to think happy thoughts and concentrate on work, but her mind returned again and again to her best friend's impending move, and that she, herself, had moved to a new town, leaving everything familiar behind. She wanted to turn the clock back to when she first joined the dinner club and she'd felt secure and rooted and that she belonged. Everything seemed to be changing too fast.

****

That night after returning home from work, she knocked on Tara's door. "Hi. Thought I'd just stop by to say hello, see how you're doing."

"I'm glad you did. How'd you like to go for a walk?" Tara sailed out her front door into the brisk, fall evening.

"I'd love, love, love that. I was just planning to unpack the boxes in my closet, but I can finish that later." Or maybe not at all, if the killer wasn't caught. But she kept that thought to herself.

Tara sounded pleased. "Great. The walking path to the pool and clubhouse leads through the woods to a large pond."

"I didn't know there was a pond back there. Let's go."

Tara walked faster than Jane's normal stride. This was just what she needed—a challenge and opportunity to increase her tempo for a more strenuous workout—while exploring the new neighborhood. Tara led her past the clubhouse, then east through the woods to a gravel track encircling a wide, clear pond edged with bursting cattails, purple cone flowers, and pink wild roses, with a faint, sweet scent in the air.

"Stop here and look west." Tara pointed through the woods. Jane spun around toward a view of Long's Peak in the distance rising up from the tops of the trees in the foreground. Its sharp, pointed top poked through a stream of white, wispy clouds; this was going to become her favorite spot.

They continued on the path looping a little over a mile around the pond. The two women stepped over black grasshoppers that jumped and flew, their wings making a rattling sound and opening to reveal a bright red color. Butterflies' soft white wings flickered in a gentle way among the reeds. On the far side of the pond, a short dock projected over the water, with two young boys fishing from the end of the pier.

Jane slapped at a mosquito. "My boys would've loved coming here to fish. What an idyllic spot."

"How old are your kids?"

"They're both grown and married."

Tara flicked a long strand of her hair behind her shoulder. "It's wonderful you've finished raising a family. Justin and I've been married almost three years. I want kids, but Justin doesn't, at least not yet. He's still a kid himself. He hangs out with his friends every weekend. They ride their bikes all day, and that's all he's interested in."

"Why not ride with him? I love bike riding. I even ride on my lunch hour downtown." Jane explained about the B-cycle passes.

"But Justin doesn't do that kind of riding. He and his friends are extremists, training for bike races all year long. It's nothing for them to ride fifty miles or more in a day. I could never keep up. And besides, he wants to go with his friends, not with me." Tara clamped her lips shut in a pout.

The path narrowed. Her new friend took the lead with Jane walking behind. Mud spread between the cattails thick along the edge of the water to their left, and low, thorn bushes crowded the path on their right. Fall-fading, yellow, black-eyed Susans dotted the field on the far side of the pond.

Jane spoke loud enough for Tara to hear, several paces in front. "It's all right for your husband to have his own interests, you know. You need to develop some friends of your own. And a hobby too." The dinner club group had helped her with the loneliness of widowhood and the empty nest, combined.

"Yeah, well, Justin doesn't care what I do."

Was Tara's marriage in trouble? No wonder she appeared as frightened as an orphan at a graveside. Jane rubbed her brow. "You and I can walk as often as you like while Justin's busy. What about this idea? There might be more women in this neighborhood who'd like to walk. We could start a walking group."

Tara appeared to brighten. "There's an HOA meeting tomorrow night. Let's go and ask around."

"Great idea." This would be an opportunity for Jane to get to know other people in this new town, too.

They finished walking the loop around the pond, paused for a last glimpse at Long's Peak, and returned to the clubhouse by the short path through the woods.

Jane hesitated a moment. "I wanted to ask you if others in the neighborhood knew Ethan Valrod well, or any of the Valrods."

"Everyone knew them. Why?"

After explaining what she'd learned at the bankruptcy court about missing company funds, Jane said, "I'd like to find out more about the Valrods' company and how the theft ties in with the murder."

Tara stopped short. "You keep saying it's murder, but how can you be so sure? Is everyone convinced that's what happened?" She turned white and put her hand out toward Jane.

"Are you all right? Let's sit down." Jane helped her to a bench surrounded by purple and yellow pansies near the clubhouse parking lot. "What's the matter?"

"I guess it just freaks me out because it happened right next door. I was probably home at the time, you know?" Tara took a deep breath. "I'm all right now, let's keep walking." They got up and trudged the few short blocks from the clubhouse to Tara's porch. She sat down on one of the Adirondack chairs, folded her hands in her lap, and said, "I did see something on the day Ethan died."

"What? Tell me!" Jane plopped into the chair next to Tara's.

"I was at the front window and saw a black Lexus drive past. It had the license plate 'VALROD3.' As I told the police, I couldn't tell who was driving, but it had to be one of the family. Ethan drove a black Lexus with the license plate 'VALROD2.'"

"Why didn't you say anything before? It could've been his twin Steven...or it could've been Gina or Kimber driving if Steven had the VALROD1 plate."

Jane sat up straight and drummed her fingers on the arm of the Adirondack chair.

"I'll bet it was Kimber."

"I don't suppose it'd be odd for one of the Valrods to be in the area, but still, it puts them right on this street on the day of the murder." Her fingers stopped drumming and flew to her mouth. "I'll have to ask around at the HOA meeting to see if anyone else saw anything."

"The meetings at the clubhouse so we can walk over."

Justin poked his head out the door. "Hello, Mrs. Marsh."

"It's Jane. How are you?"

"Good. Doing good."

Tara stood. "I need to get busy making dinner."

"I need to get going too. Enjoy your evening and I'll see you tomorrow, Tara." She descended the porch steps, but glanced over her shoulder.

Justin stared hard at Jane, as if wanting to say more, but holding back.

Chapter 4

Pacing back and forth at the front window, Jane was impatient for Tara to come by for the HOA meeting.

The newspaper was open on the entryway table. She must've left it out and just didn't remember. The twins' photographs peered at her from the front page— they were the same pictures from the company website. The article didn't give much information that was new, just their ages of thirty-six and that neither of the Valrod brothers had any children. She re-folded the paper and put it in the desk drawer in her office. Justin arrived with Tara, and the three of them made rapid strides to the clubhouse. "Why in the world is the parking lot so full?" Jane glanced up and down the two rows of cars in the tiny lot. "Why not walk over?"

"The neighborhood includes houses a couple miles away." Justin held the clubhouse door open, but Tara stopped to gawk at something. Jane stared past her friends to where someone had parked a black Lexus with the license plate "*VALROD3*" under a shade tree.

"We're going to find out who that car belongs to because the owners at the HOA meeting. Let's go in." Jane bounced on her heels, but Tara was pale and trembling. "What's the matter?"

"I'm scared, I guess." Tara's eyes were big.

"I'm here, don't worry." Justin took his wife's arm.

Tara held on as they entered the clubhouse. The roasting smell of coffee greeted Jane's nose.

They sat next to each other on folding chairs in the community room. Merrilee Eichenthal, the HOA president, discussed budgets, plans to purchase new items needed for the pool, and whether to hire a different property management company. The president was an accountant in her work life and appeared to be suited to the position, but she droned on about line items and balances. Jane stopped listening and checked out her neighbors. She drew her breath in when she saw a police officer standing at the door.

Her attention returned to the meeting when Justin raised his hand. "I'd like to know when a bike path will connect our neighborhood to the Platte River Trail."

A tall, brunette, thirty-something woman stood up. "That's not going to happen." Her face was classical, with high cheekbones and wide eyes, but the eyes were steely.

Tara nudged Jane. "That's Gina Valrod."

"I know. I recognize her from her picture on the webpage."

Gina crossed her arms over her chest. "It would be cost prohibitive and it's not in the plans for the community."

Justin's nostrils flared. "How can you just veto my idea? Why can't we discuss it?"

"Valrod Construction Company is still funding the HOA. As the developer's representative, I'm saying no."

"We'll see about that!" Justin glared around the room, but no one appeared to take his side. Tara squeezed her eyes so tight they disappeared in a straight line with her lashes sticking straight out.

Merrilee said, "Let's everyone enjoy the refreshments. The date of the next HOA meeting will be posted online." The homeowners rose from their chairs to head over to the coffee pots, teakettles, and cookies laid out on a jumbo-sized folding table at the side of the room.

Jane peeked back toward the door, but the officer had left. "I wonder why the police were here. Just observing, I suppose. And no one mentioned Ethan's death. Isn't that weird?"

Tara popped one shoulder up and let it fall back down. "I'm glad no one brought it up."

They separated at the refreshments table as Tara greeted a young mother holding an infant and Justin joined a group of men at the back of the room.

Jane strolled over to Merrilee to introduce herself. "I just moved into the neighborhood, actually on the day Ethan was found dead. Why wasn't anything said about him or his brother at the meeting tonight?" She gave Merrilee a probing gaze.

Merrilee glided close to Jane. "I'm not sure everyone knows about Ethan's death. But the police were here."

"Yes. I noticed that, too. How could anyone not know about his death?"

"Not everyone reads the paper or talks to their neighbors."

Jane crossed her arms and tucked her hands under her elbows. "Did you know the Valrod twins very well?"

"Certainly."

"Who do you think killed him? I mean, did Ethan

have any enemies?" Jane used the same line as the police.

Merrilee snickered under her breath. "Ethan was having an affair with someone in the neighborhood. Whoever it was, her husband put up a banner at the entry to the subdivision early one morning before anyone was awake. It said, 'Ethan stay away from my wife.'" She inched closer.

"Really? How long ago did that happen?" Jane clutched the edge of the refreshments table.

"It was just, let's see, four months ago, I think." Merrilee's eyes popped as she focused on something over Jane's shoulder. "That's Kimber, Ethan's wife. I knew Gina wouldn't miss a meeting, but I'm surprised to see Kimber."

Jane turned around. A thin woman with perfect makeup and expensively highlighted hair stood alone, sipping from a paper cup. For someone so young, her face bore thin lines around her eyes and mouth, like smoker's wrinkles. Jane raked her eyes up and down Kimber, then glanced away so she wouldn't appear to be rude.

Merrilee continued, "She was his current wife. He was married once before."

"You don't say?" Jane's eyes darted back to Kimber. "Does she drive a Lexus with the license plate '*VALROD3*?'"

"Yes. And I saw her Lexus in our neighborhood on the day Ethan was killed."

"You saw her car?" This time it was Jane who took a step closer. She held her breath waiting for the answer.

"That's right. It's pretty distinctive with those

plates. I couldn't tell if she was the one in the driver's seat, but it was definitely her car. You know, the Valrods own a ranch close to here, on the other side of the county road north of the subdivision."

"She lives nearby then." Jane rubbed her chin. So…there were two witnesses who placed Kimber's car on the street when Ethan was killed.

Another neighbor approached Merrilee with a question, so Jane slipped over to the refreshments table where Kimber Valrod stood alone.

"Hello, my name's Jane Marsh. I'm new to the neighborhood." She extended her hand.

Kimber gave it a brief shake. "Nice to meet you."

"Do you live in the neighborhood, too?" Jane knew the answer, but wanted to open the conversation.

"No. I'm here as a representative of the developer along with Gina."

Jane's eyes took in the black-turning-to-yellow bruises discoloring the inside of Kimber's right arm. "What happened?"

Her face clouded. "I was just heading out. See you next time." She put her paper cup on the table instead of throwing it in the trash can and walked out the door. Jane stood at the entryway as Kimber climbed into her Lexus with the license plate, "*VALROD3*."

"What were you talking to her about?" Tara appeared at Jane's side.

"I only introduced myself. I didn't get a chance to ask her anything. And look. It is Kimber who drives that Lexus."

They watched out the door as Kimber spun out of the parking lot, then they turned back to the room. Several men wearing cowboy hats and boots stacked folding chairs in a closet and others carried the industrial-sized coffee urns into the kitchen. Jane asked, "Should we offer to help clean up?"

"There's a committee for that. You can volunteer if you want. Go to the HOA website for the list of openings for committee members."

Justin joined them. "Are you two ready to leave?"

"I am." Tara gripped his arm, and he ushered her out the door with Jane on their heels.

She couldn't contain her excitement. As soon as they were away from the parking lot, she said, "Kimber had bruises all up and down her right arm—"

"She did? That's interesting." Tara met Jane's eye.

"Do you think she killed Ethan? Maybe they were in a shoving match and Ethan fell to his death," Justin suggested.

"That's a definite possibility, but one that the police must've already considered. If she did it, then what happened to Steven?" Jane asked.

"I can't imagine." Tara studied her feet as they walked along the pavement.

"It has something to do with the missing company funds. It's all related." Jane nodded to herself, her shoulders back and chin high. "But there's more."

"Wha-what else?" Tara's hand flew to her chest.

"Ethan had been married before Kimber. And get this, the HOA president, Merrilee, told me that Ethan had been having an affair with one of the women in the neighborhood."

Justin's voice came out gruff. "A man shouldn't mess with another man's wife."

Jane agreed. "That's motive. Have either of you heard any gossip around the neighborhood about that?"

Both Justin and Tara shook their heads in the negative.

Jane glanced at Justin. "Did you come to the HOA meeting to ask about bike paths?"

"No. I came because of Ethan's body being found next door, but I remembered I wanted to ask about bike paths, so I did."

Tara said, "We forgot to suggest a ladies' walking group."

"Oh, darn it. You're right." Jane snapped her fingers. They turned the corner a few steps from Tara's and Justin's house.

"We can post it on the HOA website because there's a place to announce upcoming events. We should post it anyway since the idea will get out to more people that way. Come inside and we can do it now." Tara unlocked her front door.

Justin held the door as the two women entered, then he plopped in front of the television. Tara showed Jane to her office and logged into her computer. "I can't meet this Saturday, and that's only two days from now anyway, probably not enough time to get the word out. How about meeting the Saturday after?"

"That'll work." Jane watched over her friend's shoulder as she entered the date and time for the neighborhood walk on the webpage. "Thanks for posting this and for going to the meeting with me."

Tara clicked out of the website, then turned off her laptop. "I'm looking forward to walking with a group." She gave Jane an encouraging smile.

They said their goodbyes, then Jane left to return to her own house.

She'd met both of the Valrod wives at the meeting.

Gina appeared in control of things, but Kimber seemed more vulnerable, especially with those bruises. There were plenty of motives for Ethan's murder—missing money, battling brothers, and suspicious spouses. She found a legal pad in her desk and scribbled some notes.

****

Jane joined Cheryl during lunch hour on Friday at Larimer Street on the other side of Broadway in RiNo—the River North Art District. The real estate agent greeted them at the door of the loft. Glasses of champagne and a dish of fresh strawberries sat on the kitchen counter, and they both took samples before separating to explore the rooms.

Smiling at Jane after they met in the kitchen, Cheryl said, "I love this industrial style. Did you like the solid brick walls with exposed beams and HVAC systems along the ceiling? And the bathroom. What'd you think of the glass bowls sunk into the granite countertop?"

"Loved it. I like this kitchen, too, with all the windows and the pendant lighting. Very bright and full of light. Is this what you want in Portland?" Jane sipped the sparkling wine, then put the glass back down. She needed to stay awake during the afternoon at work and not get sleepy from the wine.

"I'd love to find something just like this." Cheryl's delighted smile was contagious.

"You will. I'll have to come see it once you do."

After leaving, as they strolled together toward downtown, Jane tapped Cheryl on the arm. "That real estate agent spent a half-hour with us. Is that fair if you don't intend to buy?"

"Agents expect to get some 'looky-lous,' and

besides, I'm going to talk to Bruce about using her to sell our house. I asked, and she sells in the suburbs, too, not just downtown."

Jane had asked the realtor that same question and had tucked her business card into her pocket. "She seemed to do a good job...the strawberries and everything."

They glanced both ways at the corner of Park and 20th before crossing the busy intersection. As they meandered along Larimer Street, they came to a shop selling motor scooters. Jane stopped to admire the vintage scooters small enough to fit in the store front window. "If you and Bruce get a place in downtown Portland, you could buy two of these to commute to work."

Cheryl's eyes held a far-off gaze. "I'll ride a scooter to work every day. I'll wear a scarf around my neck, and it'll billow out behind me as I ride."

"Wear sunglasses. Big ones. I like the turquoise-colored scooter."

"I like the mint green."

They turned away from the window to walk toward the Sixteenth Street Pedestrian Mall. Cheryl asked, "Have you heard about Denver's newest commuting program called 'Car2Go?' For a small charge per minute you can drive a little Smart Car around the metro area. No cost for gas and free parking. You use a smart phone app to find one and unlock it."

"No, I haven't heard about it. But I've wondered about those tiny cars parked all over downtown."

"It's a great way to commute. Thanks for going with me. See you later." Cheryl hopped onto the Sixteenth Street Mall shuttle bus to head back to the museum where she worked. Jane waved as the bus veered away from the curb, then walked with slow steps back to her own office.

It had been fun to visit the loft, but a sinking feeling traveled from her heart to her stomach and formed a knot there. Cheryl knew the latest trends and all about what was happening in the city. Jane would have to figure this stuff out for herself from now on. She wished she'd known before moving to Limestone Heights there was a possibility the Breewoods would move, too. How long would she need to live in Limestone Heights before she could sell without a loss of equity? Likely, a "For Sale" sign would go up sooner rather than later.

Once back at her desk, she called her friend and fellow dinner club member, Olivia Ladner, and they chatted for a few minutes about the upcoming dinner party at the Breewoods. Jane didn't mention Cheryl's announcement. That was Cheryl's news, not hers, to tell. After catching up on things, Jane asked, "Can I speak to Doug?" Like Cheryl's husband Bruce, Olivia's husband, too, had been a police officer. He was now an executive vice-president in charge of corporate security at a large firm in Denver.

"Sure." Olivia handed the phone to her husband.

Jane recounted the few facts she knew about the crime scene, Ethan's death, and his missing twin. He waited until she wound down to say, "Can't you stay away from the investigation?"

"I just have a few questions. If someone accidently shoved Ethan into the foundation pit and he died, is that still considered murder?"

She could hear his deep sigh through the

connection. "It might be manslaughter, and there are different degrees depending on whether it was unintentional or premeditated. And then, some cases of involuntary manslaughter may still involve criminal liability."

"If it wasn't intentional, how could it be a crime?"

"If a person forced him over the edge, knowing there was a possibility he could die from the fall, but shoved him anyway, well, that could be manslaughter."

Jane doodled on her legal pad. "His body was partly covered in dirt and there was a tractor parked nearby. Maybe the killer used the tractor to try to cover him up. There was blood on the tractor bucket."

"That sure makes it appear intentional. Plus, if the person who knocked him into the pit didn't stick around to call 9-1-1, that looks bad."

"Thanks, Doug. It's helpful to talk about the murder with a professional."

"You need to stay out of the investigation and let the police do their job. I really mean it, Jane."

She'd heard that before. Her silence extended over a few moments.

Doug's voice sounded grim. "Jane, you don't need to investigate. You can't be falsely accused this time."

Chapter 5

On the drive home that day after work, Jane motored along the county road north of her subdivision for a glimpse of the Valrods' ranch. On both sides of the entry gate were tall wood posts joined together at the top by a horizontal pole spanning the width of the road. A sign dangled from the high beam, "Valrod Ranch." The gate was closed, so she cruised to a stop at a pull-off in the next bend and drummed the steering wheel with her fingers, then turned back onto the road for home.

After walking in the door, she gave the dogs tummy rubs, with Nora wagging her whole tail end. She changed into jogging clothes, tied her feet into running shoes, and locked up, pocketing her keys. She jogged north of the community center and pool to the county road leading to the Valrods' ranch. She ducked under a section of fence and continued jogging along the farmer's canal with giant, twisted cottonwood trees a hundred feet high and as far around as she was tall, populated with nervous squirrels and chirping red-winged blackbirds. The dead leaves rustled under her feet and gave off a loamy scent. Through the trees she could see the sprawling ranch house and several other homes dotting the flat landscape, the tall grasses dry and yellow away from a water source. Beyond that, a fenced field held horses nosing the ground.

The homes had spectacular, unblocked mountain views, and one had a three-stall garage, with a wide-open door revealing a Lexus parked inside. Jane stopped to catch her breath. She squatted near the ground, breathing hard, but as long as she dared linger, no one came out of any of the houses and nothing appeared to be happening.

Slouching as she wandered back along the trail for the long walk home, she heard a whistling sound and male laughter. She hopped off the trail into the underbrush as two bicycle riders whooshed past with a shout, "On your left!" One of the men was lean with a shaved head.

She called out, "Justin," but he was already out of sight. There must be a gate leading to the path for the riders to have access, and she made a mental note to ask Justin about it.

****

On Saturday night, she steered her car along the Breewoods' street. She'd wanted a date for the event, but her last boyfriend, Dale Capricorn, was too wrapped up in his ex-wife, so they'd broken up. She had to come on her own without a date, as she'd done all summer. In Cheryl's driveway, someone had parked a large van with lettering on its side, "Gourmet Cooking Classes in Your Home." So this was the surprise. Of course, Cheryl would think up something fun like this.

The Ladners leaned against the kitchen counter talking with the Breewoods. At the stove stood a chef wearing a white toque on his head, a white double-breasted jacket, and a white apron tied loosely around his hips over checkered pants. Jane set her wine contribution on the counter next to an open bottle surrounded by full glasses.

"Bruce knows Everett from college." Cheryl put her hand on Everett's elbow. "He's going to teach us how to prepare fish stuffed in a puff pastry, garlic asparagus with lime, and potatoes au gratin."

"And we're having flan for dessert." Bruce handed Jane one of the glasses of wine.

"Flan? What's up with flan? It must be popular." Jane scratched her head.

"Flan's featured in this month's restaurateur magazine." Everett had small, close-set, blue eyes and a strong, square jaw. The group gathered around as he distributed miniature cutting boards and paring knives. "First, we cut up the garlic and onions."

With the knives in their hands flying up and down, the group did as instructed.

He continued giving directions. "Roll the deboned pieces of halibut in the spices, garlic and onions, then wrap the puff pastry around the fish. I made the pastry from scratch in advance, but if you don't want to do that, you can purchase it ready-made at the supermarket." His long fingers enveloped the fish with the thin dough, and they followed his example. After each of them assembled their own creations, the chef slid the halibut into the oven on cookie sheets. He stirred a creamy sauce in a pan on the stovetop to drizzle over the fish once it was done broiling.

Jane wanted to wash her hands, which smelled strongly of garlic. Since it was crowded around the kitchen sink, she walked down the hall to the powder room. Peeking into the dining room and then the living room, she thought this might be the last time she'd be at Cheryl's house, which was so full of good memories—

all the dinner club events and especially the Christmas parties. She lingered over the living room for a last glimpse of the modern art, the 1960's record player console, and the abstract sculpture.

In the powder room was a lovely bar of new soap near the sink, but it turned her hands black as she rubbed the soap between her palms. The more she rubbed, the blacker her hands became. Should she use the nice towel hanging on the rack? She flicked out her fingers several times to fling the water off, then when they were mostly dry, she walked back down the hall to the kitchen and asked Cheryl for a paper towel.

"What happened to you?" Cheryl swiveled from Jane to her husband. "Bruce, did you put out that trick soap I asked you not to?"

Bruce laughed. "Gotcha!"

Olivia explained to the chef who appeared confused, "Someone usually pulls a prank at our dinners. One time someone left a fake burning cigarette on a table top."

"Oh, that's just cruel." Everett chuckled.

Cheryl pointed toward the modern table in her dining room. "You must sit down and eat with us, Everett. Look, we set a plate for you."

But he resisted the invitation. "No. It's your meal to enjoy. I'm only here for the cooking lesson—"

"You're a friend, too, not just the chef for the night." Bruce jabbed Everett in the arm.

The extra place setting was next to Jane. She patted the empty seat. "Why not join us?" He took his chef's hat off, and wavy, light brown hair tumbled down to his shoulders. Then he removed his apron and maneuvered his long legs under the table to sit next to Jane. They all held hands for the blessing. When Jane's small hand was consumed in Everett's large one, tingles ran up her arm.

Everyone released hands. Jane teased, "Did you all wash your hands before supper?" They each groaned.

"Well," began Bruce, "the cooking lesson isn't the surprise. Or, at least it's not the only surprise." Everyone turned toward Bruce, who continued, "I've taken a job at the university in Portland." Neither Olivia nor Doug said anything for a few moments as Jane surveyed their stunned faces.

"Why Portland?" Olivia put her fork down.

"It's a great opportunity. We're flying out tomorrow to view houses in the city. We want to live downtown so we can walk to work. We have an appointment with a realtor on Monday morning, then we're flying back to Denver on the red eye Monday night…"

"Congratulations!" Doug hoisted his glass of wine. "A toast to your new endeavor."

They all bumped glasses and said, "Hear, hear." Cheryl and Bruce beamed at each other.

Olivia took a sip, then set her glass on the table. "I can't imagine living anywhere but in Colorado. I was born here." She rotated her neck and preened like a cat. "I even have a Colorado 'pioneer' license plate for my car."

"I'm thinking of getting an 'Adopt a Shelter Pet' designer plate." Jane's nose twitched as she breathed in the mouth-watering smell of the broiled fish, then took a bite.

"When do you start your new job?" Everett asked Bruce.

"In ten days."

"We'll have to find another couple for the dinner club group." Olivia squinted at Jane. "Several couples have inquired about membership over the past couple of months. I'll contact one of them."

Everett plucked a piece of fish off Jane's plate and popped it in his mouth. Her jaw dropped and her fork clattered to her plate with a loud crash, then fell to the floor. "Oops. Sorry." She hid her red cheeks by ducking under the table.

"Here, let me get you a clean fork." Cheryl jumped up.

"Are you kidding? Ten second rule. I'm fine." She jolted back up and glanced around, but it didn't appear anyone else noticed what Everett had done. She peered sideways at him, and saw him staring at her with a grin. Was he flirting with her? She had no idea. If he tried it again, she'd stab his hand with her fork. To avoid the awkward moment, she said to the group, "I haven't even had the chance to have everyone over to my new house."

Doug smoothed down his mustache. "I'm looking forward to seeing it."

Olivia dabbed a napkin to her lips. "Have you found out anything more about the dead guy? And what's going to happen to your neighborhood?"

"What's this?" asked Everett, so Jane gave him a brief explanation, then told the group about the missing twin, as they listened with wide eyes. "Doug, I meant to ask you the other day on the phone, can you use your connections to find out what the police are doing?"

"If I do, then promise you won't investigate on your own. Do you promise?"

"I swear I won't interfere with the police." Her simple questions couldn't possibly interfere with anything the police were doing.

"Okay, then. I know the DA in your county, and I'll give him a call."

"Wonderful." It was a piece of good luck he knew the district attorney and had accepted her promise not to interfere. She could continue to investigate as long as she didn't get in the way of the police.

"How come you didn't ask me to check my police contacts?" Bruce had a frown on his face.

"Gosh, I didn't think you'd have time with your move and everything, but feel free. I'd love that." Jane knitted her eyebrows in puzzlement, since he'd never helped before, preferring to put his police experience behind him.

After they finished the meal and ate the delicious flan for dessert, they lavished compliments on the chef, then stole outside to sit around the fire pit and enjoy the fall evening, as was the club's usual routine. But the night was flat and the conversation lagged. The Ladners must also be thinking how the club would feel the Breewoods' absence.

When the party broke up, Everett walked out the door with Jane and leaned against her car. "That's too bad your friends are moving away."

She couldn't decide if he was irritatingly attractive or attractively irritating. "Yes. I'll miss Cheryl."

"So, are you interested in cooking?" He crossed his arms, but raised his right hand to stroke his chin as he relaxed against her car. Lounging as he was, he didn't seem quite as tall.

"Not really. It's hard work." Jane swallowed a

couple of times.

"Yes, that's true. I should know 'cause it's my job. But since you belong to this dinner club group, I would've thought you liked to cook." He slid along the side of the car closer to her.

"I like the preparations, decorating, the entertaining, and all of that." Her heart fluttered, and her hands trembled a little as she fumbled her car keys out of her purse. Everett took the keys from her hand. Jane jumped when a shock of static electricity coursed through her. He unlocked her car door, then held it open. Maybe she misjudged him. He was being such a gentleman.

"May I have your number and call you sometime?" His small, blue eyes crinkled at the corners, and butterflies fluttered in her stomach. The Ladners had left and they were alone in the street.

She faced him. Was she too trusting? Was it all right to give him her number? Well, he was a friend of Bruce's after all, so she gave it to him and watched as he punched it into his cell phone. After she climbed into her car, he gently shut the door, then walked to his van. She was a little breathless and had a lightness in her chest. It certainly appeared as if he was going to ask her out on a date.

Once home, Jane wrote down the Breewoods' menu in her hostess diary, plus she noted the clothes she wore, so she'd remember not to wear the exact, same outfit at her own dinner club event in two weeks. She made a note and underlined it twice: Met Everett.

****

Jane needed to find a new church in Limestone Heights instead of driving all the way back to Verano every week, so on Sunday morning she visited a church just a few miles from her neighborhood. The parking lot was full of pickup trucks, and the marquee announced a rodeo event for the kids that afternoon. She liked the sermon; however, the church-goers were strangers and it all seemed so unfamiliar.

Once home, Jane settled down for a quiet Sunday afternoon with a cup of hot herbal tea and her laptop. The rest of the empty day loomed ahead of her. Unpacking was on the top of her to-do list, but could wait.

She navigated to the HOA's website with the community announcements page to check if any others had joined the neighborhood walk. A few women had commented that they planned to come. Justin had posted that he wanted to see more bike paths in the neighborhood, but there were no replies to his post. A reminder popped up for new homeowners to register their appliances on the warranty page, so she tapped the warranty services menu. She entered the product numbers for her appliances to complete the registration.

A warranty request page encouraged homeowners to schedule warranty services online by clicking on a calendar. She searched the calendar back in time as well as forward.

Calendar entries for the date of his death showed Ethan had warranty appointments at two houses, one in the morning and one in the afternoon. The time slots included the addresses. She printed the calendar page, then navigated to the county assessor's website to identify the owners. Joshua and Ashley Turghart had the morning appointment, and Zachery and Kristin Gauthierville had the afternoon.

She tapped her finger against the keyboard, wondering how she could approach them. One of them was probably the last to see Ethan alive...

Another popup appeared on her laptop—an advertisement for midcentury modern replicas—so she clicked onto the link. Sitting back in her chair, she deliberated over a picture of a charcoal gray, sectional sofa with sharp angles and metal legs in the midcentury style. Yellow and teal throw pillows would look good with that sofa in her family room, instead of the old, overstuffed, brown leather sectional. Chewing on a fingernail, she clicked through the rest of the pictures of furniture. An attractive chaise lounge in a teal and gray pattern would go well with the gray sofa. She read the reviews, and the ratings were good. Jane forwarded the links to Erin to ask what she thought of the furniture.

Rubbing her hands together, she strode into the guestroom to her office area. After rooting through all the drawers and under the desk, she still couldn't find her decorating magazines. She jerked up straight and gazed around the room, circling around and around. Something was off—someone had removed the candle from the table next to the guest bed. It was now on the window sill, somewhere Jane would never have placed it. And someone had closed the window blinds—Jane always left the blinds open because she loved the light.

The hair on the back of her neck and her arms stood at attention.

She scooped up Nick, who was licking her toes, and held him in her arms, swaying from foot-to-foot, as if rocking an infant. Clutching her dog with one hand, she twirled the rod to open the blinds with the other. A group of neighbors was gathered across the street. A woman pointed toward Jane's house, and they all turned in her direction. With his fist raised in the air, a man gestured toward the crime scene. He was her neighbor to the west.

Jane dumped the small beagle onto the guest bed with a plop and yanked her phone out. She snapped a couple of photos of the man, whose face was twisted in anger, as he was now pointing at her home.

Dare she go over, introduce herself, and find out what he was saying?

Her cell phone rang in her hand. She jumped and the phone flew across the room, landing on the bed next to Nick. Diving to pick it up, she answered with shortened breath, "Hello."

"Hey. It's Erin. I saw your email. I love the furniture you picked out."

"Hi Erin!" Jane's mood instantly cleared. "You really like it?"

"Yes. You should start a Pinterest site."

"Dinner clubs at my house in two weeks and it'd be wonderful to have new furniture. Should I order it?" She turned away from the window.

"Can you get it that fast?"

"The website said delivery takes a couple of days."

"Not bad. Is the shipping expensive? Search for a coupon code. Sometimes you can find one for free shipping."

"Okay. Hang on." Jane scooted down the hall to her laptop in the kitchen. Her fingers flew over the keyboard. "I found one!"

"Good job."

"I've never made an instant purchase like this before. But I'm going to order these." Jane hit the button to confirm payment. "Do you and Caleb want to stand in as the third couple in our dinner club group? You know the Breewoods will be gone by then, and we have room, since we haven't decided on a new couple."

"We'd love to come. Is there anything we can bring?"

"Just a bottle of wine. And bring it wrapped in a brown paper bag."

"Why in a bag?"

"Oh, just something I have planned. You'll see." Jane forgot about the rearrangement of her office and didn't notice the man-sized, footprint on the carpet.

Chapter 6

It was Ethan Valrod's voice. "Hello. You have reached the Valrod Construction Company. We are unable to take your call at this time…"

Didn't anyone think about changing the recording? She waited for his voice to come to an end, then left an ambiguous message about warranty items and hung up.

An hour later, she received a call back from Gina Valrod herself. What luck! Gina said, "I understand you had a question about your home warranty?"

"Yes, I've made a small list of items that need fixed."

"I have time tomorrow morning. Shall I come by?"

"That'd be Tuesday." Jane looked at her wall calendar. "Yes, that's fine. I need to be at work by nine, but I can be a little late."

"I can be there by seven-thirty."

"All right." She was going to meet with Gina! "I'd no idea it would be this easy—"

"That what would be easy?"

"Oh, I guess I thought I'd have to fill out a request or something."

"No. Nothing's required. I'll see you tomorrow."

Jane wondered all evening if she'd be able to sneak in some questions about the business' current financial status. Could she ask about Gina's missing husband, Steven? Imaginary conversations ran over and over in her mind, but no amount of imagination could come up with a reason for asking such questions. She forgot to think up any complaints on the home warranty issue.

After awakening early the next day, she drank her first cup of coffee, read her devotional, and took a quick shower. Just as she finished drying her hair, the doorbell rang.

Gina was on time. She wore a fitted company shirt with the logo "VC" on the pocket tucked into slim jeans over stylish boots. After shaking Jane's hand, she asked, "What work needs to be done?"

"This light switch cover is not level." Jane waved at the switch plate in the kitchen—a spur of the moment excuse.

"You aren't the only one to complain about these switch plates. The electrician did a poor job installing the fixtures level and straight. I'm thinking about using a different electrician in the future—"

Jane smacked her forehead. "Don't do that! It's not a big deal. I shouldn't have complained."

"That's okay." Gina's eyes raked her up and down. "I'll have the electrician call you to schedule a time to come over."

Jane's mind searched for a diversion. "Um, I think there's a chirping sound coming from that thing attached to the high ceiling in the living room. Is that a smoke detector?" She pointed upward, where a round, plastic object attached to the twenty-foot high ceiling emitted a faint chirp.

"Yes. I'll have the electrician check the battery. I'm sure that's what's causing it."

"I don't want to bother him just to change a battery." Jane tried to give a half-hearted smile, but grimaced instead.

"The battery must've been old when it was installed because it should've lasted longer than this. It's quite all right to have it checked." Gina handed her a business card. "Call me if you need anything further."

Jane slid it into a pocket in her purse. "Do you know Ethan's voice is still on your answering machine recording?"

Gina regarded Jane. "No. I'm glad you told me. I'll change it when I get back to the office."

"Ethan had two warranty appointments on the date of his death. They're on the HOA website calendar."

Gina frowned. "With who?"

"The Turgharts and Gauthiervilles."

"The police asked me if I knew about his appointments that day, but I didn't even think to look at the website calendar."

"Gina, have you heard from Steven? You must be so worried about him."

Her eyes turned cold and she drew in a sharp breath. "Is that why you called me? To talk about that?"

"Well, um, everyone's concerned, of course." Jane drew back.

"Why can't people leave us alone?" Gina put her hands on her hips and tapped her foot on the floor. "Is there anything else I can help you with? I'm very busy since I'm running the company now."

Jane stared down at the ground like a child in the principal's office. "No. Thank you for coming over."

Gina gave her a curt nod and strode out the front door. "I'll have the electrician call to make an appointment to fix the switch plate," she said over her shoulder as she climbed into her pickup and turned on the engine.

"Don't even think of it. It's not that big of a deal," Jane called out from the front door as Gina backed down the driveway and sped down the street. "Oh dear. I hope I didn't get someone into trouble."

Jane let the puppies out for a short break and then made sure they were locked inside the house with a full water dish. She needed to leave for work. As she reversed out of her driveway, she noticed for the first time the crime scene tape was down from the lot between her house and Tara's, and several pickup trucks were parked in the street. A large semi-truck with wood trusses appeared around the corner. As she proceeded out of the neighborhood, she passed several tractors and earth movers in one of the empty lots.

Once at the office, her mind replayed her conversation with Gina as new, clever questions popped into her brain. Maybe she could find another excuse to ask them. Finally, the day was done and it was time to go home.

As she turned onto her street, lights from several police cruisers and an ambulance flashed in a harsh rhythm. She wanted to stomp on the gas pedal to hurry over, but had to slow down around the emergency vehicles. After turning into her driveway and parking, she eased herself out of the car. The crime scene tape that had been removed that morning fluttered once again next door to her house.

Not knowing what to do, she slumped against her car until a policeman marched up to her. "You live here?"

She jumped to attention. "Yes. What happened?"

"I'd like to ask you a few questions. Can we go

inside?"

"Did someone else get hurt?" Her voice quavered.

"Step inside please." He touched her elbow lightly to steady her as she punched the buttons on the garage door keypad and they entered the house that way. She perched on the edge of the sofa, and he sat down in the chair across from her. "We found Steven Valrod's body next door."

"What?!"

"Yes. Evidently his body was buried beneath Ethan's."

She gulped a few times, taking that in. "I was hoping he'd turn up." Heat flushed her face as she thought how that came across. "I mean, that he wasn't missing anymore, that he'd come back." Her widened eyes narrowed as she focused on the cop. "His body was there this whole time? It's been over a week—"

"It appears so. Have you seen anyone near that lot?"

"No. I haven't seen anyone over there until the construction work resumed this morning. It's definitely murder, right? Both twins killed..."

"We're investigating the deaths as homicides."

The officer stood up, so Jane did too. Her knees knocked together like the baby colts' she observed near the barns in the field across the main road. "Do you have any idea who the killer is?"

"I can't talk about an ongoing investigation."

"I've left you guys several phone messages, but no one called me back."

"Do you have information?"

"No. I wanted to know if you have a person of interest." She'd seen the crime shows on television and knew the terminology, like everyone else.

"If we make an arrest it will be in the paper. By the way, we found a set of house keys buried under Steven. One of the investigators remembered your keys were missing."

"I'm glad you found them, but I already changed the locks, so I don't need them now."

"We're keeping the keys with the other scene evidence anyway." The officer turned to leave. She closed the door behind him, as her head swam and her stomach lurched.

The dogs scratched at the back door, so without thinking she let them outside, where they ran up and down along the fence, barking. She opened a window on the side of the house facing the crime scene. However, she couldn't hear a thing with all the racket.

The dogs needed a walk. After snapping their leashes on, she whisked them out the door. Standing in her front yard, with the dogs tugging to head down the street, she whispered, "Nick, Nora, do your business right here, understand?"

The ambulance had left, but the scene investigators were buzzing around the construction area. The dogs sniffed the bushes and flowers, then the flowers and bushes again, as she inched closer and closer, but she could not pick up any of the investigators' words.

"Ma'am, you need to move on." One of the officers shooed her away, so she took her time walking in the other direction. Once out of sight, she circled the block fast and approached from the other side. Her neighbor to the west stood on his front porch, staring at the scene. She held the dogs' leashes tight and started toward him, but he cast her a filthy look, scurried into his house, and slammed the door.

Curious, she climbed the stairs to Tara's porch. After ringing the bell several times without getting a response, she gave up and led the puppies home.

Tara didn't answer her door the next morning either. So, Jane stopped by Tara's house the following evening after she returned home from work, but it appeared that no one was home. Alarm bells clanged in her mind. Steven had disappeared after Ethan's death, then turned up dead, and now Tara had disappeared.

Chapter 7

"What's going on next door?" Caleb asked as he stood in the doorway. Erin and Caleb had stopped by Wednesday after work with take-out pizza.

"I meant to tell you about that. I was planning to call you tonight." She'd phoned Olivia, but hadn't gotten around to calling her son, so she recounted the few facts she knew about Steven's death.

"Wow. That's a bring down." Caleb gave his mother a brief hug.

The couple sat at the kitchen counter, while Jane snatched glasses and plates out of the cabinets and poured them a cold beer. She opted for soda. They discussed the shock of another murder next door as they ate dinner, but since Jane hadn't been able to overhear the crime scene investigators, there wasn't much to tell them.

A decorator at heart, Erin spread a magazine open on the counter. "Look at these pictures of the mid-century modern style." The two women thumbed through the pages, while Caleb rinsed the dishes and loaded the dishwasher.

Jane examined the glossy photos of fiberglass shell chairs, chrome-edged dinette sets, and atomic clocks. "I'm glad you helped me decide on colors, Erin. I was so tired of the sage green at the old house, and I love this new color, teal, that's so popular with this design.

It's very cheery paired with yellow, too. But I don't know what to do with my dining room at all. My oak table with the ladder back chairs are so 1980s, but it's still a sturdy dining set in good shape. I checked the internet, and there are a ton of tables just like mine selling for really cheap. It's hardly worth the effort to sell."

"I have an idea." Erin's fingers flew across the pages, flipping them forward, then back a few. "Here. Look at this." She tapped the glossy photo of a table with black legs under a white tablecloth surrounded by red fiberglass, shell chairs. "Paint the legs of your oak table black, cover the top with a tablecloth, and buy some inexpensive chairs like those in the magazine. Not red, but teal or yellow."

"I could do that." Jane imagined her dining room with the new look, as Nora jumped up and smacked a paw in her lap.

Erin turned down the corner of the page. "Here, you can keep this magazine. If you do get some shell chairs, but it ends up you don't like them that well, you could still look for a new dining set. You'd be using something you already own while shopping around for something else."

Jane snapped the magazine shut and clutched it to her chest. "I think you're right. That's what I'll do. Because I'm not sure I'm even staying in this house long, so I might not want to invest in all new furniture."

"Really? You aren't staying?" Erin's mouth was parted a little.

Caleb stopped checking his phone messages. He raised his dark head to glance up at his mother. "It's because of these murders, isn't it?"

"Well, the murders are a little nerve racking."

"The police will solve them, don't worry." His eyes looked worried, though.

"I know, I know, but I probably won't live here forever. I'll move away someday." One day soon, she thought, but didn't voice it.

"I understand." Erin gave her a sympathetic smile. "Both brothers dead. What a tragedy. And how creepy. Like something in a Steven King novel."

After the couple departed, she pulled Cheryl's real estate agent's card out of her wallet to call her. It wouldn't hurt to check and see what price she could get for her home. She dialed the number. "I'm considering putting my house up for sale. I just moved in and it looks pristine…no, nothing's wrong with the house. It's lovely. But I knew right away I'd made a mistake. I'd be happy to get out of it what I paid for it, but I do have plenty of equity and could take a small loss." The agent promised to prepare a market analysis and stop at the house later that week.

After disconnecting, a peace settled over Jane. She was being proactive. Taking steps to move on. She ambled down the hallway, poking her head into each room. It was a beautiful home and would show well. She wasn't thrilled with the dining room, though.

As Erin suggested, she searched the internet for yellow shell chairs, found some in her budget, and ordered six. She rummaged through a couple of boxes in the basement for tablecloths that would work well—a crisp, white tablecloth and a soft, light gray one. Next, she would shop for teal, yellow, and gray napkins and perhaps matching curtains. She wanted the place to look nice for her dinner club event. And if she put it up for sale, too.

Thinking about the club, she called Olivia. "Have you found a new couple?"

"I've got some good candidates. Do you want to meet at a coffee shop tomorrow night? A new mom and pop shop opened near my house."

"Sure." Jane wrote down the address.

****

The next night after work she drove the distance to her old town, Verano, and into the parking lot at the new coffee café. Olivia's car turned in moments later.

They trooped inside together, ordered lattes, and reclined in a comfortable grouping of couches. Their hot, spumescent drinks occupied the coffee table. Olivia tucked a piece of her jet black hair behind her ear and crossed her legs. "So, I want to help."

"Help what?"

"Investigate the murders, of course. Just imagine, two bodies…" Olivia's words hung in the air.

"I thought we were going to talk about new dinner club members." Jane wrinkled her nose as she considered Olivia—the prissy one who dished out backhanded compliments with a smile. The one she'd had to win over to be accepted into the dinner club last year.

Olivia sat forward on the couch. "We'll get to that. But really, you can't find the killer on your own."

"I can't?"

"Two heads are better than one."

Jane hadn't done much investigating. Just Googling the Valrods and looking at the bankruptcy records. And she didn't get anywhere questioning Gina. "Tell me, what makes you want to help with the investigation?"

Her manicured nails a shiny pink, Olivia laced her fingers together. "This is the thing. Doug goes off by himself all the time, and he never tells me where. I know he takes long rides on his motorcycle and hangs out with his police buddies. But he's never around. So, I need to keep myself busy, too, and he doesn't need to know what I'm doing either."

Jane tried to keep her eyebrows from shooting up. "You two need to have a good, long talk."

"No! Let him wonder about me for a change."

"Olivia, he already worries about you, don't you know that? Remember how concerned he was when you had cancer last year?" Jane leaned across the table and put her hand on her friend's arm.

"That reminds me. I have a follow-up appointment with the oncologist for my six-month check-up. So far, so good."

"That's wonderful news. But see, he's acting strange because he's worried about the appointment you've got coming up, just like last time."

"I'm not so sure that's all there is to it." Olivia crossed her arms. "So are you going to include me in?"

Sitting back, Jane took a long sip of her drink. Cheryl would soon be leaving the state and a hole in Jane's heart. Olivia's offer was tempting. It would be helpful to have a buddy in on the investigation. Why hesitate? Yes, she certainly did want help. "Okay, that'd be great."

Olivia jerked up the collar of her trench coat. "Let me give some thought to the next step."

"All you need is a fedora. And a cigarette, like Sam Spade," Jane said with a smile, then sat up straighter with an idea forming. "I know what to do. My neighbor Tara and I are starting a ladies' neighborhood walking group this Saturday morning. The idea is to get to know some of the other women and ask them about the Valrods. Maybe others will be interested and we can pressure the police for an arrest. You can join us, if you want."

"Sure. That's somewhere to start, I guess."

Jane took the lid off her cup and blew on the coffee. "Be at my house at a few minutes before nine. Since you don't live in the neighborhood, I'll tell Tara you want to walk with us for exercise. She doesn't need to know you're investigating with me."

"Doug doesn't need to know either."

Jane sighed. "Should we talk about the dinner club?"

"What a shock that the Breewoods are moving." Olivia gave her a sympathetic look. "You're going to miss Cheryl, aren't you?"

Jane gazed out the window of the coffee shop. "Yes."

"Well, now I'm not volunteering as much anymore, I can come into downtown to meet you for lunch." Olivia had volunteered many hours at a facility for the homeless after she quit her job last year.

"I'd love, love, love that." Jane perked up and took a gulp of her latte. "So, tell me. Who are you considering for our dinner club?"

"There's a lot of inquiries from the Meet Up website on dinner club groups. Some of the couples sound interesting. One person's a judge. Maybe you know him, Jane."

"I don't know any personally, no." Jane laughed.

"What about some regular people? Or, are you going to invite the governor?"

Olivia's eyes lit up. "Do you know him?"

"No!"

"Well, let me give it some more thought." Olivia shifted in her seat, and Jane wondered if she'd hold out for the judge.

After finishing their coffees, they straggled out to the parking lot, and Olivia got into her car. "I promise I'll call to make lunch plans soon."

Jane opened her car door. "Great. And in the meantime, I'll see you on Saturday for the neighborhood walk." After slouching into her car, she waited for Olivia to exit the parking lot, then followed her out. Olivia turned toward her own house and Jane kept going.

Just as she was entering in the front door, her phone rang out the Elvis Presley ringtone, *you ain't nothing but a hound dog.* A male voice said, "Hey gorgeous."

"Hello…"

"It's Everett."

"Oh, hello!" A warmth spread from Jane's stomach to her toes.

"What are you doing?"

"Just walking in the door. You called at the right time."

"Great. How about a date on Friday night?"

Jane remembered Cheryl wanted to get together that night and she longed to spend time with her best buddy before the big moving day. But she didn't want to say no to Everett. "That would be nice. We could do the typical first date and meet for coffee somewhere."

She considered the coffee café where she and Olivia had just met. She could fit in a coffee date, then meet the Breewoods after.

"We've already got past that, right?"

"Yes, I suppose so." Jane was silent for a few moments, then said, "But Cheryl made plans for Friday night because they're moving so soon, gosh, in a little over a week. Would you mind if we went on a double date with them? I sort of promised Cheryl already."

"That's a great idea. I'd like to see them one last time before they leave, too." Everett suggested different possibilities and they discussed plans.

She texted her friend: *Everett just called me for a date. Can he join us Friday night?* Her phone immediately rang again, because, of course, Cheryl had to phone to discuss the new man in Jane's life.

Jane asked, "So...he and Bruce are pretty good friends, right?"

"They just recently re-connected on a classmates' website, and they've golfed a couple of times. Dating a chef could be fun. He'd know the best restaurants. And Bruce will love having Everett along Friday. They can talk golf."

"And you can tell me all about your trip to Portland. You've been back a few days now, and I still haven't heard all the details yet."

"Where should we go Friday?"

"Actually, Everett suggested grilling at my house. How's that sound to you?"

"Fantastic. See you then."

Jane's heart gave a leap. She had something to look forward to—a date, plus plans with her friends before their move. She didn't want to think about Cheryl's departure.

****

A frisson of excitement raced the butterflies around the pit of her stomach, as she put hot rollers in her smooth, brown, shoulder-length hair and applied some makeup. Her slim, blue jeans were topped with a peach, fitted blouse showing off her tidy figure. She fretted about her curvy behind, but men never seemed bothered by it. In her bedroom, she tottered around in high heels, then kicked them off for some flat sandals.

She was glad to have taken extra care with her appearance when she opened the door to Everett and saw an appreciative gleam in his blue eyes.

Cheryl and Bruce arrived after Everett started grilling tostadas on the barbeque. Once he removed them from the grill, he added the toppings—bacon, avocado, and salsa made with tomatoes, corn, green pepper, cilantro, and scallions. The smell of bacon dominated, but hints of the fresh, soapy scent of cilantro rose up from the plate of tostados. The four friends sat down at the patio table on the deck. Jane had set the table with a pale, yellow tablecloth, daisy placemats, green patio dishes, and clear plastic wine glasses. She'd opened a crisp, white Chardonnay for the four of them. A green vase with black-eyed Susans cut from the hayfield across from her subdivision sat in the center.

Cheryl finished a bite of her tostada. "It's nice the house to the west of yours doesn't obstruct your view and you can see the mountains from here. But I still don't understand why you moved all the way out to Limestone Heights, practically on the Wyoming border."

A lump formed in Jane's throat. "You exaggerate. It's not that far. Anyway, I'm still in shock about you two moving. Tell us about your trip."

Bruce said, "We found a short-term lease apartment in downtown Portland. Our house here is listed for sale, and several people have already viewed it."

"It won't take long to sell, and then we'll seriously consider buying a loft in the city. We saw several we liked." Cheryl took another bite.

Jane tried to keep her voice light and cheerful. "I can't believe you are really moving in a week."

"I have a friend who's a chef at a restaurant in Portland. You'll have to eat there and tell me what you think of it," said Everett. Jane gave him a shy smile.

After they finished their meal, the couples ambled with wine glasses in hand to the end of the deck and peered over the railing into the foundation pit to the east. "That's where the bodies were found." Jane gestured at the crime tape.

Cheryl asked Everett, "Did Jane tell you about the murders?"

"Yes. A little bit." Everett stood tall, close to Jane's side. Her head only came up to his chest, as he casually loped his arm over her shoulder.

"So, what're you doing to investigate now?" Bruce cradled his glass of wine.

"All I've done was go to an HOA meeting with my neighbor, the one right over there." Jane's eyes rolled in the direction of Tara's house as the crime scene tape flapped with clapping sounds in the breeze. They all turned around to lean back on the railing and face the other direction. "I haven't found out much."

Cheryl squeezed Jane's hand. "At least you can't be a suspect this time, since, ah…" Her arm dropped away as she darted a glance at Everett.

"It's all right. I already told him I'm twice widowed and both husbands died under unusual circumstances." Jane sighed. That was one of the first things she mentioned.

Jane's first husband, Craig, died when he fell off a cruise ship on their twenty-fifth anniversary, and her second husband, Hugh, was swept off a cliff in Ireland while taking a selfie photo of the two of them. She had become a suspect in both drownings after posting the selfie as her Facebook profile picture. That photo was her best ever. How was she to know it would go viral?

She had even changed her name back to her first married name, Marsh, in an attempt to avoid the notoriety. Would she ever get past the moniker with which she was tagged on the internet, "widow of the waves?"

"What's this? A suspect?" Everett's head tilted to one side as he surveyed her with his small eyes narrowed even farther. She hadn't mentioned that part to Everett—the part about being a suspect. Let him find it out on the World Wide Web like everyone else in the whole, wide world.

Bruce tapped Everett's arm. "Do you want to golf tomorrow?"

"Sure."

The two men extracted cigars from their pockets and lit them. They started to discuss their golf game and what new clubs were on the market.

Jane drew a deep breath through her nose, relieved Bruce was running interference. Would Everett drop her if he found out?

Cheryl pulled Jane aside. "Let's go for a hike in the mountains on Sunday, just the two of us, since it'll be my last opportunity to hike before the move to Oregon."

"I'm in!"

Jane and Cheryl bumped fists, then discussed the time and place to meet, plus what supplies to bring for a hike at high elevation in the autumn season.

After the Breewoods left, Everett set a small iPod on the table and turned on a play list that included Johnny Mathis. He inched ever closer to her on the sofa, and she could detect a hint of sage mingled with a musky aftershave, making her insides all twisted. Just when their legs touched, Jane finally realized the time. "It's late and I have early plans in the morning."

He gave her a sweet kiss goodnight. Their lips fit together like they were made for each other.

After Jane lingered at the door for another kiss or two and he left, she readied for the first Saturday morning neighborhood walking group.

She found herself biting her nails. Would Tara show up? Jane still hadn't seen her since Steven's body was found. For that matter, would anyone show up? And would she be able to uncover some clues?

****

Much to Jane's relief, Tara appeared at her door on Saturday morning.

"I've been trying to get a hold of you. I've been worried. Where've you been?" Jane asked. "I came by your house a couple of times, but you were never home. And I sent you a text."

"Justin and I took some time off and went over to

the Western Slope."

"Oh, nice. But you've heard about Steven?"

Tara's face screwed up and her lips quivered. "Yes. I heard."

"How are you doing? Ethan's death was bad enough, and now this. Shocking, right?" She reached over and tucked a strand of Tara's hair behind her ear. A calm settled on her young friend's face. At that moment, Olivia's car rolled into the driveway, so she said to Tara, "I'd like you to meet my friend. She wants the exercise, so she's joining our group."

Tara passed farther across the threshold, then shook hands with Olivia, who had reached the front door. Tara said, "I checked the website this morning. Several neighbors have joined the walking group."

Jane yanked on her hiking boots. "That's good." She gathered her keys, shooed the dogs back from the door, and turned the lock before they started out.

A group of six waited at the clubhouse steps—four young women, plus an older couple. Tara introduced herself, and everyone else gave their names, too. Among the walkers was one of the homeowners who had the warranty appointment with Ethan on the day he was killed—Kristin Gauthierville. Everybody had warm greetings for Jane's neighbor, with a "Hi Tara!" and "How are you Tara?"

After returning their greetings, she said, "So, I thought we'd just take the walk over to the pond for our first get together." They broke into formations of twos and threes as they marched down the sidewalk to the path east through the woods. Tara, then Olivia and Jane, took the front. Kristin and a married couple, Ruth and Dick, followed them.

Dick said, "I hope you don't mind me joining the ladies' walking group. I need the exercise as much as my wife."

"Of course not. I'll re-post on the website that the group is open to everyone, not just women." Tara went on to describe the pond to Olivia, so Jane stole a glance at the young woman behind her.

"Kristin, how long have you lived in the neighborhood?"

"Zachery and I moved in last fall. He's a doctor at the hospital here in Limestone Heights, and we need to live close to the hospital. Zachery works on Saturdays, and that's why I joined this group."

"So you've lived here longer than I have. I just made a warranty request."

"Why? What's wrong?"

Jane's chin dipped down. "One of the light switches isn't level." She wished she'd thought of something less lame. "Are the builders pretty quick about responding?"

"I don't really know. I've only made one warranty request. And you know what? It was for the same thing. Every time I see the switch plate, I can hardly stand it. I still haven't gotten it fixed. Ethan Valrod was supposed to come over the day he died. He never showed. I just haven't followed up with the construction company about it. I thought I'd wait a bit, you know, with all that's going on."

"Can you believe what happened?" Jane was quick to respond.

"No. First Ethan Valrod, then Steven."

"The police are treating the deaths as homicides."

Kristin nodded, but said, "I don't know anything

about it. The police stopped by yesterday and asked if Ethan came to my house that day, but I told them he did not. I don't know when I'm going to get that light switch leveled."

"That must be aggravating." Jane wondered if Gina had alerted the police to Ethan's warranty appointments.

"Well, Zachery says I'm too picky."

"Tell him I made the same complaint. I like for things to line up neatly, like when I raise the window blinds, they have to be perfectly even." Jane wondered if she had a compulsion. Must get back to the murder. "Did you know Ethan or Steven?"

"No. I never even met them. Zachery took care of everything to do with the house. I just made the one warranty request."

Jane was already tired of hearing about Zachery. "Do you know Ashley Turghart? She lives in the neighborhood, too."

"No. Should I know her? Does her husband work at the hospital? I mostly know Zachery's friends."

"I don't know what her husband does."

Kristin gave Jane a puzzled expression. They had come out of the woods to the spot where Long's Peak was revealed and the narrow path led around the pond. They could no longer walk side-by-side, which gave Jane an excuse to let Kristin fall in behind her.

When they finished the loop, several women paused to snap photos of Long's Peak in the distance. Today the peak was a bright white surrounded by blue sky. The breeze caught the cottonwood leaves, casting fleeting shadows across their faces as they stood gazing at the view. After their short break, the walking group hiked westward through the woods and gathered back together at the clubhouse.

Dick brought up what Jane was dying to ask. "What does everyone think about the Valrod boys?" Jane held her breath waiting for a response to the question.

One of the women said, "Isn't it terrible? How are you dealing with it, Tara, since it happened by your house?"

"It's been awful."

Jane lurched forward with an eager nod. "I moved in right next door on the day of the murders." A hush came over the group as waves of hostility flowed in Jane's direction. "But I, I didn't have anything to do with it, of course." Several of the walkers threw her dubious glances. Did they actually suspect her? She glared from one to the other.

Tara changed the subject. "I'll update the HOA website with suggestions for other places to hike. Is anyone interested in something longer, maybe more challenging?" Two of the young women said they would like to hike in the foothills.

After the group disbanded, Jane and Olivia walked with Tara to her house. Before Tara slipped inside, Jane asked, "Is there a bike path through the Valrods' ranch that follows the farmer's canal? I think I saw Justin on his bike over there."

Tara halted at her front step. "I don't know. Do you think the neighborhood group could hike that path?"

"I thought it might be an idea. But I'm not sure there's public access."

"I'll ask Justin. He'll know."

"There's something else. I want to show you a

picture I took last Sunday of the neighbor that lives on the other side of me." She flipped through the photos on her cell to the most recent, the angry man pointing at Jane's house. "This is him. Doesn't he seem mad about something?"

Tara sidled closer and squinted at the photo. "Oh, yes. I heard he's the neighborhood trouble maker. He's been going around complaining and demanding the police make extra patrols."

"Really? He'd be a good one for me to talk to, then. But every time I see him, he avoids me. By the way, did you notice how everyone looked at me when I said I moved in the day of the murders?"

Tara handed the phone back to Jane, but did not meet her eye. "Neighbors like to gossip. That kind of talk leads to suspicion."

Olivia piped up. "Tara, you live next door to where it happened. Yet everyone seemed friendly to you and not poor Jane here." Jane grimaced.

Tara flipped her hair over her shoulder. "They've known me longer. Don't worry about it." They said their goodbyes, and Jane walked with Olivia to her car.

"I found out Ethan did not keep his appointment with Kristin Gauthierville. Or, at least Kristin claimed he didn't show." Jane stood with her hands on her hips.

"That's a clue. We're getting somewhere." Olivia unlocked her car. "It's interesting, but who did he meet that day?"

"I've just got to find out."

Chapter 8

It was laughable how early she was—by twenty minutes—but she was always early.

She relaxed in her car with the engine idling at the trailhead, enjoying the scenery. The brilliant, blue sky filled the expanse above the high mountain peaks topped with snow. Below the tree line, groups of aspens, with their yellow leaves quaking against their white speckled branches, stood among pines marked with beetle kill, brown and bare, but upright. At the foot of the trees, the skittish, striped chipmunks searched in the layer of pine needles for food scraps left behind by tourists.

Since it was the end of September, it was chilly at this high elevation in the Rocky Mountains of Colorado. A fleece vest, water bottle, snacks, and packed lunch sat on the seat next to her. Hoping she was outfitted appropriately for this little adventure with Cheryl—one last hike—she shifted her supplies into her pack, but left her fleece on the seat. She turned off the engine since the bright sun warmed the inside of the car.

After fifteen minutes, Cheryl's SUV turned into the empty parking lot. Theirs were the only vehicles.

"Good Morning!" Jane hopped out. "Did you remember to bring the trail map?"

"Yes. Did you remember your water bottle? I

brought two." Cheryl set her day pack on the hood of her car and shrugged into her jacket.

"I just have one, but it will be enough." As she donned her fleece, Jane breathed in the cold, fresh air that smelled of pine needles. With a chirping noise and a rapid trill, a chipmunk skittered past Jane's feet. She plopped a safari hat on her head, its wide brim shielding her eyes from the sun.

They locked their cars, pocketed their keys, and started the incline up the trail. The runoff of an early autumn snowfall furrowed the ground and patches of dirty snow persisted in low spots under pine trees and behind boulders.

"I know you think this hike might be a bit advanced for tenderfoots like us," said Cheryl, "but I always wanted to take it."

"I'm good with it. It's a beautiful, sunny day. And we can always turn around if there's deep snow or it's too wet." Jane saw a flash of disappointment in her friend's eyes.

"Let's try to make it the full circle back to the trailhead. And maybe someday we can hike a '14er.' I've always wanted to."

"Me too!" Jane gave a throaty laugh since she was already huffing a little bit.

Cheryl continued, "But I don't know when we'll get another chance to hike since I'm moving next week." Jane's smile faded at the reminder.

Her friend paused, glancing up from watching her feet. "You know, I'm not moving that far away. It's only a couple hours by plane."

"I know. And I'm glad you and Bruce have this opportunity. Really."

Cheryl pointed at the tall trees across the ravine. "See the bird perched in the branches? I think it's a mountain bluebird." She plucked out a small set of binoculars from her day pack and handed them to Jane. "Look right up there. I didn't expect to see many birds this high up and this late in the season."

Jane peered through the binoculars as Cheryl jotted down notes in a pocket-sized spiral notebook. Finished, Cheryl placed the spiral and binoculars back into her pack.

They plodded on and on, dead pine needles crunching under their feet, stopping occasionally to catch a glimpse of the gorgeous views and the emerging fall scenery. The trail became steeper and narrower, turning and twisting up switchbacks, around boulders and between tall pine trees. Her breath becoming even more labored now, Jane stopped at the curve in a switchback which opened to a sunny, panoramic view of the mountain range above and a river in the valley below.

"I'll bet we've hiked at least four miles already." Cheryl drew out her trail map.

Jane retrieved her water bottle from her pack and took a long drink. She turned away from the view to study the circuitous path, expecting it to wind back into the dark woods, but it didn't. She cried out, "Look at that!"

The trail circled around a rocky outcropping, then ascended up steep steps carved into the shady side of a cliff face. To the right was a sheer drop off of hundreds of feet. At the bottom far below, white water tumbled swiftly past boulders. Jane's eyes flashed away from the water back up to the stairs. On a normal day, the steps would be daunting, but on this day doubly so, since thick ice covered the steps in the shade of the mountain. Her heart started thumping as her eyes descended once more to the bottom of the ravine.

"Let's go." Cheryl sounded resolute. "We're almost half way along the trail. To turn back now would be a shame."

Jane's heart continued to thud in her chest. The wind roared in her ears, whipping her hair around her face and up into the air, as she smiled into the camera. She brushed a wisp of hair away from her mouth when an even more powerful gust made her stumble backward a few steps. All of a sudden, the wind swept him away from her, only the camera remained with Jane at the edge of the cliff. "Hugh!"

"What did you say?" asked Cheryl.

"Oh, I said, whew!" Jane's voice quivered a little, but in a few short moments the pounding of her heart slowed down into a smooth rhythm and her ears stopped ringing. Cheryl hadn't appeared to notice anything.

She squared her shoulders as she returned her water bottle to her pack and examined the steps. Normally, one would just walk up the tall steps next to the mountain face far from the cliff edge, but ice adhered to the ubac, and bare, dry patches of rock were nearer to the drop-off. She chose to climb up on the right side near the edge where the ice was less.

Kneeling with her knees on the first step, she grabbed the notch in the rock above with her hands. It just felt safer than being on her feet. She made herself inch upward on her knees, not glancing behind or down over the edge to her right. After the first rocky step, her heart started pounding a little faster again, and her fingers turned cold.

The freezing wet stairs soaked through the knees of her khaki pants and stung her chilled hands. She waited until she had a secure hand grasp on the step above before she climbed with her knees up to the next. Even if she had a strong grip, she couldn't hold herself on the ledge with her shaky fingers if she should start to slip on the ice. Not a rock climber, she was ill equipped for this type of ascent.

Finally hauling herself up the last step, she reached the top and allowed herself to take a deep breath and a peek backward. Cheryl had chosen to follow her example and was taking the same route on her knees. After Cheryl, too, had reached the top safely, they scooted as far away from the edge of the drop-off as possible.

Cheryl rubbed her red hands together. "You know, I think it was probably easier to go up those steps than it would've been to go down. If we'd come from the other direction, we might've had to turn around."

Jane's hair stood up on the back of her neck. If they encountered any more treacherous places farther on, they would be caught between two perils. And if either of them were injured, they'd be in trouble, since coverage on their cell phones was non-existent in this remote, high mountain spot. There was no way she was going to return by going down those steps now. It was onward or nothing.

They continued their hike into an aspen grove—hundreds of aspen joined together at the roots forming one gigantic living organism over a mile in length. The trail wound through the trees that were less covered with the small, quaking leaves than the aspen at lower elevations. On the other side of the grove, they found spots to sit on fallen timber.

Cheryl examined the map. "I figure we're more than half way along the trail now." She folded it and tucked it in her pocket. "You won't believe this, but I'm actually more cautious than I used to be."

"How's that?" Jane stopped tearing the wrapper off her energy bar.

"Once Bruce and I were driving through the mountains alongside the Platte River. We pulled into a turnout near a large, flat boulder that jutted out over the water. Our daughter was about four-years old at the time. We sat on that rock and watched the water flow. It was spring and the water was high from the runoff.

"For some reason, Megan decided to run around on that rock. Maybe because of the energy of the water flowing below. She got up and ran. She ran straight toward the edge. Bruce and I both jumped up to grab her and yelled at her to stop, but she was out of our reach. My heart stood still as I imagined her running and falling into the current below. But she stopped just in time. Then Bruce got to her and yanked her back."

"That must have been horrifying." Jane's hand flew to her throat. "Then what happened?"

"We left. We've never got close to the Platte again. I was more careful after that. Megan could've been swept away by the cold, strong current. Her little body might never have been found. It seems like every year someone drowns in the mountain rapids."

"But she didn't." Jane gave her friend a comforting pat on the back.

"She could've just as easily gone off the edge into

the water. What we were thinking, stopping there and getting out on that rock?"

"We're pretty fragile beings, aren't we?" Jane knew full well how easy it was for someone to drown. She was only one small being under the large, fluffy clouds in the robin-egg blue sky over the mountain view spreading as far as the eye could see.

"Why does God allow some to perish and others to live?" Cheryl took a bite of her sandwich and chewed.

"It's a mystery we can't understand. At least, I don't understand it. I would like an answer to that myself." Jane blinked back some tears. She wrapped her energy bar in a napkin and returned it to her pack.

"I'm sorry. I've caused you to remember things you'd rather forget."

"I'm glad you don't tiptoe around my husbands' deaths. You can talk freely to me," Jane said, meaning every word.

But Cheryl, with her depth of understanding, changed the subject. "Time we start back." They stood, brushed off the seats of their pants and took a drink of water before resuming their hike.

"Have you found out anything more about those men who were killed?" Cheryl asked. "I meant to call you to talk about it, but I've been busy."

"I know you have. No worries. I haven't found out anything new. I told you I met Gina, didn't I? She made a point to say she's the one in charge now. I think the company's in bad shape with the bankruptcy and all."

"Who are your suspects?"

"I just found out Ethan didn't show up for an appointment the day he was killed. It's possible he was letting company business slide. But now, Gina's getting to run the business her way. So, she's suspect number one. Then again, maybe Ethan was meeting his lover. Kimber may have fought with him. She had all those bruises, so she's suspect number two. Or maybe she's number one." Jane drew in a deep breath full of pine scent. "But for some reason the neighbors seem to suspect me because I'm the new kid in town."

"Oh no!" Cheryl made a wry face. "How could anyone think that?"

"I know!" Jane gave her friend a grateful smile as they skirted a log that had fallen across the path. "And don't forget I offered to help you pack. Let me know what you need."

"We have a moving company and they're doing most of the work. You still have your own unpacking to do."

"True, true." Jane gave a half-hearted shrug. "I'm thinking of selling and moving out, what with these murders and everything." There, she'd said it out loud.

"You could always move to Portland." Cheryl giggled.

"Maybe I will. Who knows?"

After another hour, during which they had an extensive talk about Everett and Jane's first date, they encountered a young couple hiking from the other direction. As good mountain hikers always do, they warned the two about the icy steps on the other side of the aspens.

"Maybe we'll turn around at the steps, but I do want to see the grove," said the young woman.

Her male companion hefted his bag over his shoulder. "I've got some ropes and anchors, so we can rappel down if we have to."

Feeling confident that the hikers were forewarned and well-prepared, Jane and Cheryl continued on. The last mile of the trail climbed a steep hill. Jane trudged along, out of breath. It was a long, slow and straight incline, instead of switchbacks. She couldn't understand why she was so breathless and had to stop for a drink of water to catch her breath. Cheryl forged ahead and didn't wait for her. They were separated by a few hundred yards as they made their way to the trailhead.

It was two in the afternoon when they got back to their cars. Another vehicle was in the parking lot, likely belonging to the young couple hiking the loop from the other direction. They threw their daypacks into the backseats of their cars. Cheryl slipped off her hiking boots and nudged her feet into comfortable-looking loafers.

Jane glanced at her own footwear. "I wish I'd thought to bring a change of shoes. My feet feel tired, and though these boots are waterproof, my toes are a little damp."

"I always bring a change of shoes. It feels so good to get out of the boots."

"I wish I brought a change of pants too. My knees are still wet. Can you believe we actually crawled up that ledge? We can laugh about it now."

And they both did laugh, but Jane added in a quiet voice, "Cheryl, I won't see you again for a long while."

"It's time to move on, Jane. And remember, we'll be only a two-hour flight away—"

"I know." Jane smiled at her friend. They gave each other a quick hug and piled into their cars. Cheryl drove away first. Jane watched until she disappeared out of sight without a wave goodbye. As a lone tear ran down her cheek, Jane started the engine and turned from the parking lot onto the road home.

She thought about the Old Testament story of David and Jonathan, best friends with a close affection for each other, like brothers. They were about to be parted, and met in a field to say their goodbyes, knowing they might never see one another again. Both David and Jonathan shed tears of sadness at their parting, but David cried more.

Chapter 9

Luke's and Brittany's eager faces flashed onto Jane's computer screen, instantly cheering her up. She'd received a text from her daughter-in-law inviting her to Skype as soon as she walked in the door.

"Did you have fun at the ocean? When did you get back?" Jane adjusted the volume, then fluffed the pillows behind her on the bed. She leaned backward and pulled the laptop into her lap, to relax after the long hike.

"Got home this morning. It was nice, not crowded, since tourist season is over." Brittany sat near Luke, who had a bottle of water and a bowl of grapes.

He asked, "How's your murder investigation going?"

"I've got some suspects. I'm thinking one of the wives did it, Kimber or Gina." Jane chewed on a fingernail as her brows formed a "V" over her forehead.

"Tell me about them." Brittany slid closer to the computer screen.

"I've found a lot of dirty laundry in the Valrod family. Sibling rivalry, maybe over a dispute concerning their dad's will. There's theft of company funds and an affair, even." They discussed all the possibilities, just as Jane had done with Cheryl that morning.

"There's a lot of people with motives, sounds like."

Brittany rubbed her chin.

Luke chewed and swallowed a grape. "How do you like your new place?"

"Everyone wears cowboy hats here. It's a bit of a western town." She paused. "I don't know how long I'll stay."

Brittany said, "Gosh, Mom. I didn't know you felt that way."

"I'm not complaining. I love the house, but I feel like a guest living in someone else's home. Maybe it's just a continuation of the empty nest. There aren't any children in the house to build forts on the stairs with blankets, fill their own space in their bedrooms, spread out toys on the living room floor. You know, no family meals around the dining room table, then clearing the table to do homework. No kids making new friends on the street. That's the stuff that makes a house a home." Jane blinked a few times.

Brittany did a double take. "I thought you wanted to get away from all those memories and start fresh in a new place."

"I did. That's the irony of it." Jane was able to chuckle, and they all laughed together. "Of course, it's weird that two people were killed right next door. And I found the first body."

Brittany's eyes met Jane's in a moment of understanding. "You just need to figure it out, Mom. Like you did before."

Luke appeared nonchalant about the investigation. Of course, he was not around last year when Jane had been involved in another murder, and he didn't have the full picture of the danger. He threw his grape vines into the garbage pail. "Colorado's not going to feel like home anymore since you aren't living in Verano."

Her chest constricted. Her son was right. Soon, she would put the house on the market and start fresh somewhere else. God was a God of second chances. There was no mistake that could not be undone, except perhaps murder...

She smiled in lieu of a response. "I miss you both so much."

"Miss you too, Mom." Their voices echoed one another. Surprised they'd been talking for over an hour, they said their goodbyes and logged out.

Loud thumps came from the hallway. She drew in a quick breath, then froze. Someone was in the house, coming closer down the hall. Something hit her bedroom door. Jumping out of the bed, she landed on her feet, still holding her breath.

Then came a scratching at the door. It was the dogs, of course. Their scratches nudged the door open and Nick and Nora bounded in. They had one of her loafers in a tug of war. At seeing their mistress, both dogs dropped the shoe, which hit the floor with a loud clomp.

Returning the chewed-up loafer to the closet, Jane tripped past the unpacked boxes stacked on the floor and shelves. She wouldn't need to unpack, since she'd be moving again soon...real soon.

And yet, she'd miss her new friendship with Tara. And the kitchen—she loved the kitchen—so maybe she should stay. She hadn't signed the listing agreement or looked at the market analysis the realtor had dropped off. The unopened envelope lay on her dresser. But Luke was right, this wasn't home. She could find a house with a similar floor plan and find new friends in a new place. So maybe she should move.

Erin phoned as Jane was smoothing the comforter on her bed and unplugging her laptop. "Caleb and I have an announcement."

With the phone to her right ear, Jane carried her computer under her left arm to the kitchen. "What is it?" She held her breath as a million thoughts zinged across her brain.

"We've decided to buy a loft downtown!"

Jane sank onto a stool at the counter and laughed out loud. "How nice. Lofts must be the new trend because everyone seems to want one. And downtown, too. Have you started looking?"

"We have an appointment with the real estate agent tomorrow night. We want you to come with us."

"I'd love, love, love that!" Jane's heart soared at being included. They made plans to meet in the Ball Park District north of Coors Field the next day after work.

She kept the news of her own plans to sell to herself. No need to infringe on the kids' excitement. She didn't want to be the dreadful mother-in-law who needed to be the center of attention. It was their turn. Anyway, her house would probably take months and months to sell, so she could put it off for the time being.

****

Monday morning arrived. The beginning of the work week was always hectic, with the phone ringing and emails pinging, causing the day to fly by.

Soon it was time for Jane to meet Caleb, Erin, and their realtor.

The loft was part of what was once a ball bearings factory. HVAC pipes ran along the open ceiling throughout the rooms. The aged cement floor, with yellow lines painted in sections from its loading zone days, gave off a cool, musty smell. In the kitchen, a gas stovetop opposite a large stainless steel sink divided a length of a cadaverous gray, concrete countertop. Jane tested the tall elbow kitchen faucet with a spring spout, stream aerators, and a swiveling neck.

Behind a heavy, sliding barn door was the single bathroom. The bottoms of two large, smoky brown glass bowls disappeared into the cement countertop. The loft boasted only one bedroom, but it was large with a spacious walk-in closet.

Jane could tell Erin was enchanted and Caleb was pleased. He said, "The price is within our budget."

The real estate agent put his briefcase on the counter. "This loft will not be on the market long because a Light Rail train stop is under construction only two blocks away, so this area's going to be in demand. The owners relocated to another city several months ago, and they're anxious to sell now without waiting for the Light Rail station."

Erin and Caleb stared at each other. Erin said, "Let's make an offer." She slid onto a counter stool to complete the paperwork.

Jane tugged Caleb aside. "Wait. How many properties have you viewed? Are you sure you want to do this so quickly?" She held his shirt sleeve.

"We've been to a lot of open houses, Mom, and we've researched property values in this area. We know the realtor's right; this loft won't stay on the market. It's just what we want."

Erin darted a glance in their direction, then buried herself in the contract.

"Okay. I'm just going to walk around the block to get a feel for the neighborhood." Jane edged out the door as dusk was falling.

Buttoning her leather jacket, she strolled down the street to the west. Large elm trees stood in a uniform row along the curb, their dull yellow leaves dropping nonstop as she hurried under their outstretched branches along the sidewalk. Her feet crunched on the leaves as she left the elms behind and turned the corner to the south to find a line of historical buildings full of quaint shops and a brew pub. Light was pouring out of the storefront windows, but all the shops were closed. Peeking in one of the doorways, she was reminded of her outing with Cheryl—when they toured a loft and examined the motor scooters in a store window.

The pub was open, so she entered the dark restaurant where a young lady was stationed behind a hostess stand. "Would you like to be seated?"

"No. I'm just looking. My son and his wife are buying a loft around the corner." Jane was gushing a little. "Um, do you have any paper menus I could take with me?"

"We sure do." The hostess handed her a white, tri-folded paper. Jane retreated out the door and continued around to the backside of the block, but it was just the rear of the old factory surrounded by a tall fence. Several concrete and wood park benches sat intermittently along the well-lit sidewalk under a row of oak trees. A lone woman in a long coat walked her poodle. Around the next corner was another side of the factory, and then Jane was back at the entry door to the lofts. The sun had set in the short time she was gone, and it was dark when she returned inside.

She waited while the young couple finished signing the contract and shaking hands with the real estate agent.

"We made an offer above the asking price." Erin smiled. She and Caleb held hands.

The agent put the paperwork in his briefcase. "Expect a call from me tonight if your offer's accepted."

They stood outside the loft and watched him drive away, a grin on his face. "Do you know about the pub around the corner?" Jane asked.

"Yes. We drove by a few times in the last couple of days. I guess we've been excited to see the place." Erin put one arm into her jeans jacket.

"Let's eat dinner there." Caleb helped his wife shrug into the rest of her coat. Jane drew the paper menu out of her pocket to read as they walked around the corner to the pub.

"I'm back." Jane greeted the hostess.

"Is this your son who's buying the loft?"

"Yes."

Caleb's and Erin's faces lit up as the hostess congratulated them. "You'll love the neighborhood."

"So it's safe here, then?" Jane asked. Caleb and Erin jerked their heads toward her in unison.

"One of the cooks always walks me to my car after my shift."

"Can we get a table?" snapped Caleb.

After they were seated and explained their orders to the waiter, Jane asked, "Do you know how many lofts are in that factory building?"

Caleb sipped from his water glass before speaking. "Twenty-two. And Mom, it is safe you know."

"Well, it's certainly unique."

"We already feel at home in this neighborhood. It's just where we want to live," said Erin. Excitement was in the air inside and outside the dark pub, under the city street lights, with the noise of traffic and laughter, young people everywhere, the urban life. Jane was never going to feel that way about Limestone Heights. It was probably safer here than in her neighborhood with two unsolved murders. Decision made. She was selling. She would sign the listing agreement and send it off to the agent.

She listened to the passion in their voices as the couple chatted about the what-ifs. What if their offer was accepted? What if they could move in right away? What if they painted the living room a light gray? Soon, their food arrived.

Caleb's cell phone rang. Jane had her wine glass up to her lips and Erin had her fork halfway to her mouth. They set their glass and fork on the table, and Erin cried out, "Answer it!"

After they listened to the one-sided conversation, Caleb ended the call. "Our offer was accepted!"

Jane toasted the couple. "Congratulations on home ownership." They marveled at how fast this had come about and their enthusiasm was catching.

Rain was falling when they left the restaurant and none of them had umbrellas, so they hurried to their cars. Once Jane got home she couldn't wait to call her friend.

"Hi, Jane." Cheryl picked up.

"Well, hello. Are you all ready to move tomorrow?"

"Yes. The moving van just left. The house is

empty, and we're sleeping on a borrowed blow-up mattress tonight. The mover's planning an overnight road trip and will meet us at the apartment after we fly there tomorrow."

Jane shared the news that Caleb and Erin were going to be homeowners. After talking for a few minutes, they ended their call since it was so late. It wasn't the same as their weekly therapy walks downtown. The short phone call emphasized the emptiness to be left by her soon-to-be absent BFF.

She might as well get out of her damp clothes and into her pajamas. But before she could do that, out of the corner of her eye she saw a bright light bobbing up and down outside her bedroom window. It was not a flash of lighting; it was a flashlight. She sucked in her breath and ducked out of sight. Was the killer trying to get in the house?

After extracting her rain slicker from the closet, she yanked it on and pocketed her own flashlight and a can of pepper spray. Heart thumping, she slipped out the back door.

Lamps glowed from the windows along the back of her house, so she walked in the safety of the yellow squares of light on the dark grass. The rain had lessened, but she shook as the glacial air met her wet clothing under the raincoat. She saw nothing unusual, but what about the crime scene? Had the flashlight beam come from the building site?

Even though her heart was racing, she exited the fence by the gate, sprinted next door, and slithered under the crime scene tape. She stood on the edge of the completed foundation and darted her flashlight into the corners.

Kimber stood with her back against one of the walls. "You caught me!"

Chapter 10

"What are you doing here?"

A tear glistened on Kimber's cheek in the beam of light, and she was trembling. "I wanted to see where it happened."

Jane quieted her heart and climbed down, stretching her right foot into the open space where a basement window had not yet been installed. With both feet on a firm piece of cement, she lowered herself farther down, then jumped onto the hard basement slab.

It was freezing below ground level, but somehow the rain didn't seem to reach her.

She half-trotted over to Kimber. "That's where..." Jane shone the flashlight into the dark corner at the front of the house.

Kimber groped her way over to the spot, knelt down, and placed the palm of her hand flat against the cold floor. She said in a choking voice, "I hope the twins are at peace, wherever they are."

The basement pit was stone cold, and Kimber was wearing only a light raincoat. Jane took Kimber's icy hand in hers and hauled her up to a stand. "Come on."

Jane put her flashlight in her pocket to climb out. They planted their feet on a window ledge and heaved themselves to the top. Once out of the basement, Jane retrieved her flashlight and hit the switch.

She focused on the white face of a ghost and

screamed, "Aiieee!"

"Jane!" Justin shrieked, stumbling back a step.

Jane clutched her raincoat tighter around her neck. "Good grief, you guys—"

"What're you doing?" A vein was throbbing on Justin's forehead and his lips were pressed into a white slash.

"I thought I saw someone with a flashlight in my backyard so I came out to take a look."

"Me too." Justin's eyes flashed and darted to Kimber. "What about you?"

Kimber's eyes widened, but she said nothing, so Jane asked, "Should we get inside out of the rain and talk about this?" The rain shower had sputtered out to a drizzle, but she, for one, was bone-chilled.

"Let me get Tara. She'll wonder what happened to me. We'll be over in a minute." Justin's back was stiff as he made his way home. Kimber followed Jane into her house and Justin and Tara arrived on their footsteps.

Jane said, "I'm going to make a pot of coffee." She first wrapped Kimber in a teal throw blanket and made sure she was comfortable on the couch.

"Have you had anything to eat today, Kimber?" she asked from the kitchen. The young widow screwed up her face as if in thought, so Jane said, "I can make a sandwich. Do you like turkey? I got it from the deli." She didn't mention she kept turkey on hand to give as treats to the dogs.

"I'd love a sandwich. You don't mind?" Kimber's eyes welled with tears, threatening to spill over.

"Of course not. How about you two?" Jane pointed her face at Tara and Justin, who shook their heads no. Nick and Nora watched Jane's every movement as she assembled a sandwich on a plate and garnished it with a kosher pickle. She handed the plate to Kimber along with a napkin.

Once they all had their hands around steaming hot mugs and Kimber had bitten into her sandwich, Jane asked, "Are you doing better?" Kimber nodded and took another bite. Her pale face started to take on more color.

"Are you eating regularly? Getting enough sleep?"

Kimber inclined her head, but Jane had her doubts. "I'm really sorry this happened. I'm a widow too." She put her hand over her heart. "How are you coping?"

"It's been hard, but I'm trying to get back to a normal routine."

"That's a good idea," said Jane. The other two remained silent. Tara sank deep into the couch with her chin lowered, peering out from under her long eyelashes, and Justin had on a pinched expression. Probably he was irritated for being out on a cold, rainy night.

Kimber snuggled the blanket around her shoulders as she chewed and swallowed. "I took a leave of absence from work, but I couldn't just hang around the house, so I've gone back."

"What do you do?"

"I work in the office at the construction company. I do the scheduling for the different trades on the sites."

"I didn't know you worked there, too."

"It's a job." Kimber shrugged, but her lips quivered. "I get to drive a company car, though, so it has its benefits."

Jane took a seat on the chaise lounge. "I'm glad you were able to return to work. When my husband died, I was lucky to have some life insurance money to fall back on. Did you have insurance benefits, too?"

Kimber's neck went rigid and her voice rose an octave. "Are you asking if I got any money for Ethan's death? That's none of your business." She gripped the half-eaten sandwich in one hand.

Taken aback, Jane sucked in her breath. "Uh, no, of course not." However, she couldn't resist adding, "But did you?"

"What? Next you'll ask if I had an alibi."

There was silence for a couple of moments, then Jane asked in a quiet voice, "Did he have enemies? Anyone he argued with?"

"Of course, doesn't everyone? Ethan argued with his brother, he argued with me, he caused trouble. So he had plenty of issues, plenty of enemies, too." She swallowed the last of her sandwich in a gulp.

"Who? Who were his enemies?" Jane sat forward to catch a glimpse of Kimber's right arm, but any remaining bruises were hidden under the blanket.

Kimber wiped her mouth with the napkin. "Not me, I wasn't one!"

Tara gave her a sideways glance. "What were you doing...over there, Kim?"

"As I told Jane, I wanted to see where Ethan died. And I did have an alibi. And...and there's no insurance money!" The teal blanket fell to the floor as Kimber catapulted off the couch, then stomped down the hallway and escaped out the front door, banging it shut behind her.

Stunned, no one said anything for a moment or two. "Wow. That was abrupt. I guess I offended her." Jane winced.

Tara said, "So what? Kimber's acting guilty. Returning to the scene of the crime and all that."

"I suppose it was natural for her to want to see where her husband died. You know, like when people put up wreaths and memorials on roadsides when their loved ones die in car crashes. Is it really suspicious?"

With a stern voice, Tara said, "Yes, it is. Very. Why did she get so upset when you asked about the insurance money?"

Jane crossed over to the kitchen and fed the dogs a few pieces of turkey before returning the package to the refrigerator. "I shouldn't have. It really was none of my business."

"She just shot up and ran out of here." Justin's nostrils flared. "She was rude, after you fed her and all. It's a good thing you weren't alone with her." Justin rose from his seat and stood with his legs planted wide. "We need to head home now. It's late."

"Thanks for being here, you two."

Tara took Justin's arm and the young couple swept out the door.

Jane turned the front and back locks and checked the windows, too, before climbing into a hot shower. Was Kimber returning to the scene of the crime as Tara said, or memorializing the spot her husband departed this earth?

****

The next day, Jane had trouble settling down to her work tasks. When her lunch hour arrived, she ambled outside for a bit of sunshine. Sitting on a bench at Confluence Park watching the kayakers in the water, she was restless, so texted Cheryl. When she didn't receive a return text, she punched in Olivia's number.

"Hello, Olivia? I've got so much to tell you." Jane explained the strange encounter with Kimber.

Olivia's voice was animated. "Do you think she did it?"

"I don't really want to believe it, but I don't know her very well and she sure acted funny. It'd crossed my mind Steven murdered Ethan, then hid, but now we know *both* boys were killed, it has to be someone else. And Tara seems convinced it was her…"

"Okay, a wife kills her husband. I get it. But why kill the brother-in-law?" Olivia asked.

Jane narrowed her eyes and nodded. "Right. She had no motive to kill Steven. But Gina could've had a reason to kill both if she wanted all the shares in the company for herself. I need to find a way to talk to Gina again—"

Olivia cut in. "Me, too. I want to be there when you talk to her. But let's think some more about this. What if it was just a random thing? Some crazy person?"

"Like a twin terminator?" Jane paused and thought about how that sounded, like a cartoon character. "Can you ask Doug? Maybe there's a similar, unsolved crime, and he might know about it from his time on the police force."

She could hear Olivia's sigh over the phone. "I'm sorry, Jane, I can't ask him. You know he's not happy about you investigating. And besides, he doesn't know I'm helping and I don't want to tell him. He'll just warn me to stay out of it, too…"

"I wonder how we can find out without involving Doug." Jane slumped back on the park bench. "Hmm. Let me think." Children's laughter carried over from a sand bar on the narrow Platte River.

Olivia's voice came over loud. "Listen, I'm still going to help you. We don't need him."

"I don't want to get you into any trouble with your husband. I can manage," Jane said with false cheer.

"Absolutely not. I'm in this with you. You can't investigate by yourself, you need my help."

Sitting up straighter, Jane asserted herself for once. "I can do it on my own." Then she had second thoughts. "But I appreciate your help."

"Of course you do. We're a team."

"Let's each think about the next step. If I come up with anything, I'll give you a call." Jane said goodbye and hastened back to her office, leaving behind the bright sun on the water and returning to her tall office building. Her mind turned over the suspects again, so she shook herself, gave herself a good talking-to, and got busy with work.

And so, she was occupied the rest of the week taking care of her job during the day and preparing for her dinner club event during the evening. She'd sent an email to the club with a reminder for Saturday that included her menu, plus special directions for a blind wine-tasting contest. Each couple was to bring a bottle of wine wrapped in a plain, brown paper bag, to taste and guess the type of wine without seeing the label on the bottle. She had a prank prepared. She'd found a cheap wine for two dollars—that was the regular price—which she was going to disguise in a paper bag to include with the others. Would anyone be able to guess?

Just as she finished baking a pie and tidying the kitchen on Thursday night, Tara came to her door. "I've had trouble sleeping ever since you found Kimber in that basement."

Jane invited her friend inside. "It was weird, wasn't it? Then, Justin scared me half to death when I saw him out in the rain, too. I thought he was a ghost." She laughed and got a smile from Tara.

"Is your house for sale or did someone put that sign in your yard as a prank?" Tara sat on the gray sectional sofa and ran her hand over the material. "Is this new? I didn't notice it before."

"Yes. Do you like it?" After Tara nodded, Jane added, "I'm just trying to see how easy it would be to sell the house." Why was she having such difficulty committing?

"You're selling because of the murders."

She lifted the palms of her hands up and shrugged. "Yes. Tara, I don't feel safe here. You have to admit, you don't either."

"No, I don't anymore." Tara had a watchfulness about her. "Where are you going to move to?"

"I guess I'd like to live closer to town." Jane listened to the quiet of the country as she gazed out the window from the chaise lounge. There were no traffic noises and she could see all the way to the woods near the clubhouse.

"I guess there's no reason to keep the neighborhood hiking group going, then." Tara gave Jane a sideways glance.

Jane's eyes darted away from the window. "Oh, no. The group will want to continue, I'm sure."

Sighing, Tara said, "All right. I did find a good hike for the group, anyway, if you still want to go."

"Where are you thinking?"

"How about Roxborough State Park? From there we'd be able to see the red rocks and mountain peaks both, plus the trail is only three miles long." Tara drew her cell phone out of her pocket and tapped on the screen.

"Sounds good to me. When?"

"I'm looking at the calendar on the HOA site. Several of the women posted that they want to go Saturday, early." Tara's hair streamed down, hiding her face as she lowered her head over her phone.

"Oh, that's the morning of my dinner club event." Jane leaned back on the couch and rested her head on the cushion as she ran down her mental to-do list.

Tara asked, "What's that?"

"A club I belong to. We meet every two weeks. The idea is to try gourmet recipes on like-minded foodies. Each couple brings a bottle of wine to pair with items on the menu."

"That sounds fun. How old is everybody?" Tara had the bluntness of youth.

"My age—"

"Nice. Well, we can postpone to the next weekend."

"We don't need to. I've done everything in advance, and I'll just be waiting around all day for the party that night." She rubbed her forefinger back and forth across her chin.

"Okay, if you're sure, I'll post it." Tara looked up at Jane, her fingers posed over the screen.

Jane hauled herself off the couch and watched over Tara's shoulder as she entered the time and place Saturday morning. "Did you ask Justin about the farmer's canal trail that winds through the Valrods' ranch? I was wondering if we could hike that sometime, too."

Tara answered, "He said there wasn't public access to it. It's private property. And he's disappointed no one else in the community seems to be interested in extending the bike trails."

"Tara, could one of the Valrods have slipped over to our neighborhood from the farmer's canal trail without being seen?"

"I suppose so, but remember Kimber's car was here the day of the murders. She didn't bother to sneak around."

"Right. It was just a thought."

After they said their goodbyes and Tara left, Jane examined her to-do list one more time. She was ready, and there wasn't much left to be done, so the Roxborough hike would be a nice diversion. Remembering Olivia would want to be included, she texted her the details. After closing her text messages, she noticed a missed call from Everett and tapped in his number to call him back.

"Hello gorgeous," he answered, "would you like to go out to dinner with me Friday night?"

"Yes, I'd love to. That sounds wonderful."

"Or, I could cook you a meal instead of going out."

"Don't you want to relax and enjoy yourself? You cooked last time."

"It's what I love to do."

She hesitated, then took a bracing breath. "Actually, dinner club is at my house on Saturday night. Would you like to come?"

"Yes, I'd like that." He sounded pleased.

"All right. I'll see you Saturday night at five."

"It's a date. And what time on Friday?"

"Are you sure you want to get together both nights? I don't want to monopolize your whole weekend." She tried to sound casual and cool.

"I'm open both nights and I'd love to see you."

A rush of excitement swirled in the pit of her stomach. "All right. Let's go out to eat Friday since we're eating at my house on Saturday. My treat."

"Nah. I'd still like to cook for you on Friday."

"Well, if you're really sure, do you want to meet at my house or yours?"

"Yours. What time?" he asked. Her hardly used gourmet kitchen was suddenly going to get a lot of action.

"I get home from work around six. But what ingredients do you want? I may need to pick some things up at the store."

"Do you have eggs?"

"Yes."

"I'll bring everything else. See you at six on Friday night."

Not wanting to discuss it yet with Everett or the dinner club group, Jane plucked the "For Sale" sign out of her yard and hid it in the garage.

****

On Friday evening, Everett stood close behind Jane in her kitchen showing her how to tilt the pan to make perfect omelets. Her head fit under his chin as he wrapped his arms around her to take hold of the pan. She tried not to giggle like a school girl, but everything he said seemed so funny. Even the things she said must have been amusing, because Everett laughed along with her.

They ate dinner together at the black, high top table with the teal colored stools in the kitchen nook. Then after dinner, while she was rinsing the dishes and filling the dishwasher, Everett slid two treats out of the dogs' goodie bag for Nick and Nora. The puppies sat patiently in the kitchen with their tails thumping on the floor. Nora gulped her treat and finished before Nick.

"Okay, you each get one more. You need to wait a minute, Nora. You both get the same amount." He held two more treats up in the air as the dogs sat at his feet.

"Trust me, they don't know how to count."

Everett gazed at Jane with dancing eyes and they laughed together some more. He helped her into a jacket to take the dogs for a walk in the dark.

The double crime scene was eerily silent and empty, with the yellow tape barring entry. Everett nudged Nick away from the site. "That's so strange that not one, but two, people were killed there."

Jane told him about finding Kimber in the basement. She shuddered as they kept going. "Our neighborhood walking group hiked around the pond by the community center. Let's go that way."

"Tell me again what you found out from them about the murder."

"Not much. Only that Ethan did not show up for an appointment on the day he died. I'm not making much progress."

"What about throwing a party, an open house kind of event? The people who might have a clue are the ones who live here on your street. Ask them over."

"Would a party be a good idea since two bodies were found right next door? Sounds a bit gruesome."

"Well, your interest in the murder investigation is

gruesome." He wiggled his eyebrows up and down. "I think people will naturally talk about it. Just invite them and see what happens."

Maybe the neighbors would know someone looking for a new home. Her neighbor to the west would probably be glad to see her go. "Some of the folks in the neighborhood are not very friendly, but it's worth a try." She glanced to the right and left at the shuttered houses lining the street, with the cars locked inside three-stall garages and home security signs dotting the lawns. No voices to be heard, not even a television set from an open window.

Yanking against their leashes, the dogs led the way, hurrying with their noses to the ground past the clubhouse with the pool closed for the season. Everett and Jane were able to hold hands, since the dogs finally slowed down as they entered the woods. They turned around at the lake because the moon had gone behind the clouds and it was pitch black. Once home, they opened the door to let the dogs run inside. Jane slouched out of her jacket and asked, "Do you like old movies?"

"Yes. Love them." Everett flipped through the television channels and found an old Katharine Hepburn movie neither of them had seen.

She leaned back in Everett's arms on the new sectional sofa and watched the classic. She could smell his appealing masculine scent with its hint of sage and snuggled in his warm embrace. Near the end of the film, the impoverished Katharine Hepburn had arranged a dinner party to impress her guest, wealthy Fred MacMurray, but her dinner failed embarrassingly. Jane sobered up as she thought about her own plans for the next evening.

Everett must've noticed her scared look as he stood to leave. "Are you ready for your dinner party tomorrow?"

"I've done as much as I can in advance, so yes, I'm ready…" She gazed off, wondering where she put her to-do list. "I'm hoping my cooking's up to your standards." Rising from the sofa, she gazed into his blue eyes.

He said with a throaty voice, "Do you need me to do anything?"

"No. It's my turn to cook for you."

He embraced her by lifting her off her feet, then kissed her, and whispered hot in her ear, "I'll be there to help. Don't worry. It'll be a success."

Going out with a chef certainly had its perks.

Chapter 11

After they arrived at the South Rim Trail early Saturday morning, Tara jerked her head in the direction of the group waiting at the trailhead for the three-mile loop. "Kimber's here. She's talking with that older couple, Ruth and Dick, from the first neighborhood walk."

Jane's eyes widened. "Oooh. This is going to be interesting." She grabbed her daypack, slammed the car door shut, and hurried over with Tara to join the group. "I'm Jane Marsh and this is Tara Humphries. We're glad to see all of you."

Kimber avoided Jane's eyes as she introduced herself to the other hikers. "I'm Kimber Valrod." She pointed to the woman next to her. "This is Ashley Turghart. We rode here together."

Jane and Tara turned to get a peek at the young woman standing next to Kimber. Ashley smiled and waved a water bottle around in the air. "Hi, everyone." She was dressed in black spandex pedal pushers and a body-hugging, neon green tank top. Just then, Olivia bounded up in a pair of tan hiking shorts, lavender T-shirt, and matching sun visor. Hiking shoes with lavender laces completed her ensemble.

"Let's get started." Tara flicked a strand of her long blonde hair over her shoulder and nodded to Jane to take the lead. Jane wanted to approach her main suspect, Kimber, to ask questions, but Kimber sidled up to another hiker and they walked off together. So, Jane and Olivia fell into step with Ashley and the rest of the group followed behind.

Jane began, "It's nice to meet you, Ashley. How long have you lived in the neighborhood?"

"A little over a year."

"I just moved in, and I'm not feeling at home yet. It's a little too far out in the country for me." Jane's jaw jutted out. "I refuse to wear a cowboy hat."

Ashley glanced up at her head. "Isn't that a cowboy hat?"

"No." Jane held her safari hat tight to her head as she dodged two joggers who passed them on their left. Their conversation continued down the trail as Jane, and then Olivia too, asked the young woman about her family and job. After several minutes of chit-chat, it was time to bring up the investigation, so Jane took a deep breath and dove in. "What do you think about the deaths?"

"Awful. Just awful." Ashley pursed her lips.

"Did Ethan show up for your warranty appointment on the morning he was killed?"

"No, he didn't. But how did you know about it?"

"The website warranty page."

"Oh. The police grilled me over and over about that day. Yes, Ethan and I were an item, but that was way before he married Kimber. In fact, I introduced them. He left me for Kimber, and they ended up getting married. I explained all of this to the police." Ashley gave a curt nod.

Jane tried to keep the shocked expression off her face. Olivia piped up, "How did that make you feel?

Ethan dumping you for Kimber?"

Ashley backpedaled. "He didn't really dump me. It was more of a mutual breakup. In fact, I was getting ready to break it off with him. But listen to this, Gina actually accused me of having an affair with Ethan right before he was killed! How ridiculous is that? I'm married myself now." Ashley gave them a meaningful look with raised eyebrows. "But Gina was always a piece of work. In fact, she loves being in control of the company now that she has it all to herself."

Her breath caught in her lungs, but Jane asked, "I'm surprised Gina can function with both Valrod brothers gone, herself a recent widow. She's got to be in shock, still."

"Gina? No way. She's been mean to Kimber, trying to force her out of the company, too."

"How?" Olivia pressed.

"Kimber thinks Gina wants her to quit. Anyway, I feel bad for Kimber's sake. She's taking Ethan's death hard." Ashley's arms pumped up and down as they picked up their tempo.

Jane let her hat fall on its strings down her back. It bounced with each step. "You're good friends, aren't you? I'm sure she appreciates having a friend like you."

Ashley's eyes shone. "In fact, we are. I hope the police find who killed Ethan and Steven pretty soon, so she has some resolution. It's hard for her to be under suspicion."

Jane caught a glimpse of Kimber not far ahead. Ashley must've seen her, too, because she increased her pace even more. Jane tried hard to keep up, and it appeared Olivia was just as anxious to catch up to Kimber, so in no time they were on her heels.

A little breathless, Jane fell into step next to her. "I'd like to apologize. I'm sorry I caused you any distress the other night, but I'm glad you came today."

"I heard you practically ran out of Jane's house." Olivia stared fixedly at the young widow, as Jane made a cutting motion with her hand across her neck.

Kimber ground her teeth together. "Jane was the one who was rude to me!" She jerked her head toward Ashley, as if to say, *come on*, and then shot ahead of them, almost running along the trail.

Ashley yelled, "Wait for me." She threw Jane a questioning glance, then raced forward. Soon the two of them were out of sight.

Olivia shook her head in disbelief. "What's her problem?"

"Evidently she's still pretty mad, isn't she?"

"Tsk. Were you rude? Exactly what did you say?" Olivia's face was screwed up in disapproval.

"Nothing you wouldn't have said." Jane frowned. "And why did you bring up the other night? Kimber may have stayed and talked if you hadn't reminded her."

Olivia had high spots of color on her cheeks. "You brought it up when you apologized."

"Yes, but she ran off after your remark." Jane bunched her eyebrows together over the bridge of her nose.

They sniped at each other the rest of the way down the trail. In their excitement, they hurried along, missing the beauty of the towering, red slabs of rock, jutting skyward out of the earth, with rock climbers perched halfway to the top of the giant stones. In the short time it took to return to the parking lot, they almost caught up with Kimber and Ashley, and the last of the other hikers arrived soon after them.

Unaware of what happened, Tara's voice was cheerful. "I'll post the next hike on the website. Thanks everyone for coming." All the hikers departed for their vehicles.

Olivia unlocked her car door. "Why don't the three of us meet at a coffee shop in Littleton on our way home so we can talk further?" After agreeing upon the place, Jane and Tara piled into Tara's car to follow Olivia to the café.

It wasn't long before they were sitting down at a table with their beverages. "Tara, Ashley had an affair with Ethan," Olivia said right off.

"What? I don't believe it! When was this?" Tara's fist went up to her mouth.

Jane jumped in. "It was before he started going with Kimber. She claimed the affair was over and done with a long time ago, so she's not the recent affair." She blew on her latte, the steam giving off a cinnamon-y scent.

"Oh." Tara dropped her hands to the table and her fists unclenched.

"Another thing, Kimber wouldn't talk to Jane, here." Olivia rolled her eyes.

"So what?" Tara fiddled with her iced drink, poking her straw in and out of the plastic lid with a squeaky noise.

Jane shifted in her chair. "I'm surprised she came today."

Leaving her straw on the table, Tara scooted in closer. "Since I was the one who posted the hike, she probably didn't know you were coming."

"I'm not sure what her anger issue is. Kimber claims she had an alibi and no insurance money, so no opportunity and no motive. What's she worried about?" Jane took a sip of her latte.

"Impossible!" Tara shoved herself back from the table. "I don't believe for a minute she has an alibi."

With gold bracelets jangling, Olivia fluttered her hands around. "You could be right. Why should we take Kimber's word for it?"

Jane rubbed her forehead. "Ashley did admit Kimber's under police suspicion. They must believe she has motive and opportunity. How can we find out if she's telling the truth?"

"Gina would know about the insurance." Olivia clucked her tongue again.

Jumping up, Jane walked back and forth in small, quick steps between the tables and pounded a fist into the palm of her hand. "But what *if* Kimber is telling the truth? Gina could be the murderer. She wants control of the business, so she gets rid of Ethan and Steven, and acquires the whole company..."

Olivia's eyes followed Jane, but Tara glared down at her iced coffee and resumed playing with her straw. As Jane passed by, Olivia plucked at her sleeve. "Sit down and let's talk about this."

"Okay." Jane plopped into the chair and tapped her knuckles on her chin along with the barely audible slow jazz playing over the café's sound system. "But if Kimber didn't have an alibi, what's her motive? She might've had more money and standing in the community when Ethan was alive."

"Remember Gina inherited shares in the company and Kimber didn't. So, no money of her own." Olivia wagged her index finger in the air.

"What if Ethan was planning to leave her? That's a motive." Tara whipped a strand of her long blonde hair over her shoulder.

Olivia said, "If that's true, Kimber's not eliminated. This murder could've had nothing to do with insurance money or company control. We're back to his affair…"

On the notepad retrieved from her purse, Jane jotted a few notes. "A love triangle. That can be a pretty powerful motive. That's the theme for most of my favorite movies anyhow—"

"And what if she's lying about the life insurance policy?" Olivia tapped the pad of paper with her forefinger. "Write that down."

Jane's eyes pinged around the room as she chewed on the tip of her pen. "So, the main suspects are Gina and Kimber, since Kimber's not out of the picture. And we learned that Kimber works for the construction company. Maybe she was the one stealing the money." She scribbled another note. "This is what I've written. Gina for company control, Kimber for insurance money, potential theft of company funds, and anger over the affair. She does have anger issues."

Olivia's eyes narrowed. "You thought Ethan was stealing the company money."

"True. I did wonder…and let me write down the mystery woman Ethan was having an affair with. She might have a motive."

Standing up, Tara slam-dunked her nearly full, plastic cup into the trash can. "I don't know why you're going on about this when you're moving, Jane. Anyway, I really have to be getting home."

Olivia's head jerked around. "What's this? You're moving?"

Jane shrugged, her neck turtling between her shoulders. "Maybe, maybe. Nothing definite yet." Her shoulders fell back down as she rose, packed her notes away, and grabbed her hat from the back of the chair. "I need to get going, too." They gathered their belongings and stole out to the parking lot. Jane and Olivia carried their drinks with them for the drive home.

After Tara got into her car, Olivia stopped Jane with a hand on her arm. "Let's talk soon about what we can investigate next."

"I'd like to know what Doug thinks about these new clues. Can't you ask him?" Jane lifted one eyebrow in a question.

"I can't! He'll ask me how I found out about all this, and I'll have to tell him we've been asking Kimber questions. And he won't like that at all." Olivia's hand flattened against her throat as she gave her head a small shake.

"Oh, all right then."

The two friends said goodbye and jumped into their cars to head home. Jane focused her eyes on the tall pines at the edge of the road. "Who did you talk to on the hike, Tara? You were quite a ways behind us, and I didn't see who you were with."

"Just Ruth and Dick. We didn't talk about the murder at all, if you're wondering."

"That's too bad. They seem to know everybody, and they might have a take on the Valrods."

"Why would Olivia's husband be mad you're asking questions?"

"He used to be a policeman, and he thinks we

might interfere with the police investigation. Plus, he's protective of Olivia."

"So, she's helping you investigate, then?"

"Sort of." Jane couldn't deny it.

"He's right, you know. You really do need to quit asking questions." Tara's knuckles were white as she clenched the steering wheel and shot Jane a level look.

Jane bit her tongue as she struggled to keep the smile on her face. "Did you enjoy the hike?"

"Yes, but it wasn't long enough. Hardly worth the drive down." Tara's voice was cold, leaving Jane with an empty feeling.

****

Jane was home by eleven. She changed out of her hiking clothes and showered. Next, she checked her timetable—the list she had written to help remember everything she needed to do to make her dinner a success—and then she got busy.

But later that afternoon she was interrupted by the realtor on the phone. "I have a showing for the house. Can I bring them over, say in a half hour?"

Since the house was party-ready, it also gleamed like a showroom.

On the kitchen counter was the peach pie she'd baked on Thursday, with its golden crust sprinkled with sparkling raw sugar on a round crown peaking high above the pie dish. Jane had filled several capacious glass domes and apothecary jars with over-sized lemons she'd bought at the farmer's market along with the peaches. The jars were crowded together in the center of the dining room table, which was cheerful with yellow shell chairs tucked under the white tablecloth, and white, square dishes and gray and yellow napkins at each place setting. The yellow and teal pillows fluffed up on the new sofa in the family room pulled the style together.

"Sure. I'll take the dogs for a long walk while you're showing the house."

After hanging up, Jane hauled the "For Sale" sign back to the front yard and pushed the posts into the ground. She slipped the harnesses over the dogs' heads and fastened them around their bellies. As soon as the real estate agent turned into the driveway, Jane was out the door, the dogs trotting ahead. She allowed them to take their time, sniffing and snorting among the tall grasses and bushes near the edge of the pond. After checking the time and thinking it was more than enough, Jane turned the dogs back toward home. She dragged the "For Sale" sign back to the garage before she and the pups went in.

The realtor had left a note on the counter, reading, "The house showed well. Good job. The pie was a nice touch. They loved it. I'll call you later." She probably believed Jane had prepared the house for a showing rather than a party.

Just as she put the note down, her phone rang. It was the realtor and her voice was loud and excited. "I have an offer and it's over the asking price! But there's a condition."

"What?" Jane's mind raced as she absently opened the patio door and the dogs bounded out with their harnesses still on.

"They need possession in two weeks. They can't wait on a contingency for you to find another house to move into."

Jane gulped. "Two weeks, huh?" Most of her boxes

were still packed, so maybe it was possible. She'd use a different moving company this time, though. Her eyes darted to the clock. "I can't make the decision right this minute. I need to sleep on it."

The realtor didn't say anything for a moment. "All right, then. But think about this. They want to live in this particular neighborhood and the new builder is going to have some spec homes ready for immediate possession soon. You might miss this chance and who knows when you'll get another offer like this."

"I understand, but as I said, I can't make a quick decision on something this important."

"You already made that decision when you signed the listing agreement."

Jane stretched her neck and scratched the back of her head. She thought about the "For Sale" sign hidden in the garage. "I'll probably say yes, but call me tomorrow, please?"

"Okay. Talk to you then."

Geez. Didn't she know her own mind? Wasn't this exactly what she wanted? It was probably the two-week deadline bothering her, that's all. She opened the door and called the dogs in. After tugging their harnesses off, she tossed them in the basket with the leashes by the door. Her backyard was the perfect size for the dogs, and the walking path to the pond was their favorite. Two weeks to look for another place that suited her and her pets this well! She couldn't think about it now—her guests were soon to arrive.

Jane ran her finger down the last-minute tasks on her to-do list. She'd tossed a spinach salad with sliced strawberries and sunflower greens and organized her appetizers on serving trays—bruschetta, Crostini, and

Brie with crackers. Oversized potatoes were in the bottom compartment of the double oven on low temperature to slow cook. The short ribs were marinating in the refrigerator. The beets were a pretty color. She didn't like this vegetable, but Erin and Caleb assured her beets would be delicious drizzled with olive oil and roasted, plus they were nutritious. After taking another peek at the beets spaced evenly on the cookie sheet ready to go under the broiler with the ribs, she ticked the last item off her list.

Just before the guests were due to arrive, Jane dressed in slim jeans with a fitted, crisp cotton shirt and applied her makeup. Then she plucked the banner that read "celebrate the small things" off her refrigerator and hung it in the powder room. Yes, there was a perfect spot for it above the hand towel. Examining the printer's tray on the opposite wall, she remembered Bruce and his jokes. What would he have made of the banner's sentiment in a bathroom? Even though he wouldn't be attending tonight, she thought it best to put the banner back on her refrigerator.

Erin and Caleb arrived early. Caleb sported a T-shirt—it read, *Trust Me, I Have a Beard*—jeans, and high top, red tennis shoes, and Erin was wearing a vintage, boho, chic top and skirt, with laced-up, gladiator sandals on her feet. They set their bottle of wine in its brown paper bag on the counter.

"I love your sofa and chaise lounge. You need an atomic clock to go with it." Her daughter-in-law always had good decorating suggestions.

"And look what I've done with the dining room."

"Very nice." Erin nodded with a slow wink. The new furniture in the family room, plus the new chairs in her dining room, made Jane even more excited for the party. If her meal didn't turn out, at least her furniture would look good.

"We got something for you. Come outside to the front yard," said Caleb. They walked out the front door to the curb, where he pointed to a stone engraved with the words, "Welcome—the Marsh Residence."

"Thanks so much. I love, love, love it." A homey and happy warmth spread from the pit of Jane's stomach.

"It's so your friends can find your new house," added Erin.

"You two are so sweet. Thanks." Jane gave them each a hug. The stone looked heavy, but she could take it with her when she moved.

Everett showed up as they were about to go back inside, without giving Jane a kiss on the cheek in greeting like he usually did. Olivia and Doug arrived soon afterward. The men were dressed casually in jeans, but Olivia wore a short, melon-colored skirt and sweater.

They wandered outside to the back deck for the wine tasting contest. Jane poured glasses out of the first brown paper wrapped bottle. "I once heard wine described as 'flabby,' but I don't know what that means. How can a beverage be flabby?"

Everett answered. "That means it's not bold."

"Oh." Jane knitted her eyebrows together. Could wine be obtuse? Scary? Breezy? She was going to throw out those descriptions at her next opportunity. See if anyone agreed.

Everett's bottle was sampled next. "What do you think of the varietal I brought?"

"Is it a blend?" Caleb swished the wine around in his glass.

"No." Everett frowned. "Varietals are not the same as blends."

Jane had no idea what they were talking about. Caleb sniffed over the top of his glass. "I think I smell blackberry."

"I taste pepper and cinnamon. It's a Syrah." Doug tapped the side of his nose with his index finger. Olivia shrugged.

Jane went along with the others. "Oh yes, I taste that." But there was a harshness and an unpleasant bitterness in her mouth after she swirled the wine around and swallowed.

She was surprised and a little pleased when Everett voiced the same opinion. "It has an awkward aftertaste."

Erin put her glass down. "What do you do with the wine if you don't want to finish the sample? I know you're supposed to spit it out, but I never do."

"How do you spit it out when the bucket's across the bar? Do you ask someone to pass the bucket? Do you spew across the bar like at a spittoon in the old western movies?" Jane handed the bucket to Olivia.

Olivia made a face. "It's kind of disgusting to spit. It's easier to take just a tiny sip and dump out the rest." She emptied her glass into the bucket and passed it to Erin.

"Well, Everett guessed all the kinds of wine. So, he wins!" Jane handed him an unopened bottle, a merlot that was wrapped with a bow. "That's for you to take home and enjoy."

"I'm embarrassed that I actually liked the cheap,

two-dollar wine the best!" As Olivia chuckled, they all laughed with her.

Just then a loud bang came from inside the house. It sounded like a gunshot! A cold chill swept through Jane's heart as everyone sat frozen for a moment.

Doug jumped up and rushed indoors with Everett and Caleb on his heels. Even though blood thumped in her ears, Jane squared her shoulders and strode in after them.

Chapter 12

The men made swift steps as they separated to search the rooms. Jane, Erin, and Olivia stood close together in the middle of the kitchen, waiting.

Doug returned. "Jane, you left the front door unlocked."

"Did someone get in the house with a gun?" Jane was alert for the slightest additional sound.

Olivia gasped and pointed a shaky finger over Jane's shoulder. An odd prickling began at the back of Jane's neck, and she was afraid to turn around. Olivia trilled, "Look at the oven."

Jane spun about to see smoke curling around the seams where the door met the oven's face. Everett raced over to open it. One of the potatoes had exploded, evidently with a loud bang.

Breathing a sigh of relief, she threw what was left of it down the garbage disposal.

"Don't worry. These potatoes are huge. We can probably each split a potato in half, and there would still be some left over." Everett used tongs to remove the rest of the steaming potatoes from the baking dish.

"That mess is nasty. I don't think I've ever seen that happen before. I don't suppose this was a prank gone bad." As she peered in the oven, Olivia twisted her earring around and around prettily with her dainty fingers.

Jane answered with a grin, "Nope, the cheap wine was the only prank I planned. But the joke's on me, because I don't know how to operate the self-cleaning function in the oven. I'll have to find the directions."

Caleb rifled through the kitchen drawers, and Erin peered in the cabinets for the oven booklet.

"Let's leave the oven till later. The food's ready to be served, so let's eat." Everett had a harshness to his voice. She gave him a questioning glance, but he either didn't see it or chose to ignore her. The guests shuffled into the dining room and took seats around the table.

She and Everett bumped into each other at the sink and fridge when they were arranging the finishing touches on the plates of salad, short ribs, baked potatoes, and beets. "Even though this kitchen's so much larger than at my old house, it still seems too small." Jane laughed, trying to get a smile out of him.

"That's because there's still only the same small amount of space in front of the kitchen sink and the same for the refrigerator." Everett turned away from her and hustled into the dining room carrying two full plates to set before the guests. After another trip, everyone was served.

Olivia pointed out she'd never before seen plastic chairs in a formal dining room. She peeked over the top of a pair of orange reading glasses perched on her nose. "I've chosen a couple from those who want to audition for our dinner club, Marcy and Greg Pelican. Jane, you'll be interested to know they own a bicycle shop in Limestone Heights."

"Not the judge, then?" Jane glanced down to see Everett poise his fork over the baked potato on her plate, but he withdrew his hand. He tossed his long, wavy hair back from his face and was not smiling as usual.

"I contacted the judge's wife, but they had already joined another club. The Pelicans' bicycle shop's in the old downtown section off Fourth Street."

"I'll have to take my bike there for a spring tune-up."

"I'll ask them to come to the next event." Olivia turned to Erin and Caleb sitting together at the other end of the table. "Unless you want to try out for the club?"

"No, we're just filling in." Erin smiled as she shoved a beet around on her plate.

"Well, you're certainly welcome to try out if you want." Doug stuck his chest out as he gave Olivia a glare. Affection for him rushed through Jane.

Caleb said, "This is fun, but we can't make the commitment."

Olivia jabbed a section of ribs with her fork. "Okay. It's my turn to host next. I'll invite the Pelicans. If we think they're a good fit, we can ask them to host the event after mine. See how they do."

Jane glanced at the others across the table. It was wonderful to meet new people and make new friends. It was almost like being back in high school when your peers were the most important people in your life. Being busy raising children often shoved those friendships aside, but now the kids were grown, friends were once again important. Then, your grown children became your friends, too. She gazed at Erin and Caleb, sitting in as the third dinner couple this one time, chatting with Everett about the loft they'd just bought.

Doug interrupted Jane's thoughts. "I called the

District Attorney, and I'm having lunch with him next week. I'm sure he'll keep me in the loop when an arrest is made in the Valrod case—"

"Did he say anything about Steven Valrod? The deaths are obviously linked."

"Yes. They determined neither man fell into the foundation pit accidently. Blood was found closer to the middle of the pit, like Ethan was shoved some distance in, then his body dragged closer to the foundation wall."

"What about Steven?" Jane took a sip of her water and swallowed hard.

"He was killed by a blow to the head from the tractor bucket. The killer then buried Steven's body with dirt using the tractor. But it appeared as if he was spooked and fled the scene before completely covering Ethan."

Olivia asked, "Were they killed at the same time?"

"It's likely from the position of the bodies that, yes, they were."

A tremor shuddered up Jane's spine. She needed to accept that offer on the house, and fast.

"Do we have to talk about this during dinner?" Everett put his utensils down and crossed his arms.

"You're right, of course." Jane squeezed his elbow, then put a forkful of beets in her mouth and chewed slowly as she thought about the murders and if she could get organized for another move in two short weeks.

"It is gruesome." Erin pulled a face.

Olivia frowned. "I have to ask one more question, though. Why in the world didn't the police find Steven right after Ethan was found? It makes no sense."

Her husband answered. "It does look bad for the crime scene investigators that they didn't."

"We should go over and take a peek at the scene after dinner." Olivia's eyes appeared bright.

Doug flipped his palm upward. "No. We're not going to disturb the scene. That's why the tape's still up. You two need to stay out of the investigation."

Jane kicked her friend under the table, while fixing an innocent gaze on Doug. "Of course, Doug." She avoided Olivia's eyes while she handed around the plates of pie and Everett fed the dogs under the table from morsels on his dinner plate.

Soon everyone had put down their forks and knives. Doug patted his belly. "That was delicious, Jane."

"Let me help clean up," offered Erin.

"You go on outside with the others. I'll just be a minute, but thanks honey." Jane rose to clear the table.

The group trooped into the backyard, and Everett lit the logs in the pit with a fire starter. After a few minutes, Jane carried out a basket of chocolate bars, marshmallows, and graham crackers. "I hope everyone's not too full from pie, because I've got more sweets. Marshmallows to toast for S'mores."

Olivia reached toward the basket. "I want one."

"Me, too," said Erin and Caleb at the same time.

They speared the sugary confections onto skewers and toasted them as the fire took hold and sparks flew up into the night sky. Wood smoke filled the air and reminded Jane of camping. She turned on her iPod, and Frank Sinatra's voice sang out of the speakers, but at the same time music blasted out from the neighbor's small house to the west.

"I think there's a party next door." Caleb stood up and strained to look over the fence. "I see people in the backyard." Laughter mingled with the neighbor's music.

"Wouldn't you know it? A party on the same night as mine. And he never asked my permission," Jane joked, turning off her iPod. "We'll just enjoy his music."

Erin gave Jane a smile as a country-western tune started up.

Olivia finished toasting her marshmallow and assembling her S'more, so she adjusted her patio chair to sit back down. Once seated, she backed her chair away from the fire, but it began to topple backward off the lip of the cement slab that surrounded the pit. Even though the drop-off was only an inch or two, the ground sloped away and Olivia and the chair continued to somersault back.

Doug jumped up. "Olivia!" Everyone else gapped with open mouths. Olivia's legs splayed out in slow motion, exposing a glimpse of her underwear, white with orange polka-dots, as her legs flew over her head. Suddenly, Olivia landed on her feet, her right hand held high in the air holding the S'more intact. Even her jet black, bob hairdo remained unruffled. "I didn't drop my S'more!"

"Are you all right?" Jane asked as everyone burst into laughter. Then she started to laugh, too. Olivia and Jane laughed the longest. "I can't quit laughing," tittered Jane. "Hee, hee, hee."

"Bwahaha!" burst out Olivia.

"Give these girls more wine," said Doug.

Jane tried to explain. "It's not the wine. I'm

clearheaded. Teeheehee." It was obvious that no one believed her.

"You know that man's death could've been an accident after all." Erin wiped her sticky hands on a napkin. "What if he went backward by accident, like Olivia, here? Maybe he was arguing with his brother. They struggled. Then Ethan and Steven took a tumble into the opening, and the fall killed them both."

"How did their bodies get buried, then?" Olivia re-adjusted her chair away from the edge.

Jane agreed. "More likely his wife, Kimber, was arguing with Ethan. She had bruises on her right arm when I saw her a few days after Ethan's death. Maybe Steven happened along and witnessed the whole thing, so she shoved Steven into the hole, too, and killed him. I'm sure the police questioned her about those bruises, though."

"Can a woman really push two grown men to their deaths? And have the strength to move their bodies? Plus, if Ethan's death was an accident, why kill Steven too? And try to cover them up with dirt?" Erin gazed around the group for an answer.

"Someone in a panic who wasn't thinking straight might do that." Doug turned to Jane. "Have the police questioned you about your deceased husbands?"

"What! No. Why would they?" She flinched and squeezed her hand against her chest.

"Men falling to their deaths…"

Jane's cheeks flamed as she glared at Doug. A hush fell on the group. Everett stared into his wine glass.

Someone was moving around on the other side of the fence to the east—near the crime scene. Jane cocked an ear to listen, but Olivia broke the quiet of the night by saying, "There wasn't any water in the foundation pit, only dirt." Was she coming to Jane's defense or making an implication concerning Jane's nickname, "widow of the waves?" Jane beetled her eyebrows, then relaxed them so sharp lines wouldn't deepen her forehead.

The dogs ran barking along the property line, obliterating sounds of movement from the other side of the fence. And after Nick and Nora settled down, all was silent.

Jane set her wine glass on the cement slab. "With all your police experience, Doug, I was wondering if you knew of any similar, unsolved crimes, like when twins were both killed." She narrowed her eyes.

He stroked his bristling mustache, as if deep in thought. "No, I'm not aware of a similar criminal profile."

"You'll call me if you find out more, right?"

Doug sighed. "I will as long as you promise not to go digging around on your own." Jane's eyes flicked to Olivia.

Caleb scowled. "I hope you're listening to Doug's advice, Mom."

Erin was apparently unaware of any tension. "So you think they were killed over money or control of the construction company? Or was it the affair?"

Jane tried to put on a virtuous expression. "You're asking me?"

Putting down his drink, Caleb let out a long breath and gave Erin an exasperated glance. His young wife shrugged her shoulders and grinned back at him.

At this point the party broke up. Both Caleb and

Erin gave Jane hugs and told her what a good time they'd had. The Ladners also paid her lavish compliments. After they left, only Everett remained and the two went back outside into the night.

"Is everything okay?" Jane leaned down to pick up the marshmallow skewers from the ground near the fire pit. "Is anything bothering you?"

"Well, something did happen earlier today."

"What?" Jane straightened.

"I applied for a chef's position at a restaurant in Aurora owned by Polly Capricorn, and I had an interview with her this afternoon."

"Oh?" Jane held her breath.

"We talked about my experience, including giving cooking lessons at dinner club events, and I mentioned your name."

Jane swallowed. "What did she say?"

"She said she'd never hire anyone who's a friend of yours."

"What in the world! I only met her once. Did she say anything more?"

"She suggested that I ask you."

Jane's eyes bored into Everett's small blue eyes in his strong face. "I dated her ex-husband, Dale, for a while. That's all. We stopped going out a long time ago." She glanced away from Everett and peered up as the stars disappeared in the blackness of the night sky. "Wow. A love triangle. Just like in Casablanca when Rick says to Laszlo, 'I suggest that you ask your wife.'"

"I beg your pardon?"

"Ask your wife."

"My wife?"

"Haven't you seen that movie? I thought you liked

old movies."

"Jane, I didn't get the job." He was breathing hard.

"I'm sorry, but it's not my fault." Jane lowered her eyes in true Ingrid Bergman style. Just then, big drops of rain fell hard and fast from the sky. The two made several trips back and forth from the patio deck to the kitchen to bring in the last of the wine glasses. The rain soaked them to the skin, washing the uneasiness away, and they both laughed.

Standing inside the doorway, Everett took Jane in his arms and kissed her as the door blew open from the wind and rain. Their wet shirts stuck together. Thunder clapped in approval. She withdrew from the kiss in wonder. Should she slap him as Maureen O'Hara had slapped John Wayne?

"Shall I spend the night?" Everett spoke into her ear.

"Uh, no." Visions of the stormy scene from the *Quiet Man* movie flew out of Jane's mind.

Everett's arms dropped to his sides. He gave her a glassy stare, then turned on his heels and took flight, slamming the door behind him. It took her a stunned moment to shake herself, but he was long gone. What just happened? First Kimber, now Everett.

She snatched up her cell phone to text Cheryl. Although it was quite late, Cheryl texted back: *No mounting Everett then?*

Jane glared at the text in disbelief. Then her phone pinged again with another text: *Just kidding!*

Jane texted back: *LOL. That sounds like Bruce's golf course humor.*

Everyone told her the new dating scene included sleepovers, but she hadn't believed it until now. She took a glimpse of her middle-aged body and sighed.

She needed to quit taking her dating cues from romantic scenes in old movies.

Chapter 13

What would Ava Gardner do to win back Clark Gable's heart from that cool witch, Grace Kelly? Or going back further, what would Jean Harlow do? She shouldn't have watched the original of *Mogambo* called *Red Dust* before finally falling asleep last night at two in the morning.

She was still upset and her mind raced, so she focused again on the service at the new church she was visiting in a neighboring suburb.

A rock band covered the stage, playing worship songs. Since she'd arrived late, she'd been forced to take a seat at the front of the church where the music was loudest. Young people surrounded her, standing, so Jane stood, too. They waved their arms and danced with the music. Was this a mosh pit? Her ears rang by the time the worship team finished and the pastor gave his sermon. It was certainly different from the church last week with the rodeo event.

After returning home, she checked her pantry and made a list of things she needed. She grabbed her backpack and donned her wide-brimmed safari hat, then walked the half mile to the grocery store.

Once she was through the checkout stand, she placed the handful of items into her backpack and trailed out into the bright sunshine. On the corner near the stoplight stood a teenager twirling a sign, "Houses for sale—see showroom." Stopping to wait for the green light to cross the street, she said to the young man, "You look like you could use some water."

The teenager jerked his earbuds out. "I drank mine an hour ago and still have two hours left on my shift." Even though it was the beginning of October, it was steamy warm in the sunshine and the sweat beaded up on his forehead.

She plucked a bottle from her grocery bag and set it on the ground. "Here. You need to stay hydrated." The light turned green, and she was about to cross the street, but paused. "So, you work for the new builder?"

"Yeah. My job's called a 'human directional,' but I just tell everybody I'm a street corner twirler. It's a good job. I get to listen to music and twirling this sign works my biceps." He glanced down at his arms and flexed his muscles.

"Looks like you've been at it a long time."

"Since last year. I used to work for the Valrods, too."

Jane tipped her hat backward and let it slide down to hang by its drawstrings. "Were they good to work for?"

"Ethan was cool, if you know what I mean."

"What do you mean?" She returned his grin.

"You know, we smoked weed together. It's legal now, so no one can do anything 'bout it—"

"You did this before it was legal, then?"

He turned away to face the oncoming traffic, dancing with his feet and tossing the sign up into the air. Jane spoke louder as the roaring cars whizzed past, belching out fumes. "You liked Ethan, didn't you?"

"Yeah." The teenager caught the sign in his left

hand and twirled it fast with both hands, like a baton.

"Did you know Steven, too?"

"Yeah. But Steven was nothin' like Ethan. Stevie was one uptight guy." Sweat ran down his face as he twisted the cap off and took a long drink from the bottle. "I'd better get back to work. Thanks for the water." He set the bottle on the pavement and turned his back to her, facing the cars now coming from the other direction.

After jerking her hat back onto her head, she hurried the rest of the way home. She was not in support of the new law in Colorado that legalized marijuana, but it'd passed by popular vote and marijuana shops were popping up all over.

She put her groceries away, then mixed together a chocolate cake from scratch. While the cake was in the oven, she sent Everett a text message thanking him for coming to her dinner club party and asking him to forgive her for being so abrupt. He was the one who should apologize, but she was willing to make the first effort. She didn't receive a reply back.

As the cake baked in two round pans, she printed five invitations from a template on the computer for a come-as-you-are coffee klatch. After taking the cake pans out of the oven to cool, she breathed in the baked chocolate aroma and resisted the urge to sample a bite. Instead, she walked across the street to introduce herself to the neighbors.

No one answered at the first house, so she slid the invitation into the crack between the storm door and the door frame. At the second neighbor's, Jane held out the invitation to the elderly woman who answered. "Hello. My name's Jane. I hope you can come to my house for coffee and cake at two this afternoon."

The old lady took the invitation without a smile. "I'm Beth."

"What do you think about what happened across the street?" Jane raised her eyebrows.

"I don't know what to think." Beth wrinkled her nose.

"Did you know the Valrods?"

Beth shook her head. "I saw a 'For Sale' sign in your yard, but it's down now."

"Yes, unfortunately I need to move. I hope you can make it to my coffee klatch and I'll tell you all about it." Jane smiled as Beth shut the door.

The next resident accepted the invitation, but once questioned about the Valrods, said, "I'm too busy to talk right now. I'll see you at two."

She crossed the street to the small ranch-style house to the west of hers. The angry man, whom Jane had caught on her cell phone camera, answered her knock. Before she could utter a word, he said, "I'm not buying anything," and slammed the door. The curtain twitched as she descended the porch steps.

She scooted down the street and knocked on Tara's front door. "I'm having coffee and cake at my house at two this afternoon. Here's the invitation. I invited other neighbors, but one of them was rude and said he wasn't buying anything."

"I know which one that was." Tara chuckled. "The house on the other side of you, right?"

"Yes. What's his problem?"

"Don't worry. That's the way he is."

"I think two people might be coming, anyway. I made chocolate cake."

"Sounds great. I'll come. Are you nosing around some more?"

"Yes, you could say that." Jane's smile vanished as she pursed her lips. "Tara, I found out Ethan smoked marijuana before it was legal."

The younger woman rolled her eyes. "Big deal."

Jane breathed out a long, low sigh. "I suppose you're right. It probably has nothing to do with his death."

"Give it up, Jane." Tara shook her head.

"Okay. See you at two." After Jane left, she stopped once more at the house where there was no answer, but it still appeared no one was home.

Once back in her kitchen, she melted more of the chocolate squares, then stirred in milk, confectioner's sugar, softened butter, and vanilla. She removed the cakes from the pans onto a tiered cake platter, frosted the layers, and shook some chocolate sprinkles over the top. She allowed herself to lick the leftover frosting from the bowl.

The realtor phoned again and Jane agreed to sell. But instead of making a list of things to be done, like calling the moving company and stopping the paper, she was too busy getting ready for her coffee klatch— heck, did she need a list since she'd just done all of those things and wasn't likely to forget? She erased all signs of the party the night before, freshened the powder room and emptied the dishwasher, then made a pot of coffee and switched on some background music.

Tara and Justin knocked on the door at two. Jane's eyes roved up and down the street, but no one else was in sight. She poured them coffee, and after fifteen minutes of waiting, cut the cake.

"Two of the neighbors told me they were coming. I wonder what happened to them," Jane said with a frown as she stared down at her feet.

Tara flipped her hair back from her face. "They called me after you left my house." Jane stuck out her lower lip in an exaggerated frown. Tara continued, "They saw through your attempt to question them. They thought it fishy that you were asking about the Valrods. Beth, the one who lives in the house across from me, actually said the killer will immerse herself in the investigation. She saw that on a crime show and thinks you're selling and moving out to make your escape."

Jane kept her mouth shut and didn't mention the offer she'd accepted.

"More for us. This cake is delicious, not dry at all." Justin licked his lips and put another forkful in his mouth.

Jane scowled. "How can they think I'm the killer?"

Tara shrugged. "Who knows?"

Justin lifted another slice off the platter. "The police aren't going to catch him. I've heard if they don't make an arrest within a couple of days, the chances go down that the crime will be solved."

"It was Kimber. That was clear from the other night." Tara had a stubborn expression with a smear of chocolate on her lower lip.

Jane cut several large slices of cake to send home with her young friends. She once more glanced up and down the street as Tara and Justin walked to their own door, but no other neighbors were in sight, no one was hurrying over at the last minute. This was the ultimate insult. She was glad to be moving.

She spent the rest of the day making lists and

organizing her boxes. She called a different moving company and searched the internet for available apartments in Verano with short term leases. She didn't want to be in a rush to find a new home, so an apartment was what she needed. An apartment with a security guard in the lobby.

****

After her devotional time on Monday morning before work, she stuffed running clothes into her work satchel and hustled out the door. Once at her desk, she worked hard all morning, anticipating a chance to get outside at noon, even if it was all by herself without her former downtown buddy.

After changing into her baggy running clothes, she ran at a slow pace on the path winding from downtown Denver along Cherry Creek to Confluence Park, then forking north along the Platte River. A group of construction workers in yellow hardhats stopped what they were doing and ogled at a young woman wearing skimpy running shorts and an athletic top with a bare midriff. One of the men whistled.

Jane braced herself as her feet pounded down the path. But when she approached the workers, they picked up their shovels and returned back to their task. How many more insults would she have to endure? Wait, the young men were probably the same age as her sons, so of course they wouldn't notice her. When did she get older than everyone else?

Rejected by Everett. Rejected by the neighbors, even. Old and unloved. And soon to be homeless. She might need to join the homeless people under the bridges.

When Jane walked into the house after work that

day, she found the dogs outside on the back deck. "How in the world did you get out there?" she asked, opening the door to let them in.

She knelt down to rub their ears as they licked her cheek. Whew. Nora had bad breath. After giving the dogs breath-freshening treats, she walked from room to room, not really believing an intruder could've gotten into the house. Was it possible she forgot to make sure Nick and Nora were inside when she left for work? It couldn't have been the realtor because she would've called and left a note, and besides, the house was already sold.

Not finding anything else unusual, she shrugged into a jacket, then harnessed the dogs to take them for a walk. She may have had her exercise at noon, but the dogs still needed theirs. Nick and Nora were full of energy, so they scampered past the clubhouse and entered the short woods that led east to the pond. A flock of geese descended to the water to bed down at the end of the day. Before doing an about-face to return west through the woods, she let her dogs sniff around. The ground was hard under her boots. The cool evening wind blew along the tree tops and whispered through the tall grasses. Pink, orange and turquoise streaked across the sky as the sun set behind Long's Peak. For a moment, waves of regret rolled across her heart—she would miss the pond, the peak, the peacefulness of the woods.

The pups stiffened, then started barking and lunging on their leashes at something in the trees, but only a dry tumbleweed whisked along the path and out of sight. Jane hurried toward home, since the light was fading fast. She dashed past a Lexus with "*VALROD3*" license plates in the parking lot at the community center clubhouse, but had to stop and wait for Nora to complete her business under the pine trees.

The door of the community center opened with a loud bang. Kimber emerged with her sister-in-law, Gina. They glanced the other way and didn't seem to notice her, so Jane shot behind a tall spruce and tugged Nick and Nora in with her. While the dogs were busy sniffing the base of the tree, she cocked an ear to hear the conversation.

"That Jane Marsh has been asking questions. I can't believe her nerve." Kimber's mouth was twisted in a grim frown. Jane froze into a statue.

"What'd she ask?"

"About whether I got any insurance money! Can you believe it?"

Jane clenched her fists, but stopped herself from running out from the behind the tree and telling Kimber how wrong she was—because she never actually asked.

Gina let out a long whistle. "No...what gall. Did you tell her about the one million?"

Jane gasped out loud, then held her breath, but Nick chose at that moment to start barking at a squirrel.

After taking a few steps backward until her feet touched the walking path, she strode out from the pines into the parking lot, as if she'd just arrived on the spot. She held her head high as she motored past them. "Hello girls!" Gina and Kimber were left behind with their mouths hanging open. As Jane crossed the street, she shot a quick glance back. Gina stood with hands on hips, fists clenched.

As soon as she rounded the corner out of sight, she raced home, her nostrils opening and closing as she sucked in air and the dogs sprinted in front of her, enjoying the run. Once home, she locked the door behind her. After unhooking the dogs' harnesses and stowing the leashes in their basket, she let the dogs jump onto the new couch and sank down beside them, shivering. She tucked her feet beneath her and stretched her teal throw blanket up to her chin.

Her breathing returned to normal after a moment or two, but she kept darting her eyes over her shoulder into the dark corners of the room. Someone had broken into her house, as she was now convinced. Inside was still, quiet, and shadowy. And outside was hostility. Neither place felt safe.

She retrieved her laptop to search for an internet site on home security. She read the reviews for a tiny surveillance camera to mount on the front door and operate by a phone application. Frequently purchased with the camera were night vision goggles. What the heck, she ordered both. She still needed to live here for the next two weeks, after all.

Still a little shaky, she almost called Cheryl, but decided to call Olivia instead.

"I'm sorry to bother you…" Her tone sounded upset, even to her own ears.

"Are you all right?"

"Yes. I'm fine. Well, I mean, I'm okay now." She took a deep breath. The sound of Olivia's voice was soothing.

"What happened?"

"I was out walking the dogs when I saw the Valrod widows. I overheard Kimber tell Gina I was being nosy and had a lot of gall asking her questions. I think everyone here hates me." She sniffed, then all at once realized the significance of what she'd heard. "But before they knew I was listening, Gina said something about Kimber getting one million dollars in insurance money. So, you were right. Kimber lied to us about it."

Olivia whooped. "This is pretty exciting. And you know what, since you were only eavesdropping, Doug can't accuse you, or more importantly, me, of investigating. Let me call him to the phone and you can ask him those questions you wanted to. Be sure to let him know you overheard this clue…"

Before she could deny eavesdropping—or spill the news she'd sold the house—Jane heard her friend pass the phone to Doug, so Jane told him about the insurance.

"I'll agree with you that one million dollars is a big motive."

"Exactly. And I've been meaning to ask what you thought about Ethan as the embezzler. If it was him, why would he steal from a company he stood to inherit?" Forgotten were the scared and hurt feelings. She rose from her seat to make a hot cup of Chamomile tea.

"Criminals don't act logically. Maybe he didn't think he'd inherit fast enough. Maybe his father was tight with the money."

"Okay, I can buy that. Now we know Kimber worked for the company, too, we need to consider whether she was stealing money. She didn't inherit anything when the old man died." Jane set a mug full of water in the microwave and hit the button.

"Then there's Ethan's affair."

"Right." Jane thought about Ashley Turghart in the tight spandex outfit. Maybe he was having an affair with Ashley after all. She and Kimber might be friends, but that doesn't mean she wasn't the one having the affair with Kimber's husband, and she could've lied about Ethan not showing up for the warranty appointment.

"Murder is usually over love or money," Doug pointed out.

"It's really as simple as that?" She steeped the tea bag in the mug after taking it out of the microwave and added a dollop of honey.

"Yeah. Of course, there's also evil in the world. Some criminals don't need a reason."

"I thought at first we eliminated Kimber as a suspect, but now she's number one on my list."

"Jane...Jane...it's the job of the police to eliminate suspects. You need to stay out of the investigation and stay out of trouble."

Whoops. She'd said one thing too many, and she'd scalded her tongue on the tea, besides. As she'd heard this so many times, she paid no mind to his admonishment.

Chapter 14

The crime scene tape was down and the first floor frame was up on the foundation next door when she returned home from work on Tuesday. She slowed her car to take a long look. The truck behind gave a short beep, so she sped into her driveway, opened the garage door, and maneuvered in. She sauntered down to her mailbox. Shuffling the mail in her hands without reading any of it, she watched the construction workers packing their tools and stowing the equipment into the back of pickup trucks to leave for the day.

A tall man in his thirties or so walked in her direction, and Jane met him halfway. He offered his hand. "I'm Ned, the supervisor on this construction site." After she shook hands, he took a baseball cap off his head, smoothed his thick hair, and put the cap back on. Small clods of cement were hardened to a dirty white in places on his washed-out jeans and work boots.

"I'm Jane Marsh and I live there." She gestured toward her house. "You certainly got the first floor framing up fast. Can you tell me when it'll be finished?"

"In about two months. By Christmas at the latest."

They both eyed the skeletal structure that would soon be somebody's home. "You probably know the Valrod brothers were killed there." She met his eyes.

"Yes. Very sad." He took his ball cap off and put it

back on again. "I knew Steven pretty well."

"You did? You work for the new construction company, right? Did you work for Valrod Construction too?"

"No. I never worked for them."

"How'd you know Steven?"

"Steve and I were friends. I knew Ethan, too. Steve felt bad about the fight they had—"

"What fight?" She hoped she showed friendly concern.

"They argued because Ethan made some bad decisions. Steve blamed Ethan for running the company down. And Harold had appointed Ethan CEO over Steve. That was a rub."

"I see." She clutched the mail to her chest.

Ned ducked his head, yanked his ball cap off, and put it back on one last time. Tiny wrinkles furrowed the corners of his eyes, like those of men who worked all day outside in the sunshine. "We'll be out of your way in no time. Contact me if any of the workers are a bother."

"Thanks for letting me know when the house will be done."

Ned strode over to one of the pickups on his long legs, got inside, and turned on the ignition with a grinding sound. Several cars cruised down the street past the construction vehicles before turning the corner, then Ned drove down the street after them.

Dirt from the earthmovers speckled the pavement, and black tire marks marred the sidewalk in front of the construction site. Jane crossed the dirt encrusted road and took her dirty shoes off at the door. So, the brothers had a fight. And Steven had been friendly with the supervisor for the company that snatched up his dad's building sites.

With the new clues on her mind, she fed the dogs, then thumbed through the mail. A letter from the warranty company for the appliances she'd registered on-line encouraged Jane to send in her rebate forms. Perplexed, Jane leafed through her home warranty documents, but could find nothing about rebates. She might as well get the money, though, if she had it coming.

Jane opened her laptop to the HOA website and queried rebates, but did not find anything. When she ran her mouse over the events page, an announcement popped up for a community party at the clubhouse on Wednesday night at six. Also, Tara had posted a new hike at the Meyers Homestead in Boulder on Saturday morning. Neither the neighborhood events nor the investigation mattered as much now that her house was sold. Her time would be better spent packing.

****

When Jane arrived at her office on Wednesday, the message light on her phone was blinking. An electrician had left a message for an appointment to level the switch plate in her kitchen. She'd forgotten all about her made-up warranty complaint, but she wasn't able to get out of it now. She could picture Gina's scowling face.

Because he wanted to meet that day, she left work early in the afternoon. After he showed up, she walked the electrician into the kitchen and stammered, "Uh, this is the switch plate that's off kilter."

"Easy to fix. By the way, name's Max."

"Thanks for coming over."

He removed the switch plate and unscrewed the switchbox. With a small blade, he shaved off a section of drywall, then assembled it back together. They withdrew a few steps to survey the perfection.

"I didn't realize it was that simple. I could've done that myself. I think I have a screwdriver around here someplace." She jerked out the junk drawer. A screwdriver laid on top of the odds and ends. "Homeowners like me must drive you guys crazy." Giving a half-heartened laugh, she banged the drawer shut.

Max smiled as he put his screwdriver back into his toolbox. "No worries. Want to make it right." He consulted his clipboard. "Need to change your smoke detector battery. Hang on. Be right back."

After returning with a twenty-foot ladder, he set it up and climbed to the top rung.

She held the foot of the ladder steady. "I heard the Valrods bought last year's models to cut corners and that's why these fixtures have old batteries. And I heard they didn't agree about it. Did you ever see the brothers argue about those things?"

He eyeballed her from his perch, then gave a shrug and went back to tinkering with the detector.

She went on, "I heard the Valrod boys argued a lot. There was a probate dispute when their dad died."

"You knew 'bout that?" He twisted the cap off the detector and popped open the battery compartment. "Yeah, well, after the old man died, Ethan was mad when Gina and Steven got the most shares in the company. They got the shares, and he was made CEO. Funny, that."

"You're so right." Jane urged Max to continue.

"What do you think about it?"

He came down the ladder and folded it closed. "Don't know what ole Harold was thinkin'. Didn't seem right." He scratched his head. "Was at the construction office once and Ethan was outside with that teenager, the sign-spinner, smokin' behind the trailer. Steven and Gina showed up, so I went out back to get him. Gina was pretty harsh."

"Gina? What'd she say?"

"She wanted him out of the company, and he'd better figure a way to pay back the money he'd taken or count that money as a buy-out."

"Ethan stole money?"

"I figure, maybe, he drew more salary than she felt he should've. Never go into business with family, I always say."

Jane fell silent at this news.

But Max continued. "Ethan followed them out to the car. I watched out the window, and he shoved Steven, poor Steven who hadn't even said anythin'. Was about to run out and lend a hand, but Steven hit his brother back, punched him right in the nose. I remember Ethan acted surprised."

Leaning the ladder against the wall, Max stooped to lift his toolbox. "Sad about the twins' deaths, both of 'em gone. Tearing apart that family." With toolbox in hand, he lumbered out the door. "Got another appointment to get to, so I'll be on my way."

"Wait. What happened next? After Steven punched Ethan?"

Max paused. "Gina stepped between the twins and ordered Ethan out. Out of the construction trailer and out of the business. Just mad, that's all. They left, and

Ethan came back in as if nothin' happened. Didn't seem to take it too seriously."

"That sounds pretty serious to me. But because Ethan was the CEO, Gina couldn't order him out of the company, could she?"

Max lifted one shoulder in a shrug. "She could probably convince her husband to vote Ethan out. But, don't really know how it works."

"What happened with Gina's threats?" Jane elevated her eyebrows and gave her head a tilt.

"Nothin'. The argument happened the day before Ethan died."

Jane gasped and Max gave her a sharp look. He had a bit of a harried appearance as he said, "Really do have to get to another appointment."

"Thanks for fixing the light switch." Jane shook his hand, then Max left.

Two people had verified the brothers had a fight, Ned and now Max. Ethan was skimming company funds somehow. Gina wanted Ethan out of the business, and perhaps was tired of the brothers' fights and got rid of her husband, too. Surely the police would come to the conclusion Gina was the killer. It was solved and she could move out and leave it all behind.

****

The next day, Jane worked through her lunch hour, but needed an afternoon break, so treated herself to a coffee. While waiting for her drink order, she read the flyers on the bulletin board. She needed to get serious about moving and looked for a posting of a short-term apartment or lease takeover. There was nothing about an apartment, but there was a notice for the Downtown School for Gourmet Chefs, a cooking school in the same building as the coffee shop.

What if she became a gourmet chef? Would Everett be impressed? Would he call her back? She crossed the lobby and went inside the door to the cooking school. They had an opening in a noon class on Friday called "cooking with cucumbers." She wasn't sure she wanted to cook with cucumbers, but signed up since the other classes that week were filled. At least it was something different, and it could be fun.

That evening after work, instead of packing Jane changed into running clothes and sprinted to the farmer's canal near the Valrods' ranch. She climbed under the gate and jogged to the path at the brim of the canal. This time she kept running past the Valrods' homes and along the rusted barbed wire fence surrounding the horses' pasture. She drew near a lone woman in the field hoisting a blanket onto a horse's back. It was Kimber, and tears were coursing down her face. Jane halted in the dark shadows of the tall cottonwoods as Kimber gently butted her head against the horse's side. The horse whinnied and Kimber ran her hands lovingly over his flank.

Shamefaced, Jane turned around, her feet beating a swift rhythm on the dirt path home, allowing Kimber her private moment of grief.

She was convinced all the more Gina was the killer. Why didn't the police see it, too? Still curious, she might as well go to one last HOA meeting.

Without changing from her running clothes, she donned a jacket and walked the few short blocks to the clubhouse in the crisp night air scented with pine. She sauntered into the community room and up to a table covered with platters of snacks. After filling a plate with finger-sized sausages and cheese squares, she poured a cup of lemonade and carried her plate and cup over to a group of folding chairs. All alone, she munched on her snacks, while examining her neighbors, who walked past without a glance. Just when she was thinking about leaving after all, someone tapped on her shoulder.

Merrilee, the HOA president, said, "Jane, you know Kimber and Gina Valrod."

Jane dropped her empty plate onto the floor as she stood up, fast. She nudged the plate under her chair with her foot, brushed her hands down the front of her slacks, and stuck her hand out to shake. "We've met. How are you, Kimber, Gina?"

Gina shook her hand as Merrilee said, "Jane's very interested in the success of this neighborhood and what's happening to the Valrod Construction Company." Evidently Merrilee hadn't seen the "For Sale" sign in her front yard and now wasn't the time to bring it up.

Gina scrutinized Jane with a curious expression. "Yes. I heard about your interest."

Merrilee patted Jane's arm again. "Gina's making an announcement this evening that Valrod Construction's pulling out of new home building, so you'll hear all this in a few minutes anyway. The new builder intends to finish the rest of the empty lots by spring. This party's the Valrods' farewell to the project."

The HOA president was interrupted by a young couple who drew her away, so Jane was left alone with Kimber and Gina.

Gina asked, "Did the electrician fix your switch

plate yesterday?"

"Yes. It's fine." Her mind going blank, Jane couldn't think of the questions she'd wanted to ask. Kimber's red eyes studied her feet without saying a word. Justin and Tara caught Jane's attention as they cut across the room, then Jane remembered something. "I never received the rebate forms for my appliances. Do you know where I can get them?"

Gina answered, "No. We keep the rebates since we bought the appliances."

Jane narrowed her eyes into slits. "Don't those belong to the homeowners?"

"We pass the cost-savings on to the buyers. If you check the seller's statement with your paperwork, you'll see the money is accounted for in your discounts."

"That makes sense. Thanks." Jane thought about the oven, refrigerator, microwave, and dishwasher, all from the same manufacturer. Because of the number of appliances for each house, the rebates must add up to a significant amount. She'd find the paperwork for the purchase of the house later. "I wonder why the manufacturer contacted me."

"With all that's happened, we probably didn't send in the forms for yours yet."

Not to let this opportunity pass, Jane said more loudly than intended. "I'm sorry about Ethan and Steven. This has to be terrible for both of you. I lost my husband several years ago, and I understand your loss." She didn't mention it happened to her twice. Not knowing what to expect, she took a deep breath.

Gina's face closed. "I wish you would quit asking so many questions. We're all grieving right now. You have to understand that. And you have no right to come onto Valrod property. Stay off the ranch."

Jane's mouth opened and shut a few times. But before she could say anything more, Merrilee returned, and led Gina and Kimber away.

Feeling her cheeks burn, she retrieved her empty plate from under her chair and tossed it into a trash can. The teenager—the human directional with the advertising sign on the corner—was at the refreshments table. He and his friends swooped over to Jane.

"Hey! You're the lady with the water, right?"

"Yes. How are you?" She wrinkled her nose as she got a whiff of marijuana.

"Just leaving." The boys took off in another direction. Her gaze followed them down the hall to the restrooms. She spotted Tara and Justin at the end of the corridor with their backs to the community room. She made rapid strides toward them when Tara mumbled something out of earshot.

As she got closer, she paused, hearing Justin snarl, "What's your problem?"

"Quit pretending you care about me. You've never cared." Tara slouched away from her husband, her arms crossed over her chest.

"How can you say that? How can you believe that after what I did for you?" Justin thrust his face close to hers.

Tara swung around toward Jane, so she ducked into the women's restroom. She didn't want to walk into the middle of a marital spat, plus she needed time to digest this.

What had happened out there? What did Justin do to prove he loved his wife? They were so young, still going through the adjustment period of the newly married. She hoped they weren't heading toward divorce. Maybe her imagination was getting the better of her.

Standing at the mirror, she applied lip balm and washed her hands. Then she poked her head out the door. Tara and Justin were gone.

She tiptoed back down the hallway and re-entered the community room. Margaret Skaleop, the realtor for the subdivision, sidled over to her. "Hello, Mrs. Marsh."

"It's Jane. How're you?"

"I've started my own realty agency. Here's my card." She crushed it into Jane's hand.

"You mean, you aren't selling the houses in the neighborhood anymore?"

Margaret grimaced. "No. The new company has their own realtor. But if you know anybody looking for a new home, please give them my name."

"I wish I'd known. I would've called you, but I recently sold my house through Limestone Realty."

"I'm surprised! You just moved in."

"Yes, you're right. The nice part is, I have less to pack, since I didn't unpack everything yet." Jane wanted to point out it could hardly be surprising with two murders committed right next door, plus she was surrounded by cowboys, but instead asked, "Did you work for the Valrods long?"

"I began with Harold twenty years ago, when he started the construction company. I sold every house in this neighborhood." Margaret had a hitch in her voice. She picked up a cup of the pale yellow lemonade from the refreshments table and took a swallow.

Jane had an idea. "I have some questions, about Ethan in particular. I heard he may've been pocketing appliance rebate money."

"What? Ethan would never do that." Margaret set her cup down and some lemonade sloshed over the top. "Did someone from the new company tell you? I wouldn't be surprised if they did."

"Why?"

"They've been after this property for a long while and they took advantage of the Valrods' hard times."

Jane pressed, "What did Kimber think about Ethan's affairs?" Margaret's eyes bored into Jane's, so she back pedaled and said, "But I'm sure Kimber had nothing to do with any of this."

"No, she didn't."

"What's she going to do since she wasn't really left with much?" Jane cast a glance down but observed the realtor out of the corner of her eyes.

Margaret's lip curled. "Kimber will be fine. She's getting the life insurance money."

Jane sucked in her breath. "I suppose you know all about it, being such a good friend of the family."

"Ethan took good care of Kimber. He made certain he was insured. She wants to move away from Limestone Heights, too, and I'm going to sell her house for her."

"Where's she going?"

"She has a sister in California. Kimber's wanted to get away for as long as I can remember. Now's her chance to do it."

"Won't the Valrods be able to keep you on as the selling broker for their new projects?"

Margaret's shoulders drooped. "They won't need

me since they're moving into the commercial building market. Remember me if you hear of anyone looking for a new home." She gave Jane a stiff smile and strode off.

As she heard Gina Valrod start her farewell speech at the front of the room, Jane tucked Margaret's business card in her pocket and scanned the crowd. Justin and Tara sat in the crowded front row. Finding an empty chair in the back, Jane sat down and paid careful attention to those in attendance. Kimber was nowhere to be seen and Jane didn't recognize anyone else. Once Gina finished speaking, Jane slid her arms into her jacket and glanced around for her young neighbors, but Justin and Tara had also disappeared.

In spite of Margaret's faith in the Valrods, Jane couldn't help believing Gina killed Ethan, since he was so harmful to the company. But then, what if Kimber killed Ethan for the insurance money so she could start a new life in California? The burning questions were, why were *both* brothers killed? Which wife did it? And why should it matter to her anymore?

After returning home, she texted Olivia. *I have some news—come over for cocktails tomorrow night so we can discuss it.* After a moment, she texted Tara as well.

Chapter 15

Jane raced up the steps of the old brick building, past the coffee shop with its delicious aroma, and into the classroom with large windows full of sunshine. She was reminded of biology lab in college, with tall stools at rows of narrow, black countertops. The chef stood at the front of the classroom. Her eyes roved up from his checkered pants and white double-breasted jacket to the white toque on his head, and she did a double take. It was Everett! And he was glaring at her with a scowl on his face.

Stumbling a little, she slid onto a stool in the back row, but not before kicking it with the toe of her shoe. The loud scraping noise caused her to duck her head in embarrassment. At each student's place were ingredients, a mixing bowl and spoon, and a measuring cup, together with a high-ball glass filled with a clear liquid, ice, and several slices of cucumber and lime. She picked up her drink and took a gulp.

Gosh that was so refreshing, but it contained alcohol, so she put it back down. She plucked the recipe cards from the counter and read the ingredients for the drink—dry cucumber soda and gin, with a twist of lime. Holding the cards to block her face, she shuffled to the next one, and the next. The second recipe was for cucumber herb vinaigrette salad dressing and the third for cold cucumber soup.

She pretended to study the recipes further as other students took their seats. Though happy a large man sat in front of her obstructing Everett's view of the back of the class, she still had a hard time paying attention as he took the students through each step to assemble the cold cucumber soup and then the vinaigrette. These recipes would be perfect for a summer dinner club event, but her finished creations were not as pretty as the pictures on the recipe cards.

The students trickled out of the classroom at the end of the hour. She sat small and still, clutching her purse in front of her, until the last student left. She owed Everett an explanation for her presence today. He took off his apron and the toque from his head to shake out his wavy, shoulder length hair, before walking toward Jane.

"I didn't know you were teaching this class when I signed up for it. That's the truth." Jane fumbled with her recipe cards.

"I know. I could tell by the look on your face." Everett cracked a smile and his small, blue eyes danced. "Your expression was priceless!"

Her tense muscles eased as she grinned, too. "I could hardly follow your instructions. I'm sorry."

He examined her soup and vinaigrette, then raised his eyebrows in question. "You didn't drink your cocktail—"

"Oh no. I couldn't. I have to go back to work." The alcoholic beverage explained why Jane had to enter her birthdate on the class registration form.

"You should've sipped it over the hour like the other students. It makes cooking so much more enjoyable. Do you have to go back to work?"

"I told my secretary I'd be taking a long lunch hour today, but yes, I need to return in a little bit."

"Do you have time to go up to my apartment? I live just a few blocks from here. I'd like you to see it."

She gaped at Everett with her mouth open, then shut it with a snap.

"Just to see the apartment, Jane, and I could make a pot of coffee."

She was being silly. This wasn't a proposition. "Of course I'd love some coffee." Then she added, "And I'd love to see your apartment too."

They bustled out into the sunshine, then up the street to a modern building of condos. After Everett unlocked his door and Jane followed him in, she sat at the kitchen counter while he started coffee brewing. The kitchen was small, but efficient, with a food processor, a knife block, and a stack of cutting boards crowding the counter space. She smelled that hint of sage that seemed to linger around Everett. Once the coffee was done, he poured them each a cup and they gazed out the windows at the mountain view.

Instead of enjoying the scenery on the other side of the glass, he eyeballed her. She fluffed up her hair a little. "It's weird that our paths keep crossing. You applied for a job at Polly Capricorn's restaurant, and I happen to know her from dating her ex-husband. And then I run into you at the cooking school."

"It's not really odd. There're only a limited number of upscale restaurants. Eliminate all the other eateries and the community of fine dining is small. Same with cooking schools, and I do love to teach cooking lessons, you know that. It's how we met."

"I guess you're right. Maybe we'll cross paths

again." The cup in her hand absorbed her attention.

"I was hurt by your rejection, Jane. You seemed more interested in the murder investigation than in me. But I suppose I overreacted, and I'm sorry."

She glanced at him with cautious hope. "I'm sorry, too. And I'm not interested in the murders anymore. I've sold my house and I'm moving away from that place."

"You are? Where're you moving to?"

"I don't know yet." Her heart skipped a beat and her stomach lurched when she thought about everything she had to get done first. She'd worry about it later.

"I'm glad we cleared the air, Jane. I'd like to call you again."

"I'd like that, too." She leaned forward as if to be kissed, but drew back to swallow the last of her coffee instead. They said their goodbyes at the door.

Burning up the pavement, she rushed back to her office, wondering if she should be the one to ask him out. She could call Cheryl to discuss it. Or better yet, Olivia or Tara, as they planned to meet that evening. Dating in this day and age was a mystery. She hadn't meant to make Everett feel rejected.

A bulb exploded in her mind. Rejection could be a powerful motivator. What if Ethan wanted to break off the relationship with his lover and she felt abandoned and angry? Furious enough to shove him to his death? Mad enough to kill his brother, too. But once Jane was back at her desk, her boss interrupted her musings with a work project, so she dug in to complete it before the end of the day.

****

That night at home, Jane noticed her hairbrush

wasn't in its usual place in the bathroom. She didn't remember leaving it on the dresser, but forgot about it when Olivia and Tara arrived at the door at the same time. They passed through the house to the back deck, where Jane set out cucumber cocktails.

"This is a very refreshing drink. Where'd you get the recipe?" Olivia's beautiful black hair was brushed back into a barrette.

"I got it from Everett." Jane explained about the cooking class but didn't mention their falling out.

"When's your next date?" asked Olivia.

"I don't know. He hasn't asked me out on another one."

"You need to be more assertive. Call him up and ask him." Tara drained her glass.

"Should I do that?" This was the confirmation Jane was looking for.

"Yes!" exploded Tara and Olivia at the same time.

She nodded, but wondered if she'd have the nerve. "So, anyway, I ran into Gina and Kimber at the HOA community party. Did you see them, too, Tara?"

"Yeah. Heard the speech. Yada. Yada."

As Jane recounted her conversation with Gina, her interest in the investigation returned. "And Kimber didn't have anything to say at all."

"I think she's the killer. As you found out, she has the insurance money and can move to California now." Tara tented her fingers, leaning her elbows on the tabletop.

"It sure looks like one of the two widows." After fishing the cucumber out of her glass with a spoon, Jane set the soggy fruit on a napkin. Faint country music sounded from the house to the west.

Olivia said, "I wish I could've gone to the meeting with you. Maybe Kimber would've talked to me." Jane arched one eyebrow as Olivia continued, "I have to take off. I need to get some errands done in order to free up tomorrow for our hike." Olivia tucked her purse under her arm as if to head inside.

"So you two are going on the neighborhood hike, then?" Tara dropped her eyes.

Olivia shuffled inside to the kitchen and set her cocktail glass on the counter as the others trailed in after her. "Of course, I want to. You're going, Jane?"

"Sure, why not?"

Tara muttered, "I thought you were moving."

Olivia's head jerked in Jane's direction. "So, you really are moving, then?"

"Maybe…" She squeezed Olivia's arm. "I'm not sure about anything." She walked her friends to the door. "See you all tomorrow."

She decided to take the dogs for a short walk around the block. When she returned, she opened her pantry for snacks and a water bottle for the next day's hike.

A bang and some scuffling noises came from the basement. The puppies jumped and ran barking to the top of the stairs as the back of Jane's neck prickled. Remembering her last scare was simply an exploded potato, she steeled herself with a deep breath and headed down the basement steps.

Flipping on the light switch, she stood frozen in the doorway. There were dozens of unopened boxes with the label "basement" in black marker, and a few that read "kitchen" or "bedroom." All was still and appeared undisturbed. Her muscles eased. At least she didn't have to pack up the basement. But one of the windows caught her eye—it was open several inches. She flew over and slammed it shut, then turned with a wide-eyed stare over her shoulder. Maybe she wasn't alone and had just blocked the way for the intruder's escape.

In a quiet voice, she called the dogs to her side. "Nicky, Nora." Alert for the slightest sound, she peered behind boxes and under the antique hall tree, with the dogs sniffing and sneezing at the concrete dust from the unfinished space. Letting out a shuddering sigh, she said to the puppies, "No one here."

But there could've been someone who saw her leave to take the dogs for a walk—who knew her routine and thought she was walking all the way to the pond and would be gone longer. Perhaps Gina or Kimber had sneaked over from the ranch using the trail along the farmer's canal. And Gina told her to stay off the ranch! What nerve. If it was her, that is.

In a shaky state, she made certain all the basement windows were secured tight before going back upstairs. Whisking through the rest of the house, she confirmed all the windows were locked on the main level, too. She examined her desk and mail stack, then poked around her dresser and small collection of jewelry, but nothing was missing.

She couldn't remember having gone into the basement since the day she unpacked the tablecloths a few weeks ago. The time before was probably move-in day. It was quite possible she hadn't noticed the basement window since the day she moved in. Her knees quaked when she realized someone could've been entering her house through the open window this whole time.

Well, no more. Everything was locked up like Fort Knox now. Soon she'd be gone, maybe to an apartment complex with a security guard. Tomorrow, she promised herself, tomorrow after the hike she'd check out the available apartments she'd listed on her legal pad.

****

Early Saturday morning, Tara rode with Jane to the Meyers Homestead Trail past Chautauqua Park in Boulder.

After Jane parked, Tara climbed out and strolled over to the trailhead sign, leaving Jane sitting in the car with her door open, tying the laces to her hiking boots, listening to the *skreeka* call of the Stellar blue jays.

Setting her feet on the ground, Jane gaped at the Lexus with the vanity plate "*VALROD3*" parked on the other side of the tiny parking lot. Kimber clambered out of the driver's side, and her sidekick Ashley Turghart got out of the passenger's. Jane turned to stone as Ashley said to Kimber, "In fact, I haven't hiked this trail before." The two joined Tara and Olivia, plus others, waiting at the entrance to the trail.

Just as Merrilee strutted past, Jane grabbed her water bottle from the front seat and locked her car door. "Hello, Merrilee."

"I decided to join you, Jane." The HOA president edged closer. "I saw the posting on the website and thought I should come. You probably won't be able to keep hiking much longer since it's the middle of October already, and I didn't want to miss out. This group seems to be quite popular."

Jane took a step back from Merrilee. "As long as the weather stays warm like this, we can keep hiking for a while yet." She pointed to Kimber's car. "Do you know who has the '*VALROD1*' and '2' license plates?"

Merrilee halted next to the Lexus. "Harold bought Steven and Ethan matching cars when they turned sixteen. Steven was the older of the twins by a few minutes, so he got the plate '*VALROD1*,' and Ethan had the number two plate."

"So, Kimber got the number three plate?"

"Actually, Suzanne, Ethan's first wife, had it before Kimber. Suzanne was married to Ethan for less than a year. She was from Kansas, and no one really expected the marriage to last."

"Because she was from Kansas?" Jane thought, *but they have cowgirls in Kansas.*

"I meant, she wasn't from here." Merrilee went on in a conspiratorial tone. "He didn't even wait a year before he had an affair. That's what ended the marriage."

Jane tried to keep her eyebrows from shooting up. "So, Ethan had other affairs, not just while he was married to Kimber."

"Kimber was the one he had an affair with while he was married to his first wife, so she shouldn't've been surprised when he went back to his old ways."

Jane scratched her head. "But he went out with Ashley Turghart before Kimber."

"Yes, I think I did hear that. He must have been busy."

Jane's head swam thinking of the complications.

"Hey, you too. Let's go!" yelled Tara. A couple of hikers were several yards down the trail. Olivia waited for Jane at the entrance with the others, but Kimber and Ashley had already charged ahead.

Jane and Merrilee hurried over. She introduced Olivia to the HOA president, who didn't seem very interested in her when Olivia admitted she didn't live in the neighborhood. Merrilee soon joined two women walking behind, leaving the three friends on their own.

"This is just a five-mile hike. It's part of the Walker Ranch Open Space area." Tara waved her trail guide in the air in front of them.

"I have a map, too." Jane folded hers and shoved it in her jacket pocket. "Do you both have a bottle of water?"

"Yes," said Olivia and Tara's "yes" was like an echo.

"You sound just like Cheryl," pointed out Olivia.

"I have some gossip." Jane glanced around as they proceeded down the trail, but the hikers behind them with Merrilee were busy in conversation and the group in front were too far ahead to hear. "I feel bad about repeating this…"

"Spit it out." Olivia set a fast pace, sporting on her head a black and white plaid sun visor, which matched her earrings.

"Okay. Kimber and Ashley both had affairs with Ethan while he was still married to his first wife."

Olivia blew out a loud whistle.

"Shh, shh." Jane's eyes darted around.

Tara flicked a strand of hair over her shoulder. "Maybe it shows he's never been happy in his marriages. Some men keep picking the wrong wife."

"I agree. People tend to repeat their mistakes," Jane said in a near whisper.

Tara shrieked, "Oh, my gosh! A mountain lion!"

Chapter 16

Tara pointed with a shaky finger. "There! Look!"

Merrilee hurried up from behind, and several women a distance ahead on the trail heard Tara's yell and dashed back. They huddled together to peer around the side of a large boulder. Jane clutched Tara's arm and they both trembled.

"It's a cat, not a mountain lion." Kimber had joined them. Jane jumped at the sound of her voice.

"Really? But see how big it is," insisted Tara.

"Feral cats at these high elevations get really thick fur. It's probably not as big as it looks, it's all hair." Kimber smirked. "We're not that far from the city. It might even belong to someone."

"Hahahaha," Olivia laughed. The rest joined in the joke, and even Tara giggled as they resumed their hike down the dirt path.

"Anyone could've made that mistake," Jane said in defense of her friend.

Kimber flounced her shoulder in a huff and traipsed off ahead of them.

By the time they reached the parking lot, several hikers in their group had already departed, but a few were waiting for Tara to thank her for organizing the hike. Merrilee stood quite close to show Jane pictures of the Meyers Homestead Trail she'd taken on her cell phone. She promised to post them on the HOA website.

Jane breathed both a sigh of relief and one of exasperation when Kimber and Ashley zoomed out of the parking lot without a confrontation. There were certainly more questions to ask her, particularly about her husband's affairs, but she'd made Kimber mad enough already.

On the drive home, Tara and Jane laughed again at the mountain lion mistake. Tara peered sideways at Jane. "What did you think of Kimber showing up?"

"I'm amazed she comes to these events. I'm wondering why she does. I'm a little embarrassed that she thinks I was being nosy about the insurance money, but I didn't exactly ask, and it's weird knowing she lied to me, too."

"I told you she wasn't telling the truth."

"You don't like her."

"I think she killed Ethan."

Jane slowed at a stoplight and sat thinking as the car idled. Who was the killer? Gina, or Kimber, or…

Tara said, "Anyway, I think we should hike a 14er before the end of the hiking season. Let's hike Bierstadt Mountain on Guanella Pass. It's supposed to be the easiest 14er, even children can hike it."

"When were you thinking of?" Jane stepped on the gas as the light turned green. Was it possible she would be moving in a week?

Tara consulted her cell phone calendar. "How about the last weekend in October? Is that far enough out?"

"Isn't that too late in the season? What if it snows in the high country?"

"Let me see. I have the information in Justin's trail guide." Tara rifled through her capacious handbag, plucked out a pocket-sized book, and thumbed through it. "It says here people hike it all year round. We'll need to be prepared for bad weather, though. In late fall and winter, you need to pack snowshoes. Don't you want to do it?" Tara leaned her back against the passenger door to face Jane.

"Yes, I do. I'm in!"

****

Jane changed into old clothes when she got home that afternoon. She'd put a deposit down on an apartment at last and it was time to get serious about packing. She had just come out of the bedroom with a full box when the doorbell chimed. She set it down and swung the door open. Everett stood on the porch holding a basket of orange and yellow mums.

She said with a broad grin, "Are the flowers for me?"

"Yes."

"They're beautiful. Thanks." Jane loved fall flowers.

With one eyebrow cocked, he eyed her up and down, with her paint-stained sweatshirt and jeans with holes in the knees. "Are you in the middle of packing?"

"Yes. I move in a week. Please come in." Jane held the door and gestured for him to enter. "But first, put the mums right there." She pointed to a spot in the corner near the door.

"I don't want to keep you if you're busy." He set the mums down and took two steps backward.

Deciding not to let him get away, she grabbed his hand and tugged him inside. "Not at all." She led him into the kitchen. "There's a full pot of coffee made, help yourself."

She hurried back into her bedroom to throw on a checkered, long-sleeved, fitted blouse. She tied the tails together to cinch it around her small waist, exposing just a tiny bit of skin. When she came out to rejoin Everett, he was sitting in his jacket outside on the patio, sipping a hot coffee. A late afternoon wind blew softly across the deck. She went back for a sweater and draped it over her shoulders, then nabbed a cup of java to join him.

He asked, "So, you're actually selling your new home?"

"Yes. I don't feel like I belong. Everyone here's a cowboy. The mail's always late because, I think, they deliver it by horseback."

Everett chuckled as Jane glanced down. On her feet were the cowboy boots she'd bought at the Western Wear shop. He cleared his throat. "Have you resumed your murder investigation?"

Remembering he'd thought her investigation more important than him, she made a face, as if it was too boring to contemplate. "Sort of, but we don't need to talk about that."

"Jane, I know you're still nosing around. You might as well tell me about it."

She gave a helpless shrug. "Okay." Bunching her eyebrows together, she explained that it was possible one of the brothers was pocketing rebate money and the twins had had an argument over it.

Everett offered a new theory. "What if Ethan's first wife, Suzanne, kept those vanity license plates from years ago? Even if they were expired, she could've put the old plates on her car to drive through the neighborhood and cast suspicion on Kimber. It wouldn't even need to be a Lexus. She could've driven a black car with a similar style. Would anyone have noticed?"

Jane jerked her sweater tighter around her shoulders. "Why would Suzanne, who seems to be out of the picture, want to kill her ex-husband and ex-brother-in-law?"

"I suppose you're right. I don't know what motive she'd have."

"Hmm. I wish I knew more about her." She peered over the deck railing at the progress of the construction next door. Soon, the house would be finished; Tara would take the neighbors muffins, and Jane would need to do something neighborly, too. But of course, she would no longer be living there. Jane's eyes darted back to Everett as she rubbed the back of her neck.

"What's wrong?"

Her focus returned, but her heart skipped a beat. "Someone's been getting into my house. I found one of the basement windows wide open."

Everett gasped, "What?"

"It's okay now, no one can come inside anymore, because I checked all the windows and made sure everything's locked up—"

"Do you think the murderer was in this house?"

Jane sighed. "I don't know what to think. It might've been neighborhood kids. Or it might've been no one at all. Maybe I was imagining things, and then when I found the window open my imagination just took off. But I did buy a surveillance camera." The box had arrived the day before. "I haven't set it up yet, though."

"Let's take a look at it." Everett scanned the

camera's instructions after she'd retrieved the box from the garage. "Do you want to bother with it since you're moving so soon?"

"It's just a mounting bracket. I can take it down when I leave."

"Okay. Let's put it up. Might as well be safe the last few days you're still living here." Everett erected her aluminum folding ladder on the front porch. Hoping the neighbors were not paying close attention, she held the ladder as he brushed back a spider web and tapped in the mounting bracket with a hammer, then positioned the small camera in a corner of the eave. She flung a fall wreath on the front door in case anyone wondered what they were doing. Perhaps they would think it was only the wreath they were hanging.

After Everett stowed the ladder away, they rushed back inside to download the phone app and watch the video feed for a few moments. The space in front of her door was clearly visible, and in the background Tara's car going down the street flashed past and out of view.

"What's in the other box?" Everett tossed pieces of packing materials in the garbage.

"I bought night vison goggles, too, so I can look out in the backyard when it's dark. But, we've dealt with enough technical instructions for one day. Let's save it for later."

Everett's attention turned back to the video feed on her phone. "I should get one of these cameras, then I'd know if a salesman was ringing my doorbell."

Jane said, "Hey, this upcoming Saturday is dinner club at Olivia's and Doug's house. Would you like to go with me?"

"I'd love to. And that reminds me. Did we miss

dinner? Would you like to go out to eat tonight?" Everett asked.

"I'd love, love, love that." Jane ran into her bedroom to change out of her torn jeans into crisp, tailored ones before they took off.

Everett pulled his car into the only steakhouse in town. Not long after they placed their orders, their mouth-watering steaks arrived, nestled in red juices, with Texas fries and coleslaw.

Jane popped a piece of the meat in her mouth, chewed, and swallowed. "You don't eat food off my plate anymore."

"Did I do that?" Everett was sitting next to Jane in the booth.

"Yes. I'm wondering how you feel about me." Gosh, did she really say that out loud?

He put down his fork and stroked her face with the back of his right hand. Then, he cupped both hands around her face and inched closer. "Jane, you're fun to be with, always game to get out there and try something new. But you're hard to get close to." He gave her a light kiss on the lips, then released her chin and lowered his hands to the table.

She sat back in the booth as her expression went blank. Then, she focused on Everett. "I'll work on that."

He hesitated as he took up his fork. "Polly Capricorn offered me the job at her restaurant after all. I'm going to be head chef."

Jane's head swiveled sideways. "Congratulations! When did you find out?"

"Yesterday. I was going to tell you when I first got to your house, but I didn't know what you'd think about it."

"Are you kidding? I'm glad. No, I'm excited! This is a great opportunity." She grabbed his arm and held it. "But it's an Italian restaurant. Is that going to limit you? And when do you start?"

"Tomorrow night. They have other things on the menu, not just pasta, plus Polly and her business partner are expanding, opening a brew pub. I won't be the one brewing the beer, but I plan to learn more about beer and food pairings." He continued to chat about plans for changes to the menu as her mind wandered.

So Dale and Polly were going to open another restaurant together. Jane surprised herself when a sharp pang of disappointment shot through her at this news, although she was happy Everett got the job he wanted.

She darted a wide-eyed glimpse in his direction when he suggested, "Maybe the dinner club group can meet at Polly's restaurant. I'll reserve the large round table near the fireplace." His phone jangled and he checked the number. "I'm sorry, Jane, but I should take this call."

"Sure. Of course."

He slid his bottom to the far end of the booth. "Yes. I've been thinking about the menu and the recipes you gave me. I have some ideas, but we can discuss them at the weekly meeting. I thought I could introduce some new items by offering a nightly special, then you could see how the food is received by the customers." He paused, listening. "Okay. See you in the morning."

Jane had busied herself cutting the tender meat left on her plate to take home for the dogs. After disconnecting, Everett asked if she was done. She was, so they got going. Her heart sank with further disappointment when he dropped her off without coming in.

Was the enigmatic and interfering Polly, whom Jane had met only once, but who had managed to come between her and her last boyfriend, about to interrupt her relationship with Everett?

****

On Sunday morning, she visited a different church in Limestone Heights. The service had a harvest theme with a brunch potluck afterward. She was planning to leave since she hadn't brought a dish, but ran into the older couple from the walking group, Ruth and Dick. "Stay for the potluck," Ruth said with a broad smile. "There's plenty for everyone. We always have leftovers."

"Okay, I will. Thanks." Jane joined the line at the food-laden table and spooned a small amount of a savory breakfast casserole onto her paper plate. She sat at the banquet table next to Ruth and asked, "Do you know Kimber Valrod well?"

"Yes, dear. Why?"

"I want to find out something, and I'm wondering if you could ask her." Jane dipped her head and glimpsed Ruth from under her eyelashes.

Ruth put her fork down. "What is it?"

"I have some questions about the deaths."

"I don't know her that well! Besides, you should ask her directly or not at all."

"Yes, of course." Jane sighed, then took another bite of the egg and sausage casserole. Ruth was proving to be close-mouthed, and Jane had probably burned all her bridges with Kimber. "This is delicious. I wonder who made it." She examined the room where people greeted each other with loud voices, but didn't recognize anyone.

Ruth had a delighted smile. "I made that. I'm glad you like it."

"Can I have the recipe?"

"Of course I have it here in my purse." Ruth opened her large bag and hauled out a stack of recipe cards bound by a thick, blue rubber band, the kind that comes with a bunch of vegetables from the grocery store. "Everyone always asks for it, so I brought copies."

"Thanks." The recipe included tater tots. After finishing off the last delicious bite on her plate, Jane resisted the urge to go back for seconds. "Ruth," she hesitated a moment, then continued, "What do you think about the murders?"

"I don't have a single clue. But the police will catch up with the killer and we'll be reading all about it in the newspapers soon." Ruth patted Jane on the hand. "Don't worry, dear."

Ruth joined Dick in a discussion with the man sitting across the table. Jane listened for a moment about a 4H competition coming up, then slipped in a goodbye to the older couple and left the church to head home.

****

It was a lazy Sunday afternoon. She lay down on the couch and the puppies jumped up next to her. Folding her hands across her chest, she shut her eyes, thinking about the list of things to do before her upcoming move. In a minute she'd get up, find the empty boxes in the basement for packing the dishes, retrieve the stack of newspapers from the recycle bin to wrap around the plates…what else? She could hear the birds twittering in the trees outside the window. Her eyes were heavy. Her cell phone buzzed and she absently reached for it on the coffee table.

"Jane, I have some bad news." It was the realtor. "The buyers are backing out of the contract."

"How can they do that?" She sat up wide awake and gripped the phone tighter.

"The people who purchased their house didn't qualify for their loan, so that sale fell through. There was no contingency in the contract, though, so I don't need to refund their earnest money."

"All this rushing around and packing and getting ready for nothing!" Jane swung her feet to the floor and strode over to the counter where she'd left her to-do list. Nothing was checked off. Flushed with guilt, she said. "I'm sorry, it's not your fault."

"I'll have another buyer, no worries. Actually, I'd like to bring some prospects by this afternoon."

"Okay. Let me know the time and I'll have the house ready."

After punching the end-call button, she checked text messages and found one from her daughter-in-law, Brittany, asking if she wanted to Skype. She plopped open her laptop and made the video call. Luke started off the session with, "I'm leaving tomorrow for training. I'm going to Florida for a week."

"Can I come for a visit, Mom?" asked Brittany. "I know it's last minute, but I already checked and found a cheap flight."

"Of course. I'd love, love, love that." Jane couldn't wipe the smile off her face during their video chat. Brittany said she would text to confirm her flight information after she bought the tickets. It was a good thing Jane wasn't in the middle of a move after all, because she hadn't said anything about selling the house to Luke or Caleb. No need to bring it up now.

Chapter 17

On Monday at noon, she changed out of her high heels into flats to walk to the restaurant on the outdoor patio in Larimer Square and meet Olivia for lunch. The first thing Olivia said was, "Those cheap ballet flats are all the rage."

Jane gave Olivia a sharp glare and yanked out a chair to sit down.

"Did I just say something snarky?" Olivia had a pained expression as she tucked her chin low.

"Yes, as a matter of fact you did." Jane paused for the next blow.

"I don't know why I say these things." Olivia's voice was loud over the traffic noise. "Yes, I do. My mother was caustic. I told her I wanted to become a model and she sneered at me, said to forget it, my legs were too skinny and my face too fat."

"But you could've been a model!" Jane studied her friend's face. As waiters always do, he interrupted them to take their orders. They both requested salads and he left. "Your daughter's a model in New York, isn't she? And she looks just like you." She patted her friend's arm.

Olivia whipped her napkin open and laid it on her lap. "I hate it when I hear my mother's words come out of my mouth."

"I understand, but it's part of who we are. I have

my mother's hands." Jane splayed out her fingers, short, not long and graceful, and frowned. "Hey, do you know what's up with Cheryl? I've texted her several times, but I haven't heard back. Have you talked to her?"

"The Breewoods are probably on the cruise they planned over six months ago."

"Oh, I forgot all about it." Jane relaxed in her patio chair. "I should've remembered."

"It's hard to keep track of everything." Olivia tucked a strand of hair behind her ear. "Have you been doing any investigating on your own? You said I could help, remember? Or are you giving up since you're selling and moving back closer to town?" The waiter carried over their salads.

"No, I haven't given up. I'd like to find out more about Ethan's affair. Do you have any ideas?"

Olivia crunched on a bite of her lettuce, then swallowed. "Hmm. Someone had to know who the woman was. It's hard to keep that a secret, and it's a loose end."

"Let's think about what we do know." Jane gazed off for a moment. "The husband put up the banner in June warning Ethan away from his wife. I'd think the woman had to have lived in the neighborhood for a few months anyway, so she could've moved in in March, April, or around then."

"Or a year or two before that."

"And she'd be about the same age as Ethan, so that knocks a few off the list." Jane stabbed her fork in the air.

"Yeah, well, first you need a list."

"I can get one." Jane set her silverware down and

plucked her murder folder out of her tote bag to write on her to-do memo.

Olivia said with a hint of laughter, "You can? How?"

"The county assessor has a list of every homeowner in the neighborhood."

"How did you ever think of that?"

Jane threw her hands up. "I'm a paralegal. Finding out stuff is what I do for a living."

"Perfect. Let me know when you get that list." Olivia wiped her mouth on her napkin before returning it to her lap.

"How are you going to help me and keep Doug from finding out? I assume he's still warning us off investigating."

"I haven't told him anything about it. It's on a need-to-know basis and he doesn't need to know."

Jane shook her head. The two talked further about Olivia's last doctor's appointment—no cancer—and Brittany's visit before parting ways, after which Jane hurried back to her office.

Once at her desk, she clicked onto the county assessor website on her computer. When she entered the name for her development, the list of homeowners, addresses, and dates of purchase flashed onto the screen. After sorting the list by date, she printed an inventory of seventeen houses built in the last year and a half, but of course, there was no way to know the ages of the homeowners.

Leaving work an hour early, she headed to the airport to pick up Brittany. She talked non-stop with her daughter-in-law all the way home about Brittany's classes, Jane's new friend Everett, and Luke's military training exercises. By the time they arrived in Limestone Heights, Jane caught Brittany up to speed on the murder investigation. Her daughter-in-law was tired from the long day of travel and settled into the guest room, while Jane ordered pizza to be delivered.

"Caleb found this pizza place soon after I moved in." Jane held out the warm box containing the chicken, goat cheese, and pineapple pizza. They ate it while sitting on stools at the kitchen counter.

"I love your new home and the mid-century modern style, Mom." Brittany craned her neck to look at the high ceiling. Her long, dark brown hair was swept back into a pony tail, and she appeared young.

"I'm glad you like it, daughter." A warm glow nestled in the pit of her stomach. She'd hidden the "For Sale" sign behind the lawnmower in the garage.

After finishing the pizza and clearing up, they traipsed out to the deck to watch the sun descend behind the high peaks. Brittany said, "I've missed the mountains, but the cost of living's so much lower in Georgia, I'm not sure we'll ever move back."

Jane's heart ached at this news, but she knew Luke wanted to make a career out of the Army and had made a life for himself and his wife in Georgia. They strolled to the east side of the deck and lounged against the railing to examine the new house under construction next door. It was turning out to be a large two-story that would obviate any view.

The breeze blew Brittany's hair into her face and she brushed it aside. "It's a good thing you can still see the mountains from the west side of your deck."

"My friend Tara lives in that house." Jane pointed east across the lot under construction. "I'll have to ask her how she feels about her view being blocked. We're going on a 14er hike on Saturday at Bierstadt Mountain."

"Can I come?"

"Of course. I meant to ask you. Have you hiked it before?"

"No, but I've wanted to." Brittany stood up straight. "I'm going to call Luke and tell him."

****

After Jane returned home from work the next day, she asked Brittany, "Do you want to run to the hardware store with me to pick up birdseed? The feeders are all empty, I noticed."

"Sure. I didn't make plans for tonight." Brittany jumped off the sofa and they headed out.

After Jane rolled into the nearly empty lot at the hardware store and parked, the two strode inside. There were so many brands of seed, but Jane was impatient and just hoisted a jumbo-sized bag into a cart and sailed down the aisle to the cash register.

"Did you find everything you need?" asked the clerk.

"Yes. I only need bird seed."

"This isn't bird seed. It's chicken feed."

"It is?"

The bag read "Organic Feed." Farther down was a label for poultry. Jane sighed and asked the clerk which aisle had the bird seed. After buying the correct selection, they loaded the seed into the trunk and climbed into the car for home.

When they turned in the driveway, Brittany pointed at the front of the house. "Look. There's a note taped to the door."

A white square adhered to the dark brown paint. Brittany snagged the note while Jane retrieved the seed from the trunk, and then they both entered the house.

"It says," read Brittany in a disbelieving voice, "'keep your nose out of the Valrods' business.'" She gulped as her eyes swept up at Jane. "What's this about?"

"Let me see." Jane grabbed the hand-printed note. "It's not really a threat, more like a warning." She squeezed her eyes shut as she wondered who wrote it. A jarring thought flashed across her mind to make sure Brittany was safe during her short visit. Too bad she hadn't moved to a new place already.

"You should call the police." Brittany had a worried expression.

"Yes, I will." Jane set the note on the counter, then prevaricated. "But wait, the police might ask me what prompted the note. Let's think about this." She heaved the bird seed onto her shoulder and hauled it out the back door.

Brittany followed her. "Tell me again who you've been talking to about these murders."

Setting the bag down near the feeder, Jane checked off with her fingers. "The widows Kimber and Gina. The neighbors in the hiking group, Ned the new construction company's manager, Margaret the realtor, Merrilee the HOA president. Oh, and I talk quite a bit to Tara, who might've mentioned to someone I've been asking questions. And the two women who had warranty appointments with Ethan on the day he died, Ashley and Kristin. He didn't show up for those."

"That's a lot of people. Anyone else?"

Jane tapped her finger to her chin. "There's the kid

who stands on the corner and twirls the advertisement board for the builder. But he wouldn't leave a note like that." She opened the top of the feeder and tilted the bag for the seed to slide in. But the seed overflowed the feeder as Jane's eyes glazed over. She said, almost to herself, "My neighbor to the west is weird. I wonder if he left it."

Brittany lifted the bag from Jane's hands and set it on the ground. "It might not be a neighbor. Anyone can drive by and find out you live here, because you have the stone in your yard with your last name on it. 'Welcome—the Marsh Residence.' Maybe you're getting too close to finding out a secret someone wants kept hidden. It may not even be about the Valrod brothers' deaths."

"What kind of secret?" Jane beetled her brows.

"I don't know, but you could be stirring up trouble and don't even know it."

"You sound like Caleb." Not wanting to worry Brittany further, Jane folded the top of the seed bag shut and said in a light tone, "I promise to call the police tomorrow." She put the lid back on the bird feeder and stowed the rest of the seed in a bin on the patio.

After returning inside, she zipped the note into a plastic bag and put it in her purse, wishing with all her heart this hadn't happened with Brittany here. It was one thing to talk about suspects and try to figure out how the pieces of the puzzle fit together, but another thing to receive a warning at the same time her daughter-in-law was visiting.

Then Jane had a brain wave. "My surveillance camera! We can check the video feed to see who put the note on the door!"

"You have a surveillance camera? Did it come with the new house or something?"

"No, no. I bought it. Thought it might come in handy and it did." Jane got out her phone and opened the app. They both peered at the screen, but it only ran the current video feed.

"How do you rewind?" asked Brittany.

Jane got out the instructions, and they both read through them. "I forgot to hit record." Jane sighed.

Brittany laughed so hard she started to hiccough.

Jane gave her daughter-in-law a playful nudge. "Let's go over to Tara's. Maybe she saw who put the note on the door. It had to have happened while we were at the hardware store."

The two walked the short distance to the neighbor's house and rang the doorbell. Justin answered and invited them inside. A few moments after they sat down in the living room, Tara joined them and Justin excused himself.

"Tara, this is my daughter-in-law, Brittany. She wants to hike Bierstadt Mountain with us."

"That'd be great." Tara smiled at Brittany. The two were about the same age and probably had a lot in common.

Jane listened as the pair got acquainted. Then Brittany kicked Jane's foot. "Tell Tara about the note."

Tara's eyebrows shot up. "What's this?"

"We found a note taped on my front door warning me to stay out of the Valrods' business. I take that to mean I'm to quit asking questions. Did you see anyone on my porch within the last hour or so, by any chance?"

Tara's eyes widened as she shook her head in the

negative. "I wonder who could've left it."

"The handwriting seemed like a woman's, but it's hard to tell," said Brittany.

"Do you have the note? Let's see it." Tara reached out her hand.

"No, I didn't bring it. I put it away in case the police want it for prints. But I did bring a list of the people who bought houses in this neighborhood in the last year. One of the women had the affair with Ethan, I'm thinking." She drew the list out of her jacket pocket. "It had to be someone around Ethan's age, but I can't tell the ages of the homeowners."

Tara read through the names. "Justin and I are on here." She handed it back.

"So is Ashley Turghart. I'm wondering if there's a way to reach out to the younger women in the neighborhood. Maybe you could do that, Tara, maybe play cards or something, since you're the right age. Ask questions, ferret out this person…"

Jane and Brittany eyed her expectantly.

"I don't play cards—"

"Well, something else then." Jane crossed her arms.

"I don't know what."

"I can't think of anything else right now either." Jane glanced at Brittany who shrugged her shoulders, too.

Justin had come around the corner with his chest thrust forward. He blew out a noisy breath. "When are you going to quit investigating?"

"Of course she won't ever." Brittany chuckled.

Jane jerked her head back to take in his scowl. She shot a glimpse at Tara, who was looking down at her hands. "Let's get going, Britt." She stood up and her daughter-in-law followed her out the door.

Chapter 18

After exiting the highway to take a country road home from work the following day, she sped past fields with round rolls of hay and russet corn stalks dotting the pastures. Tractors were sitting idle since the harvest was long past. The late afternoon autumn sun fell on the earth with a bright yellow, slanting glow, so she popped on her sunglasses. The two-lane road led her into the old section of Limestone Heights, a historical western town of brick buildings with high false fronts. The city was decorated for fall, with autumn wreaths, yellow hay bales, and orange pumpkins in the store windows.

She turned into the police station and dropped the note at the desk for the detective in charge of the murder investigation. Across the street, a shop with the name, "Bottom Bracket Bicycles," was nestled between a bakery and the post office. She made a quick decision and went inside.

A woman with a long, narrow face and prominent nose was arranging a biking shirt on a rack just inside the door. "Let me know if I can help you with anything."

"Hello. I'm Jane Marsh. I hear you're going to be joining our dinner club group on Saturday."

"Oh, yes. I'm Marcy Pelican. Nice to meet you." The woman's nasal voice somehow matched her face.

Jane shook her hand. "I saw your store and thought

I'd stop in and introduce myself. Besides, I need a basket for my bike."

"Do you have it with you?"

"No. My bike's downtown right now. I'll have to bring it home."

"Just tell me what kind you have, and we should be able to help you. Most baskets have universal fittings." Marcy turned as a man came out of the back of the shop wheeling a bicycle in front of him. "Greg, this is Jane. She's with that dinner club group."

"Hello. I'll be right back." He steered the bike to the cash register where a customer was waiting. He had rolled his shirt sleeves up to his elbows and tied a work apron around his waist.

"The baskets are over here." Marcy led Jane farther into the depths of the narrow, but deep, old building with worn hardwood floors and high, tin ceilings. They stood facing a wall of shelves with at least a dozen choices of baskets.

"I really like these." Jane stepped closer and pointed to a pair of wicker hampers designed to hang on either side of the rear wheel. "Will those work on a hybrid? Mine's got straight handlebars, upright seating, and the lighter weight, thin wheels with knobby tires."

"I think I know what kind you mean. If it has a rear rack above the back tire, you just fasten the baskets to either side of the rack."

"It has one of those. That sounds easy."

Marcy found the box on the shelf and totaled Jane's purchase at the cash register, where Greg was straightening sale items around the counter. The shop had emptied of customers, and there was a lull.

Jane handed Marcy her debit card. "Why'd you

name the shop 'Bottom Bracket Bicycles?'"

"Bicycle pedals rotate around this bearing system right here." Greg touched his finger to the oily spindle of the bike on display. "That's called the bottom bracket."

"He thought it sounded better than 'Pelican Bicycles.'" Marcy rolled her eyes.

Jane pictured a long-legged pelican riding a bicycle, and thought that made a better visual image, but said, "Well, it does have a ring to it. So, I'll see you at the Ladners' dinner on Saturday?"

"Oh, is that when it is?" asked Greg, wiping his hands on a rag.

Unsmiling, Jane answered, "Yes, this upcoming weekend. I'm sure Olivia's going to have a wonderful event planned."

"I'd better make sure I've written that on the calendar." Marcy didn't seem very concerned about knowing the correct date.

The bell on the entrance jangled. Jane's eyes goggled at Justin, who entered the shop with several other young men wearing biking shorts and shirts.

"I need to help these customers. Don't leave yet 'til I can say goodbye." Marcy strolled up to the lean bicycle riders and asked them if they needed help finding anything.

Greg pointed his face at the men. "That's the guy who brought one of his tires in for repair. The rim was so damaged I couldn't bend it back into shape. I had to special order a new one."

"Oh, no. Was he in an accident?"

"He wasn't, but he said his bike was run over by a tractor. I'd never heard of that before."

Jane paused with her wallet halfway back in her purse. "A tractor? Which one of them did you say had the damaged tire?"

He nodded at Justin. "That guy with the shaved head and whiskers."

Jane's head dipped down as she peered over the top of her sunglasses at Justin, who had plucked a jacket off a clothing rack and was holding it up. She glanced away, trying to recall if Tara mentioned anything. "He's my neighbor. I should say hello." The floor creaked as she stepped over to him. "How're you, Justin?"

A startled glimmer was in his eyes. "Oh, hi. So, you ride?"

"Yes. I think I might need a new front tire because the rim is bent. I don't know how that happened." She studied him without guilt for the telling of the lie. Did he run over his bike tire while burying the Valrod boys with the tractor?

But he didn't flinch or anything. "They can fix it for you here or order a new one. So, Tara told me you two are hiking Bierstadt Mountain on Saturday morning. I'm glad you're getting her outside for exercise." He wove his fingers together and stretched his long arms out in front of him, cracking his knuckles. "I don't know why she wants to hang around the house all the time."

"Maybe you can ride bikes together."

"No way. She can't keep up." His eyes flashed with irritation. "She's not athletic at all."

One of his friends walked up and said he was ready to leave. "Well, see you later." Justin left the shop with the others without a backward glance. Jane watched from the shop window as he got into a car with a bike rack on the roof and motored out of the parking lot.

Turning to Marcy, Jane said, "I really love your shop. I'll be back soon. My bike will need a tune-up before spring…and don't forget to mark your calendar for dinner club Saturday."

They said their goodbyes and Jane left. After stowing the new baskets in her trunk, she headed home.

Rows of red maples lined the street into her neighborhood—a beautiful fall bonus of which she wasn't aware when she moved into the subdivision at the beginning of September when the trees were still green.

As she turned onto her street, the first thing she noticed was the completed second story on the house next door. The roof trusses were in place, and the siding almost up. Ned, the construction supervisor, hopped off the new front porch, and Jane waved at him. She parked her car in her driveway and zoomed over.

"It's going up fast, and it looks nice," she said. "Do you have a buyer?"

"Yes. A family relocating from Texas."

"Do they know about the history of the house?"

"Yes. We disclosed it to them." Ned frowned.

"I found a threatening note on my door telling me to stay out of the Valrods' business."

Ned took off his baseball cap and rubbed the top of his head as he stared hard at Jane. "Who wrote it?"

"I don't know. I suspect a woman because the handwriting is so neat. Do you know either Kimber or Gina very well?"

He replaced his ball cap on his head. "Yeah, sure. I knew Suzanne, too, because we went to college together in Nebraska."

"You did? What was Suzanne like?" Jane's mind raced. This young man was a fount of information, and best of all, he was willing to share.

"She was sweet. Ethan didn't treat her very well, and the marriage didn't last."

"Do you know where she's at now?"

"I lost touch with her after she and Ethan got divorced. You should ask one of her friends because they'd know more about her than I do."

"Who would that be?"

"Hello, Mom!" Brittany stood on Jane's front porch with Everett, holding a bag of Chinese takeout.

"I'll see you later, Ned." Jane bounded the few steps back to her house.

They opened the steamy containers in the kitchen. "Thanks for bringing dinner. I didn't plan anything in advance for tonight." Jane snagged plates out of the cabinet.

Everett yanked open the silverware drawer to look for a serving spoon. "Are you busy tomorrow? I was thinking of asking the dinner club group over to the restaurant."

She glanced at her daughter-in-law. "Brittany just got here, and she's only visiting for a week. Maybe, we could wait till next week?"

Brittany piped up, "Mom, I've made plans to see some friends from school tomorrow night."

"Oh, okay then." Jane stood in front of the calendar on the kitchen wall. "Let's see, that'd be Thursday. I'm wide open."

"Perfect. I'll pick you up from your office at five, Jane." Everett ripped the paper wrapper off his chopsticks. "I'll send an email to the Ladners, too."

They enjoyed their meal, then Everett left for a late shift at work and Jane and Brittany watched a chick-flick movie Brittany had rented.

****

On Thursday, Jane was impatient for the day to end, even though there was plenty of work to do until five o'clock. Everett's car was parked outside her building when she came out the door. "Have you been waiting here long?"

"No. Just pulled up." Everett was wearing a suit and tie. Jane was dressed more formally today, too, since she had been at court that morning.

They arrived at the restaurant at the same time as Doug and Olivia. "Hello, you two!" Jane greeted her friends.

Everett led them past the maître d at the restaurant's entrance to a table for four near the fireplace. A waiter, dressed in a crisp, white shirt, black slacks, and a large, pristine white apron tied around his waist, handed out the wine menus.

Everett ordered a bottle of wine to be shared. "It's a really good Chianti that goes well with pasta."

After the waiter returned to their table with the Chianti, they placed their dinner orders. Jane glanced sideways surreptitiously for Polly near the entrance or the kitchen area, but did not see her. However, she heard a man's voice behind her say, "Polly, are you sure you want to start a new restaurant on your own?" Because the man's voice sounded familiar, she strained to hear more.

The woman's words carried over. "I can't rely on you forever. If the brew pub works out, perhaps I can buy you out of this place."

Jane whirled around to catch a glimpse of Dale and Polly sitting a couple of tables away. Just then the hostess seated two couples at the table in between them, and she could no longer hear Dale's and Polly's conversation. She did see Dale's hand reach out to Polly's before she turned back to the table. Everett caught her eye, and she gave him a tight smile.

Jane enjoyed the spicy tomato bisque soup before digging into a tall square of cheesy lasagna. Everett regaled them with funny stories from the kitchen, then when they were finishing their meal, Olivia said, "I'm going to send an email with the details for dinner club at my house this weekend." She fingered the long necklace dangling near her cleavage.

Jane said, "I stopped by the Pelicans' bike shop. They acted like they weren't even aware of the date, so it's a good idea to send an email out."

All at once, Polly loomed over their table. "How'd everything taste tonight?" She was a dark-haired woman, who appeared to be in her late thirties, wearing a short black dress and very tall heels.

"Wonderful." Jane's eyes swept her up and down.

Polly prompted Everett, "These are friends of yours?"

"Let me introduce you." He stated their names and ended with, "This is my dinner club group." Jane felt proud that he took ownership of the club; he must feel he belonged. She craned her neck and caught a glimpse of Dale at his table. He winked at her, and she did a double take.

Polly didn't act as if she had seen Jane before. "Glad to meet all of you. Hope you enjoyed yourselves."

The waiter handed Everett the bill, and he began to pay for it, but Doug stopped him. "We want to pay our share."

"I get a good employee discount. Really, it's my treat," Everett insisted. But the men ended up splitting the bill and leaving a nice tip on the full amount.

"Time to head home," said Doug, and they all gathered their coats to leave. They parted in the parking lot, then Everett and Jane took off in his car with a farewell wave at the others.

Everett dropped Jane off at her car downtown where she had left it after work. "I'll pick you up on Saturday night for Olivia's dinner."

Standing at the curb, Jane leaned into the driver's window. "Remember she told us to wear old blue jeans and T-shirts. Isn't that odd for Olivia?"

"I wonder if we're going to clean out pumpkins and toast the seeds."

Jane had another idea. "Maybe there'll be a football scrimmage on the lawn, like the Kennedys in Newport on Thanksgiving."

Chapter 19

The alarm clock sounded too early for a Saturday morning. Jane sauntered into the kitchen for that first cup of coffee, having set the coffee machine timer for 4:30 a.m. Carrying her cup down the hall, she knocked on Brittany's bedroom door.

"I'm up. Be out in a sec." Brittany's feet thumped across the floor.

"Okay." Back in her bathroom, Jane brushed her teeth and swept her hair up into a barrette. After donning her hiking clothes, she had time for a few more sips of coffee before Brittany joined her in the kitchen. Tara arrived at the door a few minutes later.

Jane filled travel mugs with coffee for her and Brittany, snagged the bagels and cream cheese for breakfast on the road, and hoisted her loaded, but compact, backpack onto her shoulder.

"You all ready?" Tara appeared sleepy.

"I have two water bottles, a sack lunch, snacks, jacket, sun screen, gloves, hat, and cell phone. Plus, I found snowshoes in one of the boxes of stuff in the garage I was going to give away. Brittany has all that, too." Jane pointed to Brittany's pint-sized backpack, with water bottles sticking out of side pockets and snow shoes hanging by a clip. "Do we need anything else?"

"You've got it covered."

"Did you have breakfast, Tara? I have extra bagels

if you're hungry and there's some coffee left—"

"No, I ate already." Tara flipped her hair over her shoulder as she headed out the door. "We need to be on our way."

On the drive to Bierstadt Mountain, they talked nonstop about what to expect on the trail and the famous view from the top peak.

"This is a bucket list event for me," said Jane.

Brittany sat in the front passenger seat. "I told Luke all about it, and he's jealous because he wasn't able to come with us."

"Justin doesn't care, but that's okay. He's doing what he wants, and so am I." Tara leaned over Brittany's shoulder from her seat in the back.

Jane and Brittany exchanged glances, then Brittany turned to face Tara. "Ask to see the pictures he takes today and offer to show him yours."

"Sure, sure." Tara drummed her fingers on the seat back. "I talked to the neighbor on your other side, Jane."

Staring in her rearview mirror, Jane asked, "You did? What did he say?"

"He told me you planned a party for the same night he did, and you were mad he didn't ask your permission before he had his party."

"I never said that!" Jane's mouth dropped open. "Wait a minute. Wait just a second. I did joke about it. I said something like how he didn't check with me first, but I was kidding. He must have overheard me. Maybe that's one of the reasons he always seems angry."

They had a laugh when Tara said, "Invite him to your dinner club." They were in high spirts during the drive up the mountain.

Two hours later, they arrived at the trailhead. On this late fall morning, the parking lot wasn't as full as during the summer months. Nevertheless, there were a couple dozen parked cars. After waiting twenty minutes, they confirmed only five others from the walking group had joined them—Kimber Valrod, Gina Valrod, Ashley Turghart, Kristin Gauthierville, and Margaret Skaleop. Olivia had cancelled at the last minute, and the others must've ditched as well.

Jane whispered to Brittany, "This group is my suspect list…"

Kimber, Gina, and Ashley had driven together, but Kristin and Margaret arrived separately.

"In fact, you should've organized a car pool," Ashley mentioned as she slipped into the line to the portable restroom.

Before everyone was ready to start out, Jane had a hard time meeting Kimber's eyes, as she stood thinking about how to approach her.

Warmly dressed, they commenced up the trail with their headlamps around their foreheads, lighting the way until the sun rose fully. Kimber and Gina walked faster than the other women and had caught up with a small group of strangers ahead. Ashley, Kristin, and Margaret remained with Tara, Jane, and Brittany, as the six of them formed a little band against the loud wind, marching along single file.

The sun ascended into the sky and lit up a bleak terrain without much vegetation, except for yellow, deadened ground cover and twisted, dwarf shrubs. They kept themselves to the climbing pathway, so they wouldn't disturb the tender tundra, which took years to grow. They traversed a wooden walkway, crossed a stream, and then hiked past a mountain lake. No switchbacks and nothing narrow to cross, yet it was harder to breathe the farther they climbed.

After entering a field covered with a hard layer of snow, their feet kept breaking through the crust and sinking down into cold wetness, so they donned the snowshoes that had been strapped to their backpacks. Finally, they came across an incline of boulders and had to remove the snowshoes to scramble up and around the large, icy rocks. Plodding along toward the summit, they made more and more stops for water and to rest. Jane could only advance about ten steps before stopping to take a breath as she struggled to the top.

A strong wind blasted them at the peak where a small crowd of people were milling around. Jane had envisioned one lone, pointy rock at the very tip-top, but there was plenty of room for everyone at the large pinnacle, which was wide and rather flat, though lumpy with boulders.

"There's a register to sign-in to show you made it all the way," bellowed Kimber above the wind. She handed the torn and dirty, plastic-covered book to Gina. Ashley and Kristin stood at the marker in the ground designating the highest point of elevation. Jane took a photograph of the marker on her cell phone, and they all gathered in groups to take each other's photos. Tara's long hair whipped around viciously by the wind, disconsonant in this otherwise calm and serene spot on top of the world.

They separated to wander around the summit and gaze out at the three hundred sixty degree view, with snow covered peaks, one behind another, behind another, as far as the eye could see. Although the sky was overcast, spots of blue peeked through the darkening clouds, contrasting with the white-topped mountains. Soon, the eight women reconvened and sat on boulders to eat their lunches.

"This is so beautiful," was all Jane and the rest could say over and over. After tucking their empty sacks and water bottles into their packs, they were still reluctant to leave the peak and start back.

"I'm going to walk a little ways over there before we head down." Jane tugged on Brittany's coat sleeve and pointed to the Mount Evans wilderness area. "I'll be right back."

She clambered over boulders to the east, then slid down some rocks to a sheltered spot partially out of the wind. Perching on the edge of a boulder, she snapped more photos of God's magnificent creation before tucking her camera into her pocket. Had any human ever crossed that wild and impossible terrain?

A hard force hit the middle of her back. She flew from her roost and landed on hands and knees, then rolled into a cleft between two immense rocks.

Dazed for a moment, she laid motionless before heaving herself out and sitting up. Fear swept through her heart like the icy wind as she rubbed her right knee, which had taken the brunt of her fall. Her right wrist ached, too. She looked around, but was all alone, unable to hear the voices of the others in the crashing wind. Slowly rising to a stand, she breathed in the icy air and started to tremble.

Someone's head poked around a boulder, causing Jane to jump into a painful but defensive stance like the karate kid.

"Jane! Where've you been?" Tara's eyes were

wide. "Everyone's heading back. What's keeping you?"

Jane breathed a sigh of relief at the sight of her friend. "Someone pushed me off my rock and I fell." She grabbed onto Tara's proffered hand and allowed herself to be dragged upward, wincing in pain, heart thumping.

"What did you say?" Tara let go of Jane's hands.

"I was pushed."

Brittany rushed over. "What's the matter, Mom? Did you hurt yourself?"

"Someone shoved me off the rock!"

"Who shoved you? And are you okay?" Britt's face showed worry and concern.

"Are you sure it wasn't the wind?" asked Tara.

"No. I was shoved, hard, but I didn't see who did it." Jane's back was sore where she could still feel the imprints of strong hands. She stared at the ground as she carefully placed one foot in front of the other on the slippery rocks.

When they returned to the summit, Brittany squeezed Jane's wrist to determine if anything was broken. Jane couldn't roll up her tight pant leg to examine her knee, but said, "I think I'm only bruised. I'll be all right. And we need to head down the mountain."

Darker clouds gathered as the wind continued to blow cold. Everyone else in their group had started the descent to the trailhead. A few other stragglers took one last picture and hurried down the trail as Jane, Tara, and Brittany slung their small packs onto their backs. When her knee emitted a sharp pain with the first step, Jane kept her complaints to herself.

A few small flakes of snow drifted down from the

purple sky. Then the snow fell faster and faster as they skittered over the boulders on the pathway. A small blizzard swirled in front of their faces, with snow landing on the already slippery rocks at their feet.

Jane kept peering over her shoulder with foreboding. Her eyes searched for someone sneaking up behind them, but she couldn't see more than a foot or two. She heard voices and footfalls on the path in the howling wind. A tremor went through her body as she fought the compulsion to keep glancing back instead of watching her steps.

They stopped to regroup, so Brittany slipped her headlamp over her forehead. "This doesn't really help any. It just lights up the snow in front of my face."

Jane put on hers, too, and spun around in a slow circle, peering into the swirling snow. She saw black spots in front of her eyes, realizing she was a little dizzy.

"I can make out the rocks right in front of us," said Tara. "I can see where the path goes, so let's keep moving. We'll walk out of it."

The three friends faced forward, as Tara took the front position and Jane maneuvered Brittany between them, so she could take the rear. As the path got more difficult to follow, Tara reached behind for Brittany's hand, and Brittany took Jane's hand. Jane forced her trembling gloved hand to be still, hoping Brittany wouldn't notice. They descended in single file until they entered the field that was covered in freshly fallen snow over thick and sturdy, crusted ice. After strapping their snowshoes in place one more time, they took big footsteps, the snow crunching under their feet.

Once away from the field, the snowfall got thinner

and thinner, until they came out into clear weather.

"Gosh, I was a little scared. I've read where people had to be rescued from sudden blizzards on the peak." Tara let go of Brittany's hand.

Jane had been terrified, but for a different reason, and still wanted to bolt down the path to the trailhead. They slipped off their snowshoes and stomped their feet in the cold.

"Wasn't that exciting, though?" Brittany's eyes shone and her face lit up with a wide smile.

Jane was able to let out a weak laugh at the expression on Britt's face. She rubbed behind her neck as she rolled her shoulder to work out the knot in her back.

The snow enveloped them again, so they hurried onward. The flurries kept right at their heels until they reached the mountain lake. But by the time they crossed the boardwalk, they'd left the snow behind, and the sun was shining through the clouds.

Once they walked into the parking lot at the trailhead, Jane relaxed, but sucked her breath in when Gina, Kimber, and Margaret strode over to them. One of these women had shoved her, and she could've been badly hurt.

Margaret pointed up the mountain. "We saw the snow blow in behind us, and we were thinking of going back for you. I was trying to see if I had cell phone coverage, when we saw you emerge out of the snow flurries. I don't really know who I would've called for help, anyway."

"But we made it!" Brittany smacked Margaret's hand in a high five.

The rest of the women scooted closer and put their

arms around one another in a football huddle.

"That was fantastic."

"I had a wonderful time."

"Thanks ladies. I'll never forget this day. Just like the Ya Ya sisters."

Jane's tight chest unwound as waves of good feelings washed over her. She said with a catch in her voice, "I can cross this off my bucket list now."

Another cloud abruptly obscured the sun, so they broke apart and headed for their vehicles. The parking lot was empty, except for the other stragglers putting packs into their trunk.

"Let's get going so we can beat the snow home," said Jane, as the three piled into her car and slammed the doors shut. While Jane was navigating the entrance ramp to the highway, Tara and Brittany exchanged phones to view each other's photos.

"I'll post some of my pictures on Facebook and tag you two so the photos show up on your pages, too," said Tara from the backseat.

Brittany took her phone back. "Thanks. I'll post mine in a minute. I want to text some photos to Luke first."

"I have a suggestion for the next event. Do you think anyone'll be interested in cross-country skiing? Maybe in two or three weeks." Tara poked Jane on the back of her shoulder.

Jane widened her eyes and bobbed her head up and down. "Yes. Great idea."

"I can't go. I'm leaving tomorrow," pointed out Brittany.

"Sorry. Maybe during your next visit." Jane gave her a sad face.

"Are you coming home for Christmas?" Tara asked.

"Maybe..." Brittany was preoccupied with the text to her husband.

Tara tucked her feet underneath her bottom and sat higher on her seat. "Where do you think we should cross country?"

"I don't know."

"There're plenty of books at the library with ski trails."

"Okay. And we can do a lot of promoting on the HOA website." Jane was buzzing with plans. In spite of her sore knee, she felt empowered after conquering Mount Bierstadt. Even fearless, now she was safely on her way home. To heck with the danger. She tapped her fingers on the steering wheel. "A ski event might bring out the younger crowd...to uncover some clues."

****

But once home, the knot in Jane's stomach returned as she and Brittany discussed which of them shoved her. She asked, "Did you see anyone leave the summit and walk in my direction?"

"No. But I was busy writing in the journal." Brittany hauled everything out of her backpack and set it on the counter. "Margaret wanted to rescue us from the blizzard, so it couldn't've been her. Of course, not Tara, either. She's a good friend."

"I agree."

"I did see something on her cell phone. There were pictures of her with a man, and it wasn't Justin."

"What? Tara?" Jane jerked the zipper open on her backpack.

A troubled look passed over Brittany's face. "He

216

didn't have a shaved head like Justin. It wasn't him, and they looked real chummy."

"Maybe it was her brother. I don't want to jump to any conclusions. She's been a buddy." Jane shoved the leftover granola bars from her pack into the pantry.

"Is it time to call the cops? Remember the note and now someone attacked you."

"Yes. I think I need to."

"Don't let it stop you from going on the ski trip, Mom. But make sure to take Olivia with you, if she skis." Brittany twisted her wedding ring around on her finger.

"I wonder if Kimber or Gina ski." Jane thought about James Bond carrying a parachute on his back while skiing to escape an enemy agent. A mental image of wearing Olivia's trench coat and fedora while on skis made her give up on the idea.

Chapter 20

"And someone shoved Mom off the rock! She's getting close to uncovering the murderer." Brittany blew gently on her too-hot tea as Everett sat at the kitchen counter, his small blue eyes growing more and more wide. She'd recounted the entire story after Everett arrived that evening to take Jane to the dinner club event at the Ladners'.

"I'm going to call Luke." Brittany picked up her phone and tapped in his number.

As Britt headed down the hallway, Everett said to Jane, "Are you all right? Maybe we should cancel tonight."

"No. I wouldn't miss the Ladners' dinner for anything."

"How's your knee? Does it hurt?"

She leaned on her left hand against the kitchen counter as she rolled up her pants leg with her right to display a slim knee turning black and blue. "It looks worse than it is." Stretching her leg out straight in front of her like a ballerina, she pointed her toes then placed her foot back on the floor. "It actually feels good to move it around."

"Your feet are small, like your hands, dainty and sweet."

"You're sweet to say so." Jane ducked her head to glance down at her toes, barely peeking out from the hem of her pressed jeans. She slid her foot back into her flats. "We'd better get going." After Everett helped her out to his car, she relaxed in the heated seat. "Olivia's email said the main course tonight is steamed cod with cauliflower and saffron. I'm afraid I don't know what saffron is."

Everett watched the road. "You aren't alone. Most people don't know what it tastes like since it's the most expensive spice in the world."

"Really? Of course Olivia would serve it."

"You don't need much since the flavor's intense. You can buy it in threads, which literally amount to just a teaspoon. Then, you soak it in warm water or wine before adding it to your recipe. Soaking helps the thread break up and mix evenly with the other ingredients."

"What does it taste like?"

"It's hard to describe. Some people say like honey, but others taste a bitterness."

"Interesting. Some say bitter, some say sweet. I guess I'll find out for myself soon."

As they walked in the Ladners' door, Olivia handed them each a painting smock to put over their clothes and a glass of Chardonnay. Olivia said, "We're going to have a water color lesson while drinking wine." Standing next to Olivia and Doug was a young woman wearing a smock with 'Paint, Palette, and Pour' printed across the front. The mystery as to why they were to wear old clothes was solved.

"Appetizers now, dinner after we're done painting." Doug strode over to the wine bar which also held the appetizers. "Help yourselves. We've got Swedish meatballs, whipped goat cheese poppers, and almond stuffed dates wrapped with bacon."

"Did you whip the goats to make the poppers?" teased Everett. They laughed as they filled small plates with the appetizers.

"Where are Marcy and Greg?" Olivia asked, after twenty minutes passed and it was time for the lesson to begin. "Have you heard from them, by any chance?" Olivia's appearance was different tonight—no jewelry and she had swept her beautiful black hair back with a hairband.

"No. Do you have their phone number?" Jane glanced at the kitchen clock.

Having it handy in her phone contacts, Olivia called Marcy, only to be put through to voice mail. She left a quick message and hung up. "Let's get started. Jade's only here an hour."

The artist instructed them to choose one of the easels set up in the sun room. Thick, white canvas taped at the corners to a heavy backer board balanced on each easel. Drop cloths covered the tiled floor. They assembled at their places, the two men at the back and the women in front. Jade uncovered a beautiful watercolor of aspens with white tree trunks, yellow leaves, and blue background shades. "This is the painting you are going to create tonight. I'll take you through the process step-by-step." After removing the finished picture, she tacked up a piece of blank canvas to her easel. "First we apply the background colors." They each took up a paint brush, dipped the brush into the water, and then into the color on their palettes.

Olivia said, "It's a good thing we're painting woods because I can only draw stick people—"

"Ha. A pun!" Jane smiled.

"Actually, I wasn't intending to make a pun."

"We're going to explore your artistic side," said Jade.

"The front or back side?" teased Doug.

"The dark side." Everett twirled his paintbrush with a flourish.

Olivia paused in her painting to start some upbeat music on a CD player and refill their wine glasses.

They experimented with different amounts of water. Jane preferred the wet flowing look as she made the outline of a tree trunk on the heavy fabric, then filled in the dark places that soon took the shape of a tree trunk. Everett came up behind Jane to study her picture. "That's really good. Lots better than mine—"

"This isn't a competition," Jade said. "Because if it was I'd win!" Everyone laughed, and Everett grabbed Jane's paint brush to put a dab of paint on her nose.

By the end of an hour, they each had a painting similar to Jade's finished work of art, but marked by their own individuality.

Olivia disappeared into the kitchen for a few minutes to check on the dinner warming in the oven. When she returned, she examined Jane's creation. "Your trees look dead."

"They do?" Jane knit her eyebrows. "I guess I forgot to draw the leaves on."

The instructor took their paintings down from the easels and laid them on the drop cloth with instructions not to touch them until dry. She blew on the canvas with a hair dryer to quicken the process, then the men helped her pack her easels into her van while the ladies cleaned the paint brushes. Everyone handed in their paint smocks, washed their hands, and made sure they hadn't stepped in any paint splatters.

After Jade departed, Olivia said, "Dinner's more than ready. It's been steaming in the oven on warm. Everyone into the dining room."

They hastened to the formal table set with white china, crisp white napkins, and polished silverware, but no one was fooled by the fake wine glass spill on the white carpet. Doug frowned in disappointment under his bristly mustache. "I've been saving that gag just for tonight."

"It's been done already, Doug. I told you." Olivia rolled her eyes.

"You were right, sweetheart."

The two couples held hands, and Doug said a blessing over the meal for the four of them.

"What do you think of my choice of entrée?" Olivia glanced around the table.

"Are you fishing for compliments?" Everett chuckled.

"Don't be so koi," said Jane.

"Ho. Ho. That sounds fishy," said Doug.

"Cod that was bad—"

"No need to carp on about it."

Everyone was quiet, waiting for the next pun which didn't come. Then Olivia clapped her hands. "Oh, I thought of another. Anything new with the murder investigation? What've you been herring about?"

Before Jane could answer, a phone pinged. "I got a text." Olivia yanked her phone out. "It's from the Pelicans. All it says is, 'sorry, can't make it.'"

A moment of shocked silence hung in the air.

Jane crossed her arms. "And I was worried something happened to them. With this murder still unsolved, I'm seeing danger everywhere."

"Well, the Pelicans are not getting into this club." Olivia shook her head. "No second chances. I have another couple in mind, no worries."

Everett said, "I know several people who might be interested and one of the gals is a chef. I can ask."

Olivia just stared at him. Oh dear. Olivia would want to pick out the prospects herself. Jane said, "About the murder investigation, I thought of another suspect, the teenager who twirls the advertising sign on the corner."

"What about him?" Doug's eyes bored into hers.

"He and Ethan smoked marijuana together. Perhaps they were experimenting with more dangerous drugs, the kid went crazy on some drug, like PCP, and killed him." Jane tapped a finger to her chin.

"You never hear of PCP anymore. Is that drug still around?" asked Everett.

"It's lost popularity, but yes, it is." Doug cleared his throat. "The DA has a person of interest."

"Is it Gina?" Jane sat up straight. "Or Kimber?"

Doug raised a hand to his brow and rubbed it, as if a headache was coming on. "I shouldn't be telling you this, Jane, but the DA told me Kimber was shopping with a friend around the time Ethan was killed, which was probably the same time Steven was killed, too. She has a solid alibi."

"Really!" With her jaw dropping, Jane slouched back in her chair. "She could've faked her alibi. Got a friend to lie for her."

"Give it up, Jane." Doug wagged his finger at her.

"Okay. Okay." But Jane did not meet his eyes.

Once everyone finished, they strolled out to the patio with Irish coffees and cigars. While facing the woods in the park across from the Ladners' deck, they listened to an owl hooting among the trees. Jane couldn't help but think about Cheryl, whom she hadn't heard from for a while. Cheryl knew all about birds. A sadness grew in her heart and tightened her chest. She wanted to discuss moving with her absent friend, since the real estate agent had left her a message regarding a second offer, but Jane, for some reason, hadn't called the agent back.

She stared into her coffee cup, and swirled the rich, brown, comforting drink around, then swiveled her mug to the left and the right. "There's something in the bottom of my mug." Cigarette butts appeared to be floating in the dregs. "Yuck..."

Doug said, "Gotcha!" It was fake. She passed the mug around so everyone could get the full benefit of the joke.

Olivia left to get another coffee cup and a full pot. Returning, she said, "By the way, I have an idea for dinner club later in December. How about we all go to the 1940s White Christmas Ball? I want to wear a long, red gown with white fur cuffs like Rosemary Clooney."

"Do you have any 1940's clothes, Everett?" Was Jane assuming too much in expecting him to take her to the ball? It was over a month away, and they'd never before made plans that far in advance. She glanced down at her hands while everyone waited for Everett's answer.

"I have a fedora." He didn't say anything more.

The party soon broke up. After gathering their watercolor pictures and jackets, they headed out into the cool, foggy night.

On the drive home, Everett held Jane's hand in his

right while he competently steered with his left. Her eyes were riveted straight ahead as he drove up in front of her house. Should she invite him inside for more coffee? Yes, yes, yes, her heart sang. So she did.

****

On Sunday after church, Jane drove Brittany downtown and parked in her usual spot. They climbed out of the car and waited on the corner for a few minutes. Caleb drove up in a Car2Go and they squeezed in. Zipping the few blocks to the restaurant, they enjoyed the short ride.

"That was a hoot, Caleb. I'll never rent one of those myself." Jane took a picture of the miniscule automobile before they left it at the curb.

Erin was waiting for them in a booth for a get-together before Brittany's flight home. Jane barely recognized her. Her hair was a silvery blue—not a bright neon blue, but a long bob of shimmery, light, almost white, blue. Her new color complemented her fair complexion and blue eyes.

"I love your hair!" Brittany plopped down across from Erin.

"Thanks! So good to see you again, Britt!" Erin ran her hands through her blue strands.

"The school lets you color your hair?" asked Jane.

"Yes. There's a dress-code for the instructors, but it doesn't mention hair color." Erin giggled. "Of course, they might decide to add it to the employee manual now that I've colored my hair blue!" Caleb smiled at Erin and put his arm behind her shoulder as they sat next to each other in the booth.

Jane had almost asked if the hair color was temporary for Halloween and was glad she didn't. They ordered something to drink and sandwiches from the bistro menu, as Jane and Brittany told the couple about the hike up Bierstadt Mountain.

"My first 14er," said Jane.

Brittany tapped one finger on the table and once again told the tale. "Somebody came up behind Mom and shoved her off one of the boulders at the summit!"

"Gosh, are you all right? Who did that? And why?" Erin's hair shimmered in the light from the bistro's window. Caleb thumped his drink down on the table and gave his mother his usual stink eye.

Jane shrugged. "I don't know. But all my suspects were there, and it could've been any of them. There were plenty of other hikers at the summit, too, but I don't think it was a stranger—"

"And there was a note left on the door warning Mom off the Valrods..." Brittany must not have seen Jane's warning finger crossing her lips or hear her shushing. "Tell them, Mom."

Caleb's gaze turned cold. "What've you been up to?"

She might as well come clean. After taking a bracing sip of her coffee, Jane snagged her murder folder out of her satchel. Everyone read through her list of suspects, including motives, but no one had any bright, new ideas. Jane said, "What if the threatening note has nothing to do with the murder? Maybe the Valrods are only trying to keep me from asking questions about their business."

"From what you told me, they do seem protective of their company secrets." Brittany stirred her coffee.

Caleb could only shake his head. "Please be careful."

Jane knew her son worried about her. "Well, Happy Halloween anyway!" She cracked a smile. "Do you think you'll get many trick-or-treaters at your loft tonight?"

"We haven't noticed a lot of kids in the neighborhood, but we're prepared. We bought several large bags of candy," said Erin. "But since we just moved in, people might not know anyone's living there yet."

"Turn on your front light. If you light it, they'll come." Brittany gave her a thumbs up.

"Brittany bought plenty of candy in case I get any trick-or-treaters tonight." Jane still hadn't returned the real estate agent's call. She'd do it later.

After they finished enjoying their meal, it was time for Jane to take Brittany to the airport. Caleb dropped them off at Jane's car, which was already packed with her daughter-in-law's luggage.

They arrived in plenty of time. They checked the flight board to verify the plane was in line to take off as scheduled. As Brittany stood in the long wait at security, Jane watched from the overlook on the floor above. Brittany finally passed through to the concourse and turned to wave a final farewell.

Jane texted Luke to let him know his wife would soon board the plane for home. Luke was returning from his training the next day, and Brittany would be there waiting for him. Knowing that Luke and Brittany had each other, Jane's chest stopped aching, and she got a warm and happy, fuzzy feeling.

****

When she turned in the driveway, Everett was waiting for her.

"I thought you could use some cheering up with Brittany leaving, so I brought Chinese take-out again." Everett held up a bulging bag that smelled delicious— deep fried won tons. "I remember you liked it before."

She hugged Everett tight, grabbed his hand, and dragged him into the house with her. She never did find the time to call the real estate agent back.

Chapter 21

Jane dialed the detective Monday morning after she got to her office.

"You never called me after I dropped off the note someone taped to my door. It said I need to leave the Valrods alone. I should tell you what else happened, too. While the neighborhood walking group was hiking on Bierstadt Mountain, someone shoved me and I fell. I didn't get a chance to see who it was."

"You'd better tell me all about it. Who was present?"

Jane gave the detective the details and could not resist asking, "Are you close to catching the killer?"

"When an arrest is made, you'll read about it in the newspaper."

After disconnecting, her cell phone buzzed, so she picked up right away. Her real estate agent said, "I left you a message. Why didn't you call back?"

"I was going to call you when I had a break this morning." Jane kicked herself for not checking caller I.D.

"There's news! I have a second offer. Five thousand over asking price."

Jane's heart sank to her toes. "Don't tell me I have to move out in two weeks."

"No. Not this time." The agent chuckled into the phone, obviously delighted. "I want to hear you say you accept it."

"I need time to think about it. Let me sleep on it." She tapped her pencil on her desktop with a rat-a-tat-tat.

"Again? That's what you said last time. Jane, I'll put off the buyers, tell them you can't be reached. I'll give you twenty-four hours. If you don't accept the offer, our listing agreement is cancelled."

"I don't want you to lie. You did reach me." Jane spoke into silence. Either the call dropped or the agent disconnected. If the agent broke off their agreement, would word get out that Jane was a difficult client in this small town? If so, even Margaret may not want her listing...

Of course, she should accept the offer. How could she forget the threatening note...being shoved off the mountain top. That reminded her, the cross-country ski trip was coming up.

She turned back to her computer and navigated to the HOA website to check the tickler posted by Tara. There it was—a cross-country ski trip planned for November thirteenth. Jane needed to figure out how to include a sign-up page for carpooling. Clicking around on the site, she noticed an HOA meeting scheduled for that evening.

****

Jane threw the door open to the community center and stood aside for Tara to enter.

Gina and Kimber Valrod sat together in the back row, not speaking. Kimber appeared bored, and Gina was checking her cell phone.

"Let's go sit next to them." Jane was encouraged by the warm bond she felt at the end of the trail on Bierstadt Mountain, so she and Tara took the two empty seats next to Kimber.

Jane was a little bored herself as the HOA president, Merrilee Eichenthal, talked about the budget in confusing accounting terms. Next, she made an announcement about ordering several trees at a discount from a landscaping company, since trees needed to be replaced at the playground in the spring.

Not many people were listening and there was a buzz of chatter throughout the room. Tara pointed out Zachery Gauthierville talking in a corner with an attractive woman who was not his wife. Staring hard at Zachery, Kristin Gauthierville sat a couple of rows from the back. Ashley Turghart, alone once again without her husband Joshua, was leaning over the seat in front of her, talking to Margaret Skaleop.

The meeting finally came to an end, so people started to rise from their seats, their chairs scraping the floor. Gina glided away to talk to Merrilee, and Tara began a conversation with someone Jane didn't know.

Still seated, she turned to Kimber. "Hello. How are you?"

"Doing okay."

"I'm surprised to see you here. I thought the construction company was done with everything to do with this subdivision."

"That's right. This is the last HOA meeting anyone from the Valrod Construction Company needs to attend."

Jane took a deep breath. "Kimber, I have some questions about the twins' deaths I can't let go."

Kimber's eyebrows shot up. "What?"

"Merrilee mentioned she saw your car on my street the day Ethan died."

"What are you saying?" Kimber's tone was icy. Gone was the comradery they'd had at the end of the trail on Mount Bierstadt.

"Well, I guess I was wondering, uh, if, maybe you saw something that day."

"I wasn't anywhere near there. I told you I had an alibi." Kimber's voice was getting louder.

In for a penny, in for a pound, thought Jane. "Your car was spotted by several witnesses, and there were bruises on your arms—"

"I—fell—off—a—horse." She enunciated each syllable with loud, crisp words.

"Okay." Jane tried to keep the doubtful expression off her face.

"What about you? Were you having an affair with my husband?" Kimber shot out of her seat and glared at Jane.

With mouth agape, Kristin turned around from her seat in the row ahead.

Jane was dumbfounded. "No, of course not! For one thing, I'm old enough to have been his mother." She did a quick calculation. "Well, not quite, really, but almost…" Did Kimber think the best defense was a good offense? This was certainly offensive, causing Jane to admit her age!

"They say the murderer's usually the one who found the body. What other reason would you have to kill him? You were having an affair." Kimber gulped back a sob. Gina headed over with a dangerous light in her eyes and clenched fists, with Ashley behind her.

"That's ridiculous!" Jane also stood up, fists on hips. "You're so wrong. And you of all people probably knew who he was having the affair with, since you had an affair with him when he was still married to Suzanne. What were you doing that day? Following him? Checking up on him?"

Kimber's eyes flared, and Jane saw that she may have hit close to the truth. Kimber ripped her coat off the back of her seat, causing the flimsy folding chair to collapse to the floor with a crash. Tara appeared at Jane's side, and a small crowd formed, but others were hurrying out the door. Margaret and Merrilee stood together, and Merrilee pointed a finger in Jane's direction.

Kimber gave Jane a small shove on her left shoulder, causing her to stumble backward. "You. You. Quit bothering me!" She turned and took flight out the door past Ashley and Gina, who both stood open-mouthed.

Everyone else's eyes fixed on Jane.

"I wanted to announce that we're organizing a cross-country ski day," Jane said to no one in particular. "On November thirteenth."

"Come on, let's go." Tara tugged on her arm. Jane's heart pounded, and she was a little shaky on her feet, but she slowly put on her jacket and walked out the door, head held high.

Once outside, Tara asked, "What happened? I didn't catch the beginning of your conversation. Did you actually accuse Kimber of murder?"

"I think I may have."

Tara boomed out a laugh, then Jane joined in with a sigh of relief. She recounted the whole conversation.

"You just about got Kimber to admit she was following Ethan." Tara poked Jane in the arm.

"That's why she was there that day. But did she kill

him?"

Tara ran her fingers through her long blonde hair. "Probably."

They parted ways at Tara's house after planning to talk more later about the cross-country ski trip.

She called Everett to update him with the events of the HOA meeting, but he was at work and could only talk briefly. "Everett, I need you in the kitchen," came a woman's voice in the background. Was that Polly?

It was time for a therapy session with Cheryl, so she punched her number into the phone.

"I've been thinking about you. I've tried to call you several times, and I was wondering what was up, when Olivia remembered your cruise. How was it?"

"Lots of fun! Have you checked Facebook lately? I posted our cruise photos."

"Sorry. I haven't in a long time, but I promise to log-in soon. So do you have a cruise picture for your Christmas card this year?" she teased.

But Cheryl's voice held a serious tone. "There're so many good photos. Be sure to look at them and 'like' which is best."

Cheryl told Jane she'd been hired at a contemporary art museum. They talked about the Bierstadt Mountain hike—Jane's first 14er—and the HOA meeting. Cheryl was appropriately concerned about the shoving incident, but burst into laughter at the news Kimber accused Jane of having an affair with Ethan. After they disconnected, Jane realized there was so much more to discuss. She should've asked Cheryl more questions about her new job and how she liked the new city. And Jane didn't get a chance to complain about Everett working for Polly.

Her heart sank with disappointment, like when your favorite character in Downton Abbey dies in the season's finale.

Maybe Olivia would have a different take on things. She answered the phone on the first ring after Jane called her. "How are you?"

"Kimber accused me of having an affair with her husband."

"How on earth could she think that? You?" Olivia snorted into the phone.

Starting to pout, Jane stopped herself. It was pretty incredible, after all. She ended the call after a few minutes and trod out to her back patio to peer into the dark heavens above. Bright stars illuminated the night, and blinking lights from a plane traveled across the sky.

Nick and Nora sniffed at her feet, wondering what Jane was doing outside at this late hour. The dogs used to love to chase the squirrels running across the fence from tree to tree at the old house in Verano. Maybe if she planted more trees and bushes, the squirrels would move into the area and provide entertainment for her pups. But then she remembered she had an offer on the house.

The roof was going up next door. Most of Tara's home on the other side was now obstructed from view. Jane retreated indoors and slid the night vision goggles out of the box without stopping to read the instructions. Back on the patio, she strapped the goggles around her eyes and examined the dark depths of her back yard, then pointed the lenses toward the house under construction. Adjusting the focus, she found herself staring right through the construction site into Justin's and Tara's bedroom. And in the window, Justin scowled back at her with protruding eyes.

She jerked the goggles away and dodged back in the house. What must he think of her? Heat flushed her face. Would he think she was voyeuristic? Most likely he would just believe she was a middle-aged snoop. She comforted herself with the intention of simply explaining it to Tara later.

****

As soon as Jane entered her home Tuesday after work, someone banged hard on her front door. Jane checked her surveillance camera app, thinking of some kind of excuse to give Tara, but it was her real estate agent. Jane swung the door open. "Hi, there."

The agent had uprooted the "For Sale" sign from the front yard. Dirt clods fell from the unearthed posts and spotted the porch steps. "Consider the listing agreement cancelled." She did an about-face and stomped to her car while Jane leaned against the doorframe, hands hanging limply at her sides.

Jane fretted the rest of the week about that awful real estate agent. Really, how could she stay in business turning away clients? What was the matter with her?

On Friday night after work, Everett climbed into Jane's car, and they cruised the highway to Fort Collins for the microbrewery tour. The scent of grain in the brew pubs brought back memories of hayfields and corn silos and whole wheat bread in the oven. Everett explained it was the smell of the barley and hops in the fermentation process. Jane also learned the distinction between ales and lagers—different yeasts and fermentation temperatures. She'd tried a small sip of a lager, but still could not accept the taste. Everett raved about it.

"You're a good sport, Jane," he told her during the drive home. "It must have been hard not to sample more of the brews."

"No, it wasn't hard for me. Did you learn a lot?"

"I did. People think a chef should be knowledgeable about all things consumed. And they ask about which beer to pair with different foods."

After they arrived back at her house in Limestone Heights, Jane made a pot of coffee. Caleb and Erin arrived as the coffee finished brewing. They brought empty packing boxes to store in Jane's basement. Everett and Caleb hauled the containers down the stairs, while Jane and Erin sat at the high-top table in the kitchen nook.

"So, you're done unpacking?" Jane peered over her steaming mug at her daughter-in-law.

"Yes. What I didn't unpack, I gave to charity. We're settled in. How about you?"

"Uh, no." Her eyes darted from the door to the garage over to the stairs leading to the basement. "I still have quite a few full boxes, but maybe I don't need that stuff and I'll give it away, too." Pack or unpack, move or not move, that was the question. "I'm going to the landscaping nursery tomorrow to order trees for planting next spring." Jane thought the trees would add value to her home when she got around to putting it back on the market.

Walking in the room, Everett said, "If you want some company, I'll go with you."

"That'd be great."

"Do you know which nursery you want to go to?" asked Caleb.

"I saw an ad in the neighborhood flyer for one

outside town. I have the directions."

Caleb and Erin said they wanted to go, too, so they discussed a time to meet in the morning.

Early the next day, they piled into Jane's car to drive to the landscaping company. They cruised a few miles north on a country road past farms with fields of yellow stubble and rolls of hay. Jane almost missed the entryway, but swerved at the last moment, and parked the car.

Enjoying the late fall day with a cool, crispness to the air and a contrasting warm, bright sun, they walked between the rows of trees. Jane's cowboy boots kicked up the scent of turned earth and mulch. She chose two blue spruces, Caleb suggested a red maple, and Erin found a choke-cherry cluster in the discount area. A nursery worker wrote up her order—at a two-for-one price and free planting—then strode into her office for a schedule of delivery dates in the spring.

A man, who seemed familiar, meandered along the dirt path between the maple trees a couple of rows over. It was the angry neighbor from next door. Turning her back to him, she ran right into Gina Valrod. "Oh, pardon me."

"Humph!" Gina threw her a filthy glance and kept walking.

The nursery worker returned, gave her a receipt, and explained delivery could be as early as March, depending on the weather.

They all climbed back into Jane's car, and she drove out of the parking lot past Gina, who was getting into a pickup truck. Jane pointed her car toward the coffee shop in Limestone Heights.

While the other three sat down at a table, Jane

hurried to the restroom. She ran a comb through her hair and put on some lip gloss before returning to the group.

"Are you following me?" came a harsh voice to her left. It was Gina.

"No!" Jane stopped in her tracks.

"You were at the nursery. Now here."

"I could ask you the same thing."

"Kimber told me you accused her of murdering her husband, and she saw you spying when she was outside with her horse at the ranch. You need to leave her alone. She's grieving for her husband. Just stay away from us and quit following me." Gina breathed hard, and her hands closed into tight fists. She was thin and willowy, but tall, and loomed over Jane.

"What's the matter, here?" Everett stood even taller.

Gina turned on her heel and hurried out.

Jane and Erin eyeballed each other in alarm as they all sat back down in their chairs. Conversation resumed at the tables nearby.

"That was Gina. She was at the nursery, and she thought we'd followed her here," Jane said in a near whisper.

"That's quite a coincidence," said Everett.

"What did she mean you were spying on them?" Caleb pursed his lips. "You're not doing your own surveillance?"

"Of course not. I was jogging near their ranch, that's all." Jane put an innocent expression on her face and gave an elaborate shrug.

Caleb seemed appeased. "Do you think she followed us instead?"

"Well, I know the HOA was purchasing trees. Perhaps all the construction companies shop the discounts this time of year. That probably explains why she was at the nursery. And this coffee shop is a popular place. It's the only one in town." Jane scratched her head. "But I did ask Kimber about the bruises on her arm and told her she was seen driving down my street on the day the twins were killed."

"Did she explain the bruises?" Erin's blue eyes showed concern, glancing out from under her silvery blue bangs.

"She said she fell off a horse. At the time I didn't believe her, but maybe it's true…"

"That's fin," was Caleb's comment. Jane was proud of knowing that was 'lame' in hipster-speak.

"Gina has quite a temper." Everett's eyes twinkled with interest. "She seemed protective of Kimber."

"Right. Yet I heard she was trying to force Kimber out of the business." Jane chewed on a fingernail. "Maybe that was a ruse. Maybe the girls were in it together."

"Remember what Doug said…that Kimber had an alibi," Everett reminded her.

"Yes, so he did. Anyway, I've decided just to avoid the Valrods." Jane glanced at her son.

"Say that again." Caleb flopped back in his chair and took a sip of his latte.

Jane added, "Except the walking group's planning a cross-country ski trip. It's open to everyone. If you're interested, it's on November thirteenth."

"Staff meetings at the restaurant are in the middle of the month, so I need to check my schedule and let you know," said Everett.

Erin scrolled through her calendar on her cell phone. "Sorry, Jane. We have plans that day."

"That's fine. We'll probably go again some other time." Jane tried to keep the disappointment from her voice.

"I hope Gina doesn't show up there. Like today," said Caleb. They all turned to Jane.

She reassured them, "I don't expect her to, but I'm not worried. There'll be a large group, plus Olivia and Doug will be there." But she kept the thought to herself someone had shoved her on Bierstadt Mountain, even though there was a crowd at the summit.

Chapter 22

Excitement gurgled in the pit of her stomach. Jane stood at the beginning of the cross-country ski trail at the Mountain Nordic Center in her rented ski bibs, holding her rented ski poles. She took a few practice steps in the ski boots, watching her heel lift up and down in the correct free-heel method.

The robin egg blue sky was without a cloud, the sun shone, and fresh powder covered the ground, since it had snowed for a short time the previous day. Even at this high elevation, the snow pack was not deep this early in the season, so patches of bare ground stuck out in places.

She'd been taken aback when they'd run into Kimber and Gina Valrod in the Nordic Center parking lot. Kimber had been standing shoulder-to-shoulder with Gina, then they both flounced away to head into the center.

Jane asked Margaret Skaleop, who was standing nearby, "Why did Kimber and Gina come today? I thought they were done socializing with the HOA group."

"They didn't want you to keep them from neighborhood events." Margaret shot her a level look.

Jane took a bracing breath before they joined Ashley Turghart, Kristin Gauthierville, Merrilee Eichenthal, Ruth and Dick Nelson, along with several others from the neighborhood, at the trailhead. Before long, Olivia and Doug skied up to the group.

Tara reiterated what was posted on the HOA website. "We're planning to ski this twelve kilometer trail to the warming hut and back. If anyone's not up for the entire loop, there are other trails you can take. Did everyone pick up a trail map?" She flicked her map open and held it up. Several in the group nodded. Jane had a map in one of her capacious jacket pockets along with snacks and water.

"This trail's fairly easy. Not a lot of uphill terrain, but it's long. If you want to take another one, go ahead, but some of them are rustic and less groomed. Be careful to choose a trail at the level of your abilities."

In spite of Tara's advice to pick their own trail, everyone decided to ski the twelve kilometer, even the older couple Dick and Ruth. Tara and Jane stood to the side as the other skiers set out ahead, their excited voices filling the air. Jane snapped some photos of the trailhead sign on her cell phone, then gave Tara an excited grin when they took their places at the end.

As they skied into a serene forest of tall spruce trees, the crunch of their skies sliding across the snow interrupted the silence. The sun's rays glared down between the branches and spackled the ground with spots of sunshine in the mostly shady glen. The trail took many twists and a couple of sharp corners, but they could always see several other skiers ahead. Although cold under the trees, the brisk movement of her arms and legs kept Jane warm.

Soon they found themselves crossing a wide-open, snow-covered alpine meadow with distant, white-topped mountains forming a dramatic backdrop. They stopped at a gathering of other skiers taking photos and snapped pictures of their own. A group of snowshoers, with two German shepherds and the smell of wet dog, passed the lingering group. Tara drew her map out. "It says this meadow is four kilometers into the trail."

"Wow. We got here fast." Jane gulped a drink of water and tucked the water bottle back into her pocket. As they started up, she gushed, "This is so fantastic. It's like riding a mountain bike through the woods and fields. But in the winter."

Tara agreed. "It's rejuvenating with all this fresh air and wide open space."

After crossing the meadow, they entered an aspen glade, the trees denuded of all foliage, standing with large, black-freckled, white trunks stretching up into the blue sky. Jane paused at the base of an aspen and gazed up the tall trunk waving in a high breeze she could not feel at ground level. It gave her a dizzy sensation.

Another two kilometers and they reached the warming hut. Tara had been right—this was a popular trail and the hut was full. Leaving their skis outside, they entered the primitive building, which had a fireplace at one end where several in their group were gathered. Kimber sat with Gina and Ashley on a bench near the door, but as Jane entered, the three of them got up and left. Jane assumed they wanted nothing to do with her and were going to start back to the Nordic Center.

Ruth and Dick called her over to join several strangers who held skis like staffs in their hands. The skis were quite a bit shorter than cross-country skis. "I want you to meet these skate skiers. It's the new thing," said Ruth.

"What's skate skiing? Is it the same as cross-country?"

"No," a young man answered. He was wearing expensive, name-brand ski clothing and had a high-powered camera around his neck. "Skate skiing uses lateral movements, like inline roller skaters. It's not the same as the step and glide cross-country method." Everyone scrutinized his skis as he rotated them left and right, obviously a proud owner, and not a renter like Jane.

"Interesting. I've never heard of it before."

"It's so much more fun."

As the skate skiers hurried over to take a spot near the fireplace, Jane sank onto a wooden bench to wait for her turn in front of the blaze. Doug and Olivia joined her, and they drew their snacks and water from their pockets and packs. "Are you having a good time?" she asked.

Olivia answered, "Yes. We decided to ski regularly from now on. I don't golf with Doug, but this is a sport we can do together in the winter when Doug can't golf." Her husband stroked his bristling red mustache, wet with melting snow, then he put his arm around Olivia's shoulder. Jane wondered if they'd resolved their little differences. Her mind flashed to Tara and Justin, and she hoped they would be able to do the same.

After eating, they packed up what remained of their food and water bottles, then Olivia stood to zip closed her pink ski jacket that matched her bibs. The hut cleared, then filled again as newly arriving skiers came inside.

"We're heading out to put our skis on." Doug took

his wife's elbow, and they turned toward the door.

"Okay. I'll be out in a few minutes, too." Jane slipped into an empty spot in front of the fire to wait as Tara talked to a few stragglers from their group. After several minutes she was quite warm, so she threw her empty water bottle into a recycle bin and took a peek out the door of the hut. Olivia and Doug must've left, but Kimber was there, sitting alone, fitting her boots back into the clips on her skis. She had an ugly twist to her mouth.

"Are you ready?" Tara asked from behind. Determined not to let Kimber ruin her day, Jane nodded, and they walked out of the hut together. Kimber shot up from the bench and whisked down the trail, snow flying out behind her.

"I just know it was Kimber who killed the Valrod boys," hissed Tara as the two of them steered toward the loop that would take them back to the Center. "She's acting very suspicious."

Jane skied close to her friend and said in a low voice, "I'm not supposed to talk about this, but the DA confirmed Kimber has a solid alibi."

Tara stammered, "Really? I can't believe it! What's her alibi?"

"She was shopping with a friend during the time of the murders...although I don't know how she proved it. Maybe she had her credit card receipts or the store clerks remembered her."

Their skis swished through the snow as they glided forward in the quiet woods. Tara's voice rang out, "But if Kimber's the murderer she'd arrange for an alibi, wouldn't she? She could've given her credit card to a friend and asked her to go shopping with it."

They rounded a corner to find Kimber skiing just ahead of them, so they fell silent. Did Kimber hear them talking about her? A chill traveled up Jane's spine, and it wasn't from the cold, mountain air. She wondered what had happened to Kimber's friends, since they were nowhere in sight.

She slowed her speed, and Tara followed suit, but after Kimber once again passed out of view, the two resumed their pace. Was she letting her imagination get the best of her? Was Kimber really the villain here? Or the victim?

She turned her head toward Tara. "I've been focusing on Kimber and Gina, but what if the deaths had nothing to do with the family or the business? I've neglected Ethan's affair. I want to find out who he was sleeping with. It could be the key to everything."

That was the true mystery. Why hadn't Tara made any real attempt to investigate the other young women in the neighborhood?

Jane stared hard at her friend and was about to inquire when Tara bellowed, "Why are you glaring at me like that?"

Speechless, Jane came to a halt and Tara stopped, too. Jane glanced around. Had they skied away from the groomed trail?

Rocks stuck up through the snow in the middle of the forest glen, and no other ski tracks but theirs marked the ground. The untouched layer of snow in front of them disappeared over a steep incline.

"Did we get off-trail? We'd better follow our tracks back." Jane turned around and caught a glimpse of another skier through the trees some distance away. "Look, I think that's Kimber over there. We're pretty far off, but it should be easy to find the way back."

Just then the snow gave away behind her right foot, causing her ski to skid backward. She fell forward, letting go of her poles to catch herself. When she landed on her hands and left knee, her right ankle jolted with a sharp pain as the boot popped away from the ski. Slithering backward a few feet down the embankment, she crashed to a stop as her right boot collided with a stone embedded in the side of the steep incline previously hidden from view. A shot of sharp pain went up her leg.

"Pull me up! I hurt my ankle." Her knee throbbed, too, as did the palms of her hands, and her left ankle was in a stretched, extended position with her foot trapped in the boot attached to the ski under her body. Vulnerable on her perch on the mountainside with Kimber just along the trail, she extended one hand out to Tara.

The snow-covered earth loosened and the stone under her right foot rolled downward. Her fingers grabbed tight onto roots poking through the snow as she nosed the toe of her right boot around for a foothold. She lodged her foot into a tree root poking out from the earth.

Tara lifted a grapefruit-sized rock up from the ground, her face flushed with rage.

"What are you doing? Help me up!" Jane's jaw dropped.

"I'm waiting for you to ask me about my affair with Ethan. I know you've figured it out."

Jane was stunned beyond words. They were alone, and her cell phone was in an inside pocket of her ski bibs, out of reach. She could no longer see Kimber or any other skiers, and the woods held a deep quiet. An adrenalin rush of fear swept over her as Tara continued, "I kept suspecting you were close to the truth. I was hoping you'd hit your head on a rock on Mount Bierstadt. If your body had wedged into a crevice, you wouldn't have been discovered until the next day, and you would've frozen to death."

Jane found her voice and it came out shrill. "It was you who pushed me?" Her heart thumped as the top layer of snow around her formed little snowballs mixed with scree and tumbled down the slope.

Tara just frowned, instead of making a reply.

"Brittany would never have left me on Bierstadt Mountain. What were you thinking?"

"Well, I couldn't get rid of you after that, with her watching you the whole time. Admit it, you thought it was me from the first day. Justin said you were spying on us the other night through some kind of binoculars."

"I wasn't spying." Panicking, Jane tried to wriggle her body up the embankment, but only managed to shift backward a few inches.

"Your basement window was always open, so I sneaked into your house to poke around. Justin came with me once, too, but he wasn't careful enough, so he only went inside the one time."

"That was you guys? But I never suspected you were the one having the affair. What happened? Did Ethan break it off?" Jane shivered as the shock set in.

"Yes. I threatened to tell Kimber, but he just laughed at me. I didn't know he'd had many other affairs until that day. He said Kimber was the forgiving kind." She tucked the rock in the crook of her left arm, then tore off her gloves and ski cap with her right hand.

She ran her fingers through her blonde hair cascading over her shoulders, looking wild. "Ethan stopped by my house that morning. He broke up with me and walked out the door. Just like that. I followed him out, but he kept going. I was so mad! He was standing on the edge of the foundation pit when Justin came around the corner on his bike and saw us."

"What did you do, Tara?" Jane's voice was ice cold.

"It wasn't me. It was Justin. He knew about the affair, but I'd told him it was over. I didn't know it really was…" She laughed, but without smiling.

Jane's body slid down the slope a few more inches.

"And…and…Justin jumped off his bike and ran up. Ethan said, 'You can have her back,' and Justin shoved him, hard. Ethan flew out over the edge and into the pit."

Chunks of frozen dirt skidded down the long slope, gaining speed and bouncing out of sight, as Jane glanced around for a sturdier branch to grab onto.

"We both ran inside the house hoping no one had seen us. But I started to worry and thought I should check to see if Ethan was all right. I went back outside to look. It was quite a shock to see him lying there, dead. I had no idea he'd died from the fall. So I panicked and told Justin he'd better get rid of the body… Justin got on the tractor and turned it on. Just then Steven walked up and asked me what happened, and Justin punched the button to operate the shovel and…and hit Steven with it." Her voice cracked and her staring eyes bulged.

Jane hung onto the mountain in her awkward position as Tara kept on. "Justin dug a hole and shoved

Steven's body in…and used the tractor to cover him over with dirt. Then he rolled Ethan's body on top." Tears coursed down her cheeks. "I just couldn't watch, and I guess he didn't cover him completely. Ethan! Ethan!" she sobbed, as her hands flew to cover her face.

Brushing the tears away with the back of her hand, she stared into the trees, a vacant gaze about her eyes. "I was friends with Suzanne, Ethan's first wife."

Jane clung to a dead branch, but it started to bend with her weight. "You told me you didn't know he was married before."

Refocusing on Jane, Tara smirked through her tears, and then laughed out loud. "I lied! We all went to college together." She yanked her stocking cap back onto her head and tucked blonde strands of hair underneath. "In spite of our friendship, Suzanne never admitted to me Ethan had been unfaithful. She'd surrendered her rights to the vanity license plates when she didn't re-register her car in Colorado, but didn't destroy them. She'd given me the plates, '*VALROD3*.' I took them with me to rent a black car that looked a lot like a Lexus. I put the '*VALROD3*' plates on it and drove up and down our street and through the neighborhood. Then I returned the rental car and hid out at home."

"You wanted to throw suspicion on Kimber, so it'd seem as if she'd been near the scene."

"Yes. I thought someone would just report the brothers missing, but if their bodies were discovered, Kimber would be the obvious suspect. I hated her." Tara's tears had dried. Now she looked like she could spit nails.

"You had me convinced she was there, following

her husband, but her alibi was true." The root gave way under Jane's foot, which was suddenly dangling in midair. She instinctively shifted her weight to her left, but her body sank a few more inches down the hill as she hung onto the bowed tree root with both hands.

"I thought Ethan would leave her, but he laughed at me for suggesting it. Suzanne was my only friend until she moved away. I don't have a lot of friends like you do, with your dinner club and all." Her mouth twisted into an ugly snarl.

Jane was astonished at her venom. "Why, I thought you and I were friends. I invited you and Justin to the 1940s White Christmas Ball!" Not only was her life in danger, but her feelings were hurt.

"I might just go to the Christmas Ball, but you won't be going."

"So, Justin was the one who put up the banner."

"Yes. But our marriage was in trouble long before that."

"Did the police find out about the affair?"

"No." A flash of victory crossed Tara's face. Didn't she realize there was a paper trail from the rental car agency? The police only had to check with Suzanne to verify the extra set of license plates. It was merely a matter of time before they found out about the affair.

Jane slid down a few more inches, her body hugging the earth. Her hands clutched the loose root. Her heart thumped in her chest.

"I'll tell everyone how we accidently skied off the trail. You went over a cliff and hit your head on the way down, so I skied out for help." Tara inched closer and raised the rock in her right hand.

Jane thought about letting go of her tenuous hold

on the side of the hill. She pictured her body sliding on the fresh but shallow snow, gathering speed, tumbling into tree trunks and rocks. She could hope to survive the fall, battered and left with a broken bone or two. Her mind flashed back to Mount Bierstadt, and then farther back to her hike with Cheryl when they climbed up the dangerous steps. The most common mountain dangers were getting lost or caught in bad weather. But this was the third time she was in the freakish danger of falling—a trifecta. Bad things came in threes, and she was determined to survive this last one.

Tara skied close to the verge and raised her arm high above her head, but her skis slid forward and she fell onto her back, joining Jane on the slippery slope. She dropped the rock to grab at her own branch.

Jane snagged Tara's left arm in a tight grip at the edge of the steep precipice. Tara's face was only inches away. "Don't let go of me."

"I won't." Jane's arms ached, but she was determined to hold on. "We were friends. You led Brittany and me down from Mount Bierstadt during the mountain top blizzard. And you saved us."

"I told you. I couldn't hurt you with Brittany right there." Remorse, then fear, flickered across Tara's face.

"Can you get your feet on solid ground? We need to get off the side of this cliff."

Tara kicked her feet, her skis popped off her boots, and the skis sailed into the air, bounced off a tree, then a rock, and broke into pieces. "I can't get a foot hold." Tara's eyes were so wide Jane could see the whites. Then, her body began to slip and loosen from Jane's grip.

"Jane!" Doug popped out of the trees with Olivia

right behind.

"Help! Help us!"

He jumped out of his skis and dug his boots into the snow. He reached his hand out to Jane, and Olivia held onto Doug's belt to steady him from behind. Jane held tight to Tara, and that way Doug dragged them both to safety.

Olivia hugged Jane close. "We heard everything."

"Good. And I'm going to need a ride home."

Chapter 23

"You're going to walk back to the Nordic Center while the rest of us ski back." Doug gave Tara a stern nod.

Jane's left ski was somehow still on her left foot. She skied on one foot over to her right ski lying in the snow and popped her boot back into the bindings. Doug hesitated with his lips sucked in, then stated to the other two, "Actually, I'll walk with Tara to make sure she gets back safely."

"Are you okay to ski?" Olivia gripped Jane's arm.

"It only hurts a little." She tried a few gliding movements. "I'm okay if I just slide my foot forward and not move it sideways." She gave Tara a filthy glance. "I'm sorry you have to deal with her, Doug."

He stabbed his skis into the snow, tips pointing skyward. "The police will want to examine this scene, and my skis will identify the spot." He extracted his cell phone from his pocket and called 9-1-1 to request a police officer to meet them at the Nordic Center.

Jane glanced from one to the other of her friends. "Thanks so much for rescuing me and managing Tara, too."

"Of course. Doug realized we hadn't seen you for a while, so we came back for you. You don't have to thank us. You would've done the same thing. Let's get going. It's cold in these woods." Olivia dug her poles into the snow and nudged off. Following her, Jane glided down the trail. They soon left Doug and Tara behind.

Traversing the end of the loop quickly, the women approached the Nordic Center where the hiking group was waiting for everyone to return. Olivia yelled out, "Tara tried to attack Jane!"

Margaret charged forward. "What? Why?"

Dick and Ruth hurried over, too, and Ruth put her hand on Jane's arm.

"Justin's the murderer and Tara helped him cover it up," Olivia rattled on excitedly as everyone gathered around and followed the two friends into the building. Jane sat by the fireplace and rubbed her ankle while Olivia answered their questions.

A police cruiser arrived a few minutes before Doug led his prisoner out of the woods. Tara was placed in the back of the police car, as Doug gave the officers the facts. One of the policeman rode the Nordic Center's snowmobile out to the site to take photos of where Jane almost met her death on the side of the mountain.

She completed a handwritten statement describing Tara's attack and confession. She was sure to include the information on the rental car. The two rescuers also completed written accounts, while the officer in charge called the Limestone Heights police detective, who requested them to stop and give recorded statements at the station on their way back to the metro area.

Margaret, Kimber, and Gina were waiting when they walked out of the Nordic Center.

Kimber strode up to them. "Do you have a minute, Jane? I want to talk to you to clear the air." Jane hesitated, but Kimber said, "I purposely stayed back at the warming hut to talk to you, but I lost my nerve."

"What about?"

"I knew you suspected me for Ethan's death, but I didn't know why. I thought I should talk to you about it after all." Kimber's face was fierce, then softened as she continued. "The best day I ever had since Ethan died was on Mount Bierstadt. I wanted another day like that. To feel a part of a group who cared about me, experiencing things together. Anything to take my mind off Ethan's death."

"I can relate to that, Kimber. I'm a widow, too."

"Yes, I know."

"Let's sit down," suggested Jane. They scooted away from the others to sit on a bench near the flagpole. "I'm twice widowed. And both of my husbands died under suspicious circumstances. I was a suspect after the second one died. I suppose that's why I was so curious about the twins' deaths, because I know what it's like to be under suspicion."

Kimber sniffed as a tear rolled down her cheek. "You, a suspect?"

"I sure was. The news of my last husband's death, and a photo, went viral on the internet. I had to change my last name back to my first husband's name because of the notoriety."

"In spite of the pain, there's relief that Ethan's murder is solved. It's finished. You and I can be friends now." A weak smile showed through Kimber's tears.

She held out her hand to shake Jane's, but Jane gave her a hug instead. "I'm sorry I ever suspected you, Kimber. I don't know how I could've, especially after my own experience." Kimber hugged her back, then Olivia insisted on getting Jane home.

****

The next day her right ankle throbbed in pain. She awoke early to apply ice for twenty minutes, then wrapped her ankle in a heating pad. She didn't want to miss church so she could see Dick and Ruth again, and Everett agreed to go with her.

She dressed in casual slacks, a sweater, and a scarf. After sliding her feet into ballet flats, she shrugged into her leather jacket, and let the dogs into the backyard so they could perform their duties and a quick perimeter check before Jane locked them inside the house. Everett was soon at the front door, and it was time to leave for church.

Jane enjoyed the sermon, which seemed to carry a special meaning just for her. The pastor explained that this Earth was not their home, this life being temporary and fleeting. Her new house may never feel like home, but that was okay, since her true dwelling place was in Heaven. She'd been lucky to get her deposit back on the apartment she'd leased.

Everett held her arm as they strolled out of the sanctuary with the rest of the congregation, and Jane tried to catch a glimpse of Ruth or Dick. Sadly, all she saw were strangers. She limped to the entryway table to read the bulletins before heading out.

"Jane!" Ruth was on one side of her and Dick on the other. "How are you feeling today?" Ruth's face displayed care and concern.

She introduced Everett, and the older couple insisted on taking them out for coffee. They drove to the coffee shop, and Jane ordered a new drink—a nonfat, double shot latte, sprinkled heavily with cinnamon.

"Kimber told us Gina left a threatening note on your door. Why didn't you tell anyone about that?" Ruth asked.

"I did tell the police, but I didn't know it was her." Jane thought about Gina's controlling manner, even to the point of protecting her sister-in-law.

Dick had news to contribute as well. "The note had nothing to do with the murder. She felt you were stirring up bad feelings about the company and bringing Ethan's problems to light. Ethan was stealing the rebate money. He cashed the checks instead of depositing them in the company account."

"So, you've talked to Gina?"

Ruth answered, "It was Kimber who told us. Gina always looked after Kimber, encouraging her to move on with her life."

Jane went on to discuss Justin's guilt and how surprised she was, but Everett stopped her after several minutes. "Jane needs to get home and prop her ankle up."

She acquiesced. "But I'm sure I'll be able to make plans for the walking group in the next couple of weeks."

Ruth said, "Kimber wants to open the farmer's canal trail and make it a public bike path. She invited the neighborhood walking group to stop at the ranch for refreshments if we hike it."

"Justin would've liked that." Jane's heart dropped a bit, thinking of the young man, who let his anger get the best of him and was now suffering the consequences.

They said their goodbyes, and Everett helped Jane into his car for the short drive home. He came inside the house to make sure she was sitting comfortably with the heating pad before he left for work at the restaurant.

Jane's ankle felt better in just a few days, and she didn't miss any work. Life was soon back to its usual routine.

One day in the following week, Olivia met Jane for lunch downtown. As they settled in with their salads, Olivia announced, "Doug talked to the DA this morning. He offered Justin a plea, and he took it. Second degree murder, a class three felony, because his actions weren't pre-meditated and were in a sudden heat of passion. Tara took a plea, too, for aiding and abetting."

Jane crunched on her salad. "I'm still trying to wrap my head around Justin being the killer."

"The DA claimed they had been investigating Tara's relationship with Ethan, since they had gone to college together and known each other well, but the police didn't have enough proof to make an arrest before the day of the cross-country ski trip—"

"I wonder if it's true or if the DA's office is just trying to save face. Does Doug believe it?" Jane set her fork on the table with some force.

"Actually, Doug was wondering the same thing. Justin may've gotten away with it, if not for you," Olivia agreed.

"Or you and Doug. Who knows what would've happened if you two hadn't shown up in time to rescue me. Everyone might've believed Tara that I simply skied off the trail over the precipice." She grabbed her fork and jabbed it into a tomato.

"I'm glad we turned around to look for you, too." Olivia wagged a finger. "I also wanted to tell you I found out what Doug was up to all those evenings he took off on his own. He was at the cigar lounge."

Jane cracked a smile. "That's all it was!"

"All? What do you mean, all?" Olivia huffed out a big breath. "I put an end to it. I don't mind if he smokes one rarely, but how can a man develop a smoking habit when his wife's had cancer?"

Swallowing, Jane murmured, "I see what you mean." Changing the subject, she asked, "Is your daughter coming home for the holidays?"

"No."

Her friend's face was sad, so Jane didn't press further.

****

Thanksgiving arrived, and Erin and Caleb came to Jane's house for the holiday meal as planned. "I thought you might want to have Thanksgiving in your loft, but I'm glad we're having it here." Jane opened the top of the double oven, and the savory aroma of turkey floated out. Urban and country collided, because Jane was wearing authentic, worn-out cowboy boots with her knit dress.

"It's your first big holiday in your new home, same as us. We'll host the next one." Erin was gracious, as always. "I see you have a new plaque." They peered up above the refrigerator at Jane's new decoration. Yellow letters on a teal background spelled out, "It is well with my soul."

The young couple had brought steamed squash. Although Jane missed the traditional mashed potatoes loaded with butter, the yellow vegetable was pretty on the table and a healthier choice. As was their family tradition, while they passed around the sliced turkey and cranberries, Jane brought up the subject of thankfulness. "I'm thankful for my home and family. I've finally finished unpacking."

"Talking about the fam', when are Luke and Brittany going to get here?" asked Caleb.

"The night before the 1940s White Christmas Ball. I bought extra tickets for them. And you guys, too."

Erin said, "I don't have anything to wear. Let's go shopping at the vintage stores in the SoBo District, you know, South Broadway."

"I can go shopping tomorrow." Jane added, "I'm thankful for my daughters-in-law."

"My internship at court ends next week." Caleb smiled with relief.

"Just in time for you to start studying for finals." Erin turned to Jane. "By the way, have you heard anything more about your neighbors' arrests?"

Jane repeated what she'd found out from Olivia. "Justin entered into a plea bargain for second degree murder."

Caleb swallowed a bite of squash. "You were lucky your friends came back to find you on the ski trail."

"I'm thankful for my friends." Jane slipped the puppies a piece of turkey. "And I'm thankful for my dogs, too."

"Is Everett coming by for dessert?" Erin touched her napkin to her lips.

"Yes. His new job as head chef means he'll miss most holidays. Restaurants are always busy on Thanksgiving and Christmas."

"Did you make pumpkin pie?" asked Caleb, as they put down their forks.

"No. I know you don't like pumpkin. Everett said

he's bringing dessert." Jane gathered the dishes to put in the sink full of hot, soapy water. "I'm thankful for Everett."

"And I'm thankful he's such a good cook!" added Erin.

Chapter 24

Luke and Brittany weren't the only ones in town visiting in December. Cheryl and Bruce Breewood flew to Colorado to spend time with their daughter at college and go to the 1940s Christmas Ball with the dinner club group at the Wings Over the Rockies Museum. The theme was "White Christmas" from the holiday movie with Bing Crosby and Rosemary Clooney.

Olivia wore a vintage, long, slinky red dress. None of her black hair showed under her blonde wig, styled to match Clooney's locks. Doug sported a Santa Claus suit, his red mustache hidden beneath a long, white beard. Bruce wore his same newsboy outfit from the summer ball, but Cheryl had on a vintage dress and fur stole with the intact head of a little fox. Jane drew back, but Cheryl explained it was fake, only a reproduction. Wasn't that a hoot? But Jane could hardly look at it.

She and Everett were a hit in outfits from the movie scene with Bing Crosby and Danny Kaye lip-syncing to the musical number, "Sisters." Trousers rolled up to their knees exposed men's sock garters, and they carried large blue, feathery fans and had blue butterfly barrettes pinned to their hair.

Their photographs were taken in front of the sign, "Pine Tree Ski Lodge, Vermont." Jane also posed with just her daughters-in-law, then her two sons with their wives, then the dinner club group as a whole—true

Christmas card-worthy photos.

"I know you've taken dance lessons, Jane. I don't know how to dance, but I'm willing to take a spin around the floor," Everett whispered in her ear to be heard above the Christmas music and loud buzz of the crowd.

"I'd love to dance. Let's go."

They joined the dancers on the ballroom floor and worked their way to the middle. Everett put his arms around Jane and held her close. The top of her head came to his chest. She pressed her nose against his tight muscles and breathed in his scent, so familiar to her now. They danced a simple waltz step as others around them performed fancier footwork. With her cheek lying on his shirtfront and her hands resting on his shoulders, Jane studied the crowd to see Luke and Brittany dancing a few feet away and Caleb and Erin a few feet farther. And Dale and Polly a few feet farther yet. Dale and Polly?

"Everett, your boss is here."

"I didn't know she was coming. But I didn't tell her we were, either. We should probably say 'hello.'"

"No. Let's forget about work for tonight." Jane turned her face the other direction and gripped his shoulders tighter.

"Okay. I'm fine with that."

When the song ended, they made their way back to the table, where Bruce showed Everett the bow tie he'd purchased at one of the vintage clothing booths along the back wall of the museum hanger.

Cheryl said, "I'm not surprised you solved the murder, Jane, but I would never have guessed Justin."

"I didn't guess it either, and I can't take the credit

for solving it. But I should've known something wasn't quite right with Tara. She was always trying to throw suspicion on Kimber, that's for sure. The first time we met, she brought a flan over as a welcoming gift. Isn't it tradition to bring a cake? That seemed a bit off."

"Nobody brings a cake anymore."

Jane frowned, thinking about the cake she had taken last week to her neighbor to the west. He seemed to like it and smiled at her for the first time. "I'm wondering if Tara made the flan for herself, then later decided to bring it over as an excuse to meet me and make sure I didn't see anything. You know, that I didn't see Justin shove Ethan into the pit."

"But it didn't go according to flan." Erin peered at Jane with a smile.

"Oh, I get it." Jane smiled, too, and they all chuckled.

"How's the dinner club group?" Cheryl stared from Olivia to Jane.

Olivia readjusted her blonde wig. "I think I've found a third couple who will fit well. Their names are Wes and Libby Powell. Wes was in the military, and they've lived all over the world, quite the world travelers."

Bruce interrupted. "Instead of dinners in your homes, you could plan an evening out each month. Like the 'Paint, Palette and Pour' event at your house you told us about. They have places that host those kinds of classes. Or, you could turn the club into a dining-out club and try new restaurants every other week."

"No." Olivia's jaw was set and her lips squeezed together. "The idea behind the gourmet dinner club originally was to entertain in our homes. I want to continue like we started."

Cheryl stood behind Olivia's chair. "Everything has its season, and all things come to an end. Maybe it's time to move on." They all gazed at her.

Doug smoothed his mustache. "We're not ready for the dinner club to end. Let's give the Powells a chance."

"I've received requests from several others, too. The club is still in demand." Olivia narrowed her eyes as she craned her neck to shoot Cheryl a look.

Jane was comforted by the Ladners' insistence the club remain as originally planned, but had a moment of doubt it would continue. She turned to Everett for his opinion, but he was checking his cell phone. Her own phone vibrated from inside her clutch purse.

She dug it out, squinted at the screen, and saw a text message from Dale. The phone slipped out of her fingers onto the cement floor. She glanced around the table, but no one was paying her any attention, and Everett had risen from his chair, one finger stuck in his left ear, trying to listen on his cell phone with the other.

Picking the phone off the floor, she noticed a crack across the screen. Not caring, she opened the text message from Dale. *I've missed you. Let's get together.* Jane quickly tucked her phone back into her purse. She jumped as Cheryl plopped down in the chair next to her.

"My feet hurt," Cheryl complained.

"I'm so glad you and Bruce came back for the holidays. There's so much I've been wanting to talk to you about. I miss our therapy sessions on our lunch hour walks."

"I miss you too," Cheryl said with a smile.

"We aren't keeping in close touch like we used to. I know you're busy, but we aren't talking as often."

"I disagree. We talk all the time—"

"No. There are periods of radio silence," Jane insisted. Cheryl cocked her head and raised her eyebrows. Bruce, in the chair on the other side of Cheryl, said something to his wife. She leaned into him and turned away. Jane sat alone, studying the room.

The colossal museum hanger was mostly in shadows, but spotlights shone on the vintage airplanes along the back wall. The brightly lit bandstand showed off the musicians in matching white suits with their brass instruments gleaming. Sparkling lanterns edged the bandstand, and twinkling lights above reflected off the glowing faces of couples below.

Everett put his phone away. He bent over the back of her chair as she tilted her head upward and reached with her fingers, ruffling his hair. He leaned in and kissed her.

No Grater Evil

by

Karen C. Whalen

The Dinner Club Murder Mysteries
Book Three

Chapter 1

A whisper of movement stirred the woods on the other side of the canvas. Were the mother bear and her two cubs in the campsite? The movement flitted away in the direction of the pond. Tightening the sleeping bag around her neck, Jane tensed and wiggled deeper into the down-filled flannel. When the wind rattled the dry evergreen boughs releasing the sharp pine resin, her eyes darted around in the dark, but they must have dropped closed as her mind fell into nothingness.

A fearful scream jerked her back from sleep. She scrambled out of her bag and tore the tent flap open, but hesitated, crouching low. "Olivia? Are you awake?"

"Yes." Olivia and Doug stood with flashlights outside the tarpaulin. "What was that?"

"Did a bear get somebody?" Jane's voice came out as a squeak.

They flicked the light at Jane's face for a moment, then pointed their flashlights into the woods, the light beams throwing shadows around. Jane stretched behind for her flashlight and bear repellant, then emerged from her minuscule tent, shivering in the cold night air. They leaned together without speaking, listening to the blowing wind for several heartbeats, then Doug spoke, making her jump. "I'm going to look around." He strode off in the direction of the latrines.

She squinted at Olivia, who was holding a brave face while flinching at every gust of wind. Both women were middle-aged, but Olivia managed to look youthful with smooth, olive skin and her thick, black hair in perfect place. Even while camping. And in the middle of the night. She said, "I'm going back to the tent."

"Wait for Doug." Jane aimed the flashlight in her friend's direction.

"All right, scaredy-cat." Olivia trembled.

"Like, you're not scared." Jane's knuckles showed white as she gripped the flashlight tighter at the sound of crunching footsteps on gravel. "Who's that?" she shrieked. The hair on the back of her arms stood at attention, and her heart thumped.

Doug popped out of the dark. "The campsites look quiet, and I didn't see a thing. Someone was probably having a nightmare."

Jane let out a long breath, as Olivia asked, "Do you want to bring your sleeping bag over? We have plenty of room."

"Thanks, but I'll be fine." Jane fluttered her hands around. "See you in the morning."

She had not camped since her first husband passed away a few years earlier and had never slept alone in a tent, but wasn't going to be afraid of the dark. With the bear repellant clutched in her right hand, she fell sound asleep.

It seemed like only moments later, her eyes opened. She peered out the mesh fabric that served as a window. The sun had not yet topped the mountain range on the horizon, but in the twilight-before-the-dawn she was able to make out her friends' palatial tent on the other side of the old, weathered picnic table. A welcome mat for wiping dirty camp shoes lay on the ground in front of the zipped-shut awning, and a bright red hummingbird feeder swayed from one of the stately tent poles.

The temperature was chilly outside her warm bag. After climbing into her worn blue jeans and a T-shirt, she grabbed her fleece jacket and stepped out into the brisk, fresh air. A beautiful day in the Colorado Rocky Mountains was about to begin.

Coffee first. She pumped up the gas on her Coleman stove. Something grabbed her, and the pot slammed down on the burner.

"Jane, it's me. I need some coffee." Olivia was outfitted in L. L. Bean camping apparel.

"Good morning, Miss Fashonista." Jane lugged her giant cooler from the secure, bear-proof, metal container. She lifted out a jumbo-sized plastic bowl of chopped jalapeño peppers, bell peppers, onions, and tomatoes.

"Hmm. I'm hungry." Olivia eyed the plastic dish. "What's all that for?"

"Huevos rancheros." Jane held out a block of cheese. "Darn! I meant to pack *shredded* cheese. How am I going to grate this?"

"I've got a grater."

"You do?" Jane peeled bacon out of its wrapping, as her friend went to get it. "Of course, she does," she said under her breath.

Olivia returned with a compact grater that had sharp, stainless steel ridges. "Give me the cheese. I can do this while you fry the bacon." Jane handed her the cheese block, then banged an over-sized, cast iron

3

skillet down on the stove. "Ouch!" Olivia yelled, "I just shredded my knuckles instead of the cheese."

"Oh, sorry." Jane grabbed antibiotic ointment and Band-Aids from the first-aid kit and treated her friend's cuts.

Olivia surveyed her bandages. "That grater's evil."

"Or the cook's not fully awake." Jane adjusted the camp stove knob, and the blue flames leapt higher. She dumped the slab of bacon into the pan, and soon the aroma of bacon, mingling with the fresh-air scent of the pine trees, filled her nose.

Doug poked his head out of his tent. "That smells wonderful."

"Good Morning." Wes strolled into the campsite, rubbing his bald head. He was wearing brown camping pants with endless pockets and a camouflage jacket. His wife, Libby, cruised up behind him in blue jeans and a flannel shirt, her chin in the air, nose quivering. A sun visor topped her short, spikey blonde hair.

Doug said, "Morning," as his full body broke away from the tent. He brandished a pistol in his right hand. Everyone gaped at him. The jalapeño pepper mixture slid from the bowl into the pan with a plonk.

"Jane, I want you to go to the firing range with us after breakfast." He handed her the gun, and she numbly took hold of it, as Wes and Libby lowered themselves onto the picnic bench, their eyes wide.

With the revolver in her left hand, Jane stirred the huevos rancheros with a spatula in her right. "Take this back, Doug. I'm not going." She stuck her left arm out straight, dangling the gun from the trigger guard pinched between her fingers.

4

"Did you get up at the crack of cranky? After all the danger you've put yourself in over the past couple of years, you of all people should learn how to shoot. Especially since you live alone."

The revolver still dangled from her fingers. "I'm never going to own one of these things, so why should I learn to shoot?"

"That's not how to hold a gun!" Doug's hand whipped around, snatching the pistol from her. "It's not loaded, but still, you have to be more careful." He rechecked the safety before sliding the revolver into its leather holster and snapping the buckle shut over the barrel. He returned the gun to his tent, while Libby poured coffee for herself and her husband.

Jane removed the heavy, steamy skillet from the stove to the table. Olivia sprinkled the grated cheese on top and jabbed a large spoon into the pan. "Everyone help themselves." The hungry campers dug in without much to say this early in the day. The chill burned off as the morning sun ascended higher into the sky.

Soon, Doug threw down his napkin and stood. "I'm heading over to the firing range. You coming, Olivia?" To Jane's surprise, his wife nodded. "Anyone else want to come?" Smiling, Doug glanced around the group.

"I don't think so," said Wes, "but if you'd like to shoot a 9-millimeter, you can take mine. It's kind of unusual, a Ruger."

"Sure." Doug clapped him on the back.

"I'll stay and help you clear, Jane." Libby wiped the table with a damp, checkered dish cloth, as Wes trotted off. He returned in a matter of moments, with a gun case the size of a trade paperback.

"Thanks." Doug extracted the pistol, checked the safety, and tucked the gun into his pocket.

Jane scraped the plates into a garbage bag while reminding him, "We're taking the short hike to the fishing pond and amphitheater this morning. Don't be long."

"You three go ahead and we'll catch up to you." Doug tugged on his wife's arm.

"All right. The trail marker's over there." Jane motioned toward the signpost, as Doug and Olivia gave a farewell wave.

A few minutes later the campsite was tidy and clean, with the garbage bag deposited into the rusty iron dumpster and the food locked inside the metal bear-proof container. Before long, the crack of gunshots sounded in the distance. Wes's body twitched, and a vacant, distant look came over his face. Libby's hand flew to her husband's shoulder. "You okay, honey?"

"I'm fine. Leave me alone." His voice was fierce.

Jane sucked in a breath. "Is everything all right?" Wes rarely lost his temper for no reason. He was like a big teddy bear.

Libby shook her head and mouthed, "I'll explain later." She rose from her seat and trailed after him toward their site.

Jane filled a squeeze bottle with water and a miniature backpack with raingear, listening to the shots resounding from the range. Yes, she had taken risks in the past, walking into danger because she was too trusting. But maybe there was something else she could do—self-defense classes, perhaps.

She banished those thoughts as she breathed in the fragrance still in the air, a pine and bacon blend. This was a day to enjoy and savor, no worries in the world. After only being gone a short while, Wes and Libby reappeared, backpacks on their shoulders. Jane unfolded herself from her seat. "Let's go. The Ladners can catch up later, like they said."

"Sounds good." Wes looked to be back to his normal self. Their feet carried them over the stone-peppered path. They trudged along in single file until they reached the pond. Wes said, "Let's take a break. Maybe Doug and Olivia are on their way and will meet up with us here." He gestured to a spot in the shallow water. "See all the fish just below the surface?" He stepped onto a fallen log to get closer, but the log rolled, and his feet went out from under him. With a splash, he went down on one knee in the cold, glacier-fed water.

"Wes! Look what you've done." Libby grabbed hold of his hand, but he was wet all over by the time he sloshed out of the pond.

"You're going to freeze. Should we turn around?" Jane tried to hold her lips still, so she wouldn't burst into laughter.

He shook himself like a dog. "Nah. It'd be quicker to keep going."

Libby brushed some of the moisture off his sodden pant legs, but he pushed her hands away, then took the lead as they continued past the pond. The sun traveled behind a low cloud and the wind kicked up, as they climbed upward. Soon, large, icy drops of rain sprinkled onto their heads and shoulders and made circles in the dirt on the trail.

"Did you bring rain gear?" Jane opened her small pack.

Libby slung her pack off and unzipped the pocket. "No, but I did bring a hoodie." She dragged the gray sweatshirt over her head and fitted the hood around her face, while Jane slipped into her thin plastic poncho.

A flat cap with a brim covered Wes's bald head. "The storm will pass quickly, you'll see," he said.

He was right. They only hiked about a quarter of a mile more before the rain stopped. The quick-drying drops spotted the otherwise dusty ground, giving off an after-rain, wet-earth smell. Jane shook her rain gear to shed the few beads of water clinging to the plastic before stuffing the poncho into her pack. The three friends soon emerged from the piney woods and paused at a rock outcropping near a bend in the trail. Jane's chest expanded as she took in a deep breath of the crisp mountain air. "Someone lives over there." She shielded her eyes with one hand and pointed with the other across the narrow box canyon to a log cabin nestled in a fluttering aspen grove.

Smoke puffed in white clouds out of the short chimney stack and sailed to the east. A lone man with a German shepherd lumbered out the door. She waved both arms above her head in greeting, but the man was staring the other way, down into the short ravine.

"What's he looking at?" Jane's gaze fell to the bottom of the gully just a few more steps down the path. Next to the shallow, winding creek, an amphitheater with rows of gray, splintered wooden benches encircled a smoldering fire pit.

Near the pit, a man lay still, his legs crumpled underneath his body.

Her heart flew into her throat. She raced down the steep trail, her friends on her heels. "Are you okay?"

she shouted as she drew near the man. Jane recognized him as the campground host.

Libby drew in an audible breath, and Wes mumbled, "What the heck?"

Dark red blood stained the man's light jacket and pooled beneath his back. Tracked in the blood were several large animal prints.

Jane's Dinner Club Suggestions

Planning in advance is key to a successful gourmet dinner club group.

Put some thought into making a list of potential participants. Which of your friends enjoy entertaining in their homes and would be willing to commit to an every-other-week or once-a-month event? Remember that Marcy and Greg were not willing to commit. Three to four couples comprise the best number. If you include too many, you won't find dates each month when everyone is available. In addition, you won't be able to seat everyone around your dining room table!

You can invite people who have never met before, but your guests should be compatible. You want a cohesive, committed group. Your club members may not see each other outside of dinner club, yet by coming together every other week or so, they will find themselves forming a bond with everyone having something to say to "catch up" from the last dinner club event.

Explain that the idea of a gourmet dinner club is to try new recipes, something outside of the normal, everyday family dinner. Don't serve the meal home style. Instead, fill the plates in the kitchen and add garnish to make a beautiful presentation. Bring the plates from the kitchen and set them in front of your guests once they're seated around the dining room table. To make everyone less anxious when it's their turn, be sure to leave an "out." Jane always tells her guests if her meal burns in the oven they're having pizzas delivered!

If you plan to serve alcohol (I can't picture a dinner

party without wine) be sure everyone is comfortable with imbibing and ask each couple to bring a bottle of wine. This helps everyone learn more about wine, plus is easier on the budget.

Invest in a good set of white dishes that can be mixed with a variety of placemats and napkins depending on the season and the party theme. Don't spend money on disposable decorations, but make wise purchases on quality table coverings that are timeless and can be used for many years. Prepare centerpieces for a gorgeous table and organize a playlist of background music.

Don't plan every minute of your party, but do plan your menu, theme, decorations, and what you'll wear in advance. Do your shopping ahead of time, and if you can prepare any part of the menu in advance, by all means do so. Remember Jane's timetable: write down when each item on the menu goes in and comes out of the oven, when to pour water in the glasses, and when to turn the coffee maker on.

Set the dates well in advance for each hosting couple. If you have four couples, plan two to four months of dates in advance. A month before the last couple's turn, schedule the next two to four months out. That way, every couple has the dates on their calendars and can plan ahead. Don't spend time during the dinner club with calendars and planning—that should take place in email communications or phone calls beforehand, so that scheduling doesn't take away from your evening. Send out email reminders a few days before each event. Adding the menu to the reminder helps guests to know which wine to bring to accompany the meal.

Be the first to host your event so everyone knows what to expect. What makes the party memorable is keeping the conversation moving (drinks help) and enjoying your own party since your guests will follow your lead.

If you add a theme to your dinner club event, remember it's only a tool to help you pull your menu and decorations together and provide an ice-breaker for your guests.

~*~

Here are some theme suggestions to get you going:

Time Change Dinner Club—for when the event occurs near the "time change" in the spring or fall—gather all the clocks from your house and arrange them as centerpieces in the middle of the dinner table—even hourglasses (some board games come with hourglasses, so think about what you have on hand). If you don't have enough timepieces and don't want to buy any, print pictures of clocks and hourglasses from the internet and scatter the pictures along the middle of your table, like a table runner. Play a game after dinner called, "Times are a-changin'," and ask each guest to write on a piece of paper what they would like to change about themselves. Jane always wished she could sing. The host reads the papers out loud and the guests try to guess which person filled out the paper.

Pizzas on the Grill—take Everett's suggestion for grilling gourmet pizzas on the grill, each person choosing their own toppings and grilling their own pizzas. Serve home-brewed beer or beers from your local micro-brewery.

Scavenger Hunt—use song lyrics for clues and play

those songs on your iPod over a wireless speaker during your party. Examples: Hand out the first clue written on a piece of paper: "Strawberry Fields Forever" by the Beatles. That should lead to the pot of strawberries growing on your patio where the next clue is hidden, "I was born with a plastic spoon in my mouth" from the song, "Substitute," by The Who. That clue will lead people to the next one hidden among the plastic spoons sitting at places on your patio table. Plan at least eight to ten clues for each team. The final clue leads to a nice bottle of wine in your wine cooler.

Dinner Club at the Park—everyone should bring their hibachis, spread a table cloth on the ground, and the host provide the meal to be grilled, plus bouche ball or other games to play for an old-fashioned picnic. Bring your iPod and play summer music, like "Saturday in the Park" by Chicago.

A word about the author...

Karen C. Whalen is the author of a culinary cozy series, The Dinner Club Murder Mysteries, the first of which was *Everything Bundt the Truth* also published by The Wild Rose Press, Inc. She has hosted gourmet dinner club events for a number of years.

And a word from the author herself...

Would you like to be a member of my "street team"? A street team is a group of volunteers who love an author's books and want to assist in promotion. Members of my team are those who like to read cozy mysteries and are willing to commit time to promote on social media.

And, if you would like to receive notice of new release dates and be the first to see new book covers, please subscribe to my newsletter.

Sign up for the newsletter and street team today by contacting me at http://www.karencwhalen.com/.

Thank you all! Karen